Simon Cleary was born in Toowoomba in 1968, and attended university in Brisbane. He has lived in Sydney and Melbourne and travelled widely in Europe, Africa and North America. He lives in Brisbane. *The Comfort of Figs* was published by UQP in 2008. *Closer to Stone* is his second novel.

CLOSER
TO
STONE

SIMON CLEARY

UQP

First published 2012 by University of Queensland Press
PO Box 6042, St Lucia, Queensland 4067 Australia

www.uqp.com.au

Cover design by Design by Committee
Cover photograph © Corbis
Typeset in 12/16 pt Bembo by Post Pre-press Group, Brisbane
Printed in Australia by McPherson's Printing Group

This project has been assisted by the Commonwealth
Government through the Australian Council,
its arts funding and advisory body.

National Library of Australia cataloguing-in-publication data
is available at http://catalogue.nla.gov.au/

Closer to Stone / Simon Cleary
ISBN: 9780702239229 (pbk)
        9780702247651 (pdf)
        9780702247668 (epub)
        9780702247675 (kindle)

To Sue Cleary and in memory of John Cleary

And of course
Alisa

'You almost expect,
when you touch this body,
to find it warm.'

Auguste Rodin

What went wrong, Sergeant Logan?

I don't exactly know, sir.

You were together six weeks. You knew him well?

We knew each other from before that, sir. We've known each
other since we joined.

You're friends?

Yes, sir. He's a fine soldier, sir.

In your opinion, Sergeant Logan, what happened?

There are so many possibilities, sir.

Go on.

I don't know . . . all sorts of things.

What are some examples, Sergeant?

He could have got separated from his lift, sir . . . he could have
got lost, or been killed, or had an accident, a mine . . . it
could easily have been a mine, sir . . . or taken prisoner . . .

Do you really think so? Seriously, Sergeant Logan. What else?
Give me something else, something plausible.

Anything's possible, sir. It's the desert after all.

PART ONE

ONE

I was petrified when the plane finally landed at Casablanca's Mohammed V airport. It was four o'clock in the afternoon on the second of February, 1993. I had some photos of Jack, a few names, a crude plan and more responsibility than I could bear. At twenty I'd barely ventured beyond the quarry-town where I'd been born. Now I was in Africa. The size of the thought! Casablanca, a city of God knows how many million, and there was not a soul I knew or knew me.

Somehow I got myself by train from the airport to the central railway station. I only have snatches of memory of that darkening city – images that collide and fragment as I try to recover them. I recall a sign beneath the carriage window, a lit cigarette trapped in a red circle: *Ne pas fumer.* My six months of grade eight French was so slight. And the Arabic scrawled below those words like scribbly-gum markings was unintelligible. I didn't know if it was even language back then, though it wouldn't have mattered – half the carriage was smoking anyway.

Then the chaos as I stepped out onto the tiled platform at the Gare du Port, and the madness of searching the crowd for

Jack's face. Knowing it was impossible he'd be there, but unable to staunch the hope. Standing there helpless, till I surrendered to one of the hundred taxi drivers crowding round me, pulling at my bag. A dizzying journey through the streets followed, the headlights not only the wrong colour, but the current of them coming from all the wrong angles. The entire world spun round wrongways. Flashes of light picked out curiosities, all unsettling: children selling chewing gum in the traffic, men holding hands as they walked, all the bent and faceless shuffling-veiled women, the palm trees and the rubbish swept into the gutters, a rampant Peugeot lion blinking in neon above a building. I wrote down a street name before it flashed past – Rue Laalouj – a futile attempt to get my bearings.

At some point the taxi passed through what seemed like a giant keyhole in a high wall, and a band of shadow fell across us like a guillotine blade. On the other side was the medina. The cab slowed and there were voices and hands and shoulders of men brushing against the vehicle in the tight alleys, and all the while my bag was in the boot. The noise which burst through the window when the driver wound it down to ask for directions was no sound I'd heard before, not yet something I knew to call music. Finally we stopped at the Hôtel de France where the driver handed me over to the innkeeper, some arrangement between them, a wad of *dirham* changing hands beneath a portrait of their king on the wall.

When the driver left, the innkeeper lifted a guestbook from beneath the reception desk and opened it on the counter. Muttering some terse instruction, he swivelled it round and pushed a pen towards me. I followed the pattern of entries already there – name, address, nationality – and obediently wrote. My passport hung around my neck in the money pouch my step-mother, Em, had bought me before I left. I opened the little navy blue booklet with its gold coat of arms, and its kangaroo and its emu facing each other, and copied down the number. After completing the final column on the page – profession – I slid the register back across the counter to the innkeeper. He checked without interest what I'd written until he reached that last entry. He leant forward, peered closely at the word before tapping it with his finger and looking up at me.

'*Cela*,' he said. '*Qu'est-ce que cela signifie?*'

But how could one explain the work of a sculptor?

When at last I got to my room on the third floor I locked the door, dropped my duffel bag beside the bed, and hurried to open the shutters. I closed my eyes and breathed, all the air my lungs could hold. I had no chisel I could take in my hands to feel its comforting weight, no stone to calm me. When I looked out across the city I saw a bright blur: strings of bulbs, neon street signs, the interiors of nearby buildings lit up, red warning lights on the tip of each of the cranes down at the port, flickerings in the darkness near the horizon which might have been tankers at sea. I heard my heart beating in my ears and exhaled. A swallow stirred from its roost nearby and darted through the night air, its dark shape lifting with each wing beat, rising through the scales of some invisible night-music, before abruptly turning and swinging back the way it had come, a moth now pincered in its beak.

I lay on the bed but didn't sleep. What I'd left behind was as foreboding as what might be ahead: the trajectory of my life had been blown so totally off course. I'd had to turn my back on my first commission, the bearded dragon I was cutting from a great block of pink sandstone in the backyard of our home at The Springs. His collar of rust, his head and neck, the ridgeline of his back already broken free, his shoulders muscling their way out of the stone. Just three nights earlier I'd been standing before him, working by makeshift floodlight, my mallet and point-chisel flying, scattering sandstone chips on the ground – so many shards of cream and pink and brown – desperate to finish him before I had to go. But it was no good. Despite those late nights I'd still had to abandon him on a platform of temporary railway sleepers at the back of the yard, sweating under a sheet of dark tarpaulin, while my father sent me to Africa to find my brother.

The screeching started near midnight. The streets below the hotel teemed with cats, the narrow alley outside my room funnelling their hissing up to the window and through the shutters to echo around the walls. An incessant howling, wild with hunger or mating instinct or territory marked. I hung a blanket from the top shutter-slats to muffle the sound, returned to bed, shivered and checked my wristwatch every fifteen minutes.

I lay exhausted until dawn was surely not too far off. Then a new sound, entirely foreign, broke open the night. It was a wail, neither strong nor delicate. Even whether it was near or far I couldn't tell, the sound distorted by whatever distance it had to travel, an inconstancy on the gusting ocean winds. My first thought was of a rabid dog losing itself in fever. But there was no agitation in this whining. It was more like the sound of dingoes beyond a campfire, flat and controlled. Then, from another compass point, a second wailing began, as if in answer to the first, and I understood they were not dogs, but men calling into the night. Two men, droning away in the dark. And then a third voice, and a fourth, perhaps more. Some ritual was taking place out there. I imagined Aborigines chanting through the darkness around the tentative encampments of The Springs' first settlers, *unsettling* them. The stories our father told Jack and me when we were kids.

I crept from my bed, lifted the hanging blanket, and peered sideways through the slats at the faded stars and all that lay beyond. Now the chanting was like warrior calling warrior out there in the night, warning the city of an intruder, planning their assault. Because on that first night I was just a boy, a country child who knew nothing of Muslim calls to prayer. Wide-eyed, I listened to the wailing city, my cheek pressed against the cold plaster of the wall. The moon, visible near the roof-line at the end of the street, was many days from full, a mere sliver of crescent. In time the last echoes of wailing stopped, there was silence, and I crawled back to bed, curled tight, and waited.

Finally dawn broke. Everything was so still, all so quiet, the cats and demons vanished, the world fresh again. I pulled the blanket down from the window, opened the shutters, and looked out at the city's scalp, the strange geometry of its roofscape. The layering of building upon building: square, whitewashed, paint-peeled, each set close beside the other, cascading down to the port. Antennae rose above the roofs, waves of satellite dishes all facing the same direction, as if having turned as one. There was the shimmering Atlantic I'd smelt the night before, the tips of the harbour cranes, egg-yolk yellow, a ragged army of them turned against the prevailing sea breezes.

A tower out there among the squat white buildings caught my eye, each of its four sides green-tiled. There was a brilliance in it, some calmness of form in the midst of that intimidating sprawl. A golden orb and crescent were mounted on its tip and rose towards the sky, the crescent cupped just so, as if inviting the entirety of the sky to rest in its arc.

TWO

A taxi dropped me at the *gare routière* before dawn on my third day, to catch the long-distance bus to Western Sahara.

I'd spent the previous day holed up in my hotel room, venturing out only to stock up on food and to buy my ticket. Because Casablanca's medina wasn't the exotic place Jack had described on his first weekend's leave there. It wasn't *an extravaganza of colour and fragrance and sound,* as he'd written in that confident hand of his on the postcard he sent home of Humphrey Bogart and Katharine Hepburn. Instead, the carved fretwork he'd described, the minarets and the ancient fountains and the narrow alleys – they all seemed so threatening. The donkeys pulling carts of vegetables, the old men and the henna-palmed old women, the swirl of Coca-Cola signs in Arabic, the plastic teapots, the strange-shaped watermelons, and the hands of dates hanging dark against white-washed walls . . . I know there are people who say it's just another Mediterranean city. That Europeans have taken their annual holidays there for years and that students at the Université Hassan II were probably wearing Levis just like me. I know that *now.* But back then the city was utterly foreign. I could have drowned in it.

The *gare routière* was no better than the medina, probably worse in the darkness, but I had no choice. I joined the current of people outside the gates of the walled compound, my duffel bag slung over my shoulder, moving with them towards the entrance, and the sound of the bus engines starting inside. Bodies pressed against mine, bodies and bags and boxes and sacks of hessian. In front of me a shrouded figure balanced a crate on her head. I watched it rise and fall with each step, its rhythm hypnotic. As I passed through the gate, the woman and I were momentarily pushed against each other by the crowd and I saw the crate was a cage, and that inside it were three hens, their beaks glinting in the light of a kerosene lantern hanging from a nearby pole. One of the birds squawked, its frightened eye fixed on me until the tide of people pushed us apart once again.

Inside the compound voices were calling. Men began pushing close, tugging at me, shouting through white-specked moustaches. Over the din men yelled the names of towns. Fez, Marrakech and Rabat I'd heard of, the other names mere syllables slurred together, the entire country named in the dimness.

'*Non, non, non,*' I said to the first, shaking my head.

'Where you go? Where?' he demanded.

I ignored him, but others came. Their intensity grew, the way they pushed close, two or three of them together, blocking my way, insisting I answer.

Eventually I took the ticket from my pocket and lifted it into the air. This must have looked foolish, but it worked because when the men saw it they melted away. I passed through the crowd like that, the ticket raised before me, Moses and the sea, kids pointing the way.

The bus was idling when I reached it, though the driver's seat was empty. A young man with a short beard was throwing luggage to another, even younger, who stood on the roof of the bus, legs astride, like he was riding some beast. He had the poise of an athlete, catching the suitcases as they were thrown to him. I showed the bearded man my ticket. He grunted and reached for my bag. For a moment I hesitated, worried about parting from it, some security in having it close, slung over my shoulder or resting in my lap. But he insisted and I let him throw it with the rest, a fluid movement of arms and shoulders and chest and head. As my bag was packed away in the tray on the roof of the bus I remembered a trip we'd made to the beach one summer when Mum was still alive, how our father had loaded the suitcases on the roof-rack of our Kingswood the same way. The skill it took, the satisfaction it gave him.

Some women were seated inside, sleeping already, veiled heads pressed against the windows, blankets close around their shoulders. A rough semicircle of men squatted on the tarmac near the front of the bus, impassive faces lit by cigarettes. I stood nearby and watched a mother and her children climb the stairs, watched the luggage being thrown. I hugged my smaller daypack to my chest, to keep warm as much as anything else. A young man with a woollen hat pulled tight around his ears offered me a smoke. I shook my head.

The first wave of the day's buses began to reverse slowly from their bays, headlights still off but horns blaring. Exhaust fumes came off the rear of the buses in clouds. A man walked in front of each bus like a goatherd, yelling at the crowd, banging the palm of his hand loudly on the side of the vehicle, pushing people out of the way, leading his charge through the compound and into the street, the opaque dawn.

Then it was our turn. The change in the pitch of the engine, the driver in his seat, the youth on the roof pulling a tarpaulin over the mound of suitcases and boxes and cases and crates. The one who'd thrown my bag yelled into my face, his breath foul, and motioned his head to the door of the bus. The men tossed their cigarettes aside and we filed on. I took the last window seat, near the back. An old man stood in the aisle beside me. He wore a large brown coat which fell long around his legs, hid his wrists in its wide-looping sleeves and covered his head in a deep hood. A strange skin so many of the old men here wore. Then he sat down next to me, his face set back in his hood and its shadows. I pulled my own jacket tight.

The bus nudged its way through the gate of the *gare routière*. I became aware of a clicking, close to me and not quite rhythmic. Prayer beads were moving through the old man's thick fingers, his wrists still. I turned away and pressed my cheek against the glass. The young man who'd stood on the roof of the bus was now jogging beside it, waving at people he knew, calling out their names, before he leapt on as it picked up speed – a readiness for action that reminded me of Jack.

But Jack wasn't just athletic. Though he'd won every race there was to win, captained every football side he ever played in, and crammed the sideboard with trophies Em will have kept somewhere, there was more. The way he strode along the cliff-tops of the family quarry after school, his gait so confident, as often as not out in front of our father, ready to make a glorious success of the business when it was time for him to take over. Ultimately though, it was his composure more than his confidence. *That* was the thing that made you believe there was nothing he couldn't do: he was out ahead of everyone else and could see things coming a mile before anyone else did. The sense you got that time somehow paused for him, that he shaped the world more than it shaped him.

You can cling to people like that, hope they'll look after you. Sometimes they do.

★

13

It was a Saturday not long after the fire that took Mum, and our father hadn't yet worked out what to do with us. We were young – I was seven, Jack nine – and there was still a quarry to run. Our father left me with someone in town that day while he took Jack out to the quarry with him. There were orders that needed filling, stone to cut, and he'd spent so much time away in the weeks after Mum's death he must have been worried about the business. He would have been exhausted too. That probably accounts for it, because it usually took two men to operate a channelling machine, one to turn the wheel, the other to clean away the mud.

Jack was playing among the blocks when it happened, jumping across the gaps between them – when he heard our father yell. It would traumatise most boys to hear their father scream like that, to see his arm hanging, all that blood. But not Jack. Not then, and not later either, as far as anyone could tell. He was a young boy who'd lost his mother a month before, but was calm as could be. He led our father by the hand – the one still there – up to the office, and got him into a chair before he fainted. Jack rang triple zero and did what the operator told him. Took off his own small t-shirt and held it to the wound. His nine-year-old's hand staunching the blood like that Dutch boy with his finger in the dyke, the channeller's engine still thrumming away in the distance, Jack waiting calmly for the ambulance to arrive.

Even as a kid, Jack had stood between us and ruin – our father's one consolation in all the broken years that followed.

Outside my window the city began to unravel. We'd left streets lined with colonial buildings and their wrought-iron balconies, the intersections and traffic lights, the restaurants and the businesses with their sheen of modernity. Soon carpet emporiums were replaced by petrol stations and mechanics' garages. Then even that order petered out, as if it was all pretence and the effort of keeping it up was too great.

Next were the unfinished buildings, deserted entirely or surrendered to some different purpose. New structures abandoned, their concrete walls only half-poured, the incomplete second floors open to the weather, steel reinforcing rods thrusting out like barbarous spikes breaking from dusty grey concrete. Some were now homes, with curtains covering open windows, soccer-balls left on vacant lots, and people living between the steel spears.

Then came the *bidonvilles*, the slums. Shanties set one beside the other, so close that the sheets of roofing iron from one overlapped the next. Like a vast contagion, coloured pieces of plastic covered holes in this sweep of corrugated roofs, the corners of each splotch of colour weighed down by broken bricks. Metal cylinders were cut roughly through the corrugations, and in the early light these crude chimneys blew thin runs of smoke. The slums stretched for miles. Along unguttered roads and unpaved paths women trudged with water containers hanging from each arm. In places I saw burning sewage: thin towers of smoke linking city and sky. Dogs raking piles of rubbish with their front paws. Barefooted children balancing on the tops of overflowing industrial bins, their splayed toes holding fast to the steel edges while they paused in their rummaging to watch the bus pass.

We reached the end of the city, beyond the last broken settlements, where the countryside began. But there was no relief from the haggardness. A littered no-man's land, the detritus of the city collecting at the margins, blown out by the prevailing winds of the place. The land was strewn with black plastic bags. Every stump, every low-growing bush, every branch of every tree had, wrapped around it, a plastic flag of flapping black. I saw a coloured inversion of the photos on the mantelpiece at home, the white crosses of the war cemeteries in northern France where my great-grandfather was buried. But where there was stillness in those white limestone crosses, here the black bags fluttered, like cindered effigies, waving.

THREE

So I looked away. I took solace in my guidebook, in the familiar shapes of the English words, the way they fitted together into sentences, and paragraphs and created images, and communicated information, even ideas. The way they gave order, and beauty, the way one of my people, in *my* language, had sought to describe this place. But more than comfort, I was reading out of need, taking it all in, everything these pages had to say about this country, these people. I had this chance, this opportunity for the hours or the days I was on this bus, to read and learn, and to try to make sense of the place.

I began at the start, like it was an instruction manual. As if I wouldn't be able to build the thing which came with the manual if I skipped a section, or read it out of order. So I started with *Facts About the Region*, and *Facts for the Visitor*, before moving on to *Getting There and Away*. There were sections on *Arts and Crafts* and *Getting Around*. Next I read chapters – a few pages each – headed *History* and *Religion* and *Language*. I gripped the guide as if it was a key I couldn't afford to lose.

★

'So,' I had said, 'Africa.'

'The Sahara,' Jack replied, all that nonchalance of his. 'A peace-keeping mission.'

It was the last time I'd seen him, the night he'd come home to tell us the news, two years after he'd enlisted. Our father's surprise at him joining up in the first place had long since passed. He'd had faith that Jack would do his time in the army like they all had – him in Vietnam, his own father in the second war and his grandfather before that at the Somme – and that the quarry would wait. All the stories coming back to us about Jack's nights on the town, his rolled ute at the Birdsville races, or the book-makers he'd stared down, just added to his reputation at home. This son who could mix it with the world.

So the night Jack announced he was serving overseas our father was overcome with pride. He brought out the family atlas after dinner, and rested his hand on the northern fringe of that continent. Jack's precise destination, Western Sahara – a place none of us had heard of – was obscured under his index finger. In that glowing moment, it didn't matter much exactly where Jack was going. It was enough it was North Africa, and as our father said, pointing at Libya and Egypt, 'It's where your grand-father fought.' As soon as our father started telling the stories once again of *his* father, the Rat of Tobruk, I retreated to my bedroom. They weren't for me, those tales of valour. They were for Jack to take with him, letters of recommendation, guarantees of safe passage.

Later Jack saw the light still on in my room and came in, stood there in the doorway looking around. My bedroom shrank under his gaze. The way the army had trained him to look, the fullness of his eye. Though he'd *always* been like that, calmly absorbing everything there was to take in without any-one realising.

I watched him looking, tried to see what he saw. The pictures I'd cut from magazines and tacked to the walls, objects that had caught my attention, things I planned to sculpt one day. The photos of *David* and *Moses*. *Night* and *Day* and *Dusk* and *Dawn*. But not just Michelangelos. There were Rodins up there too. And the classics, *Venus de Milo* and *Laocoön* and *Samothrace*, pages from old *National Geographics* or a book on Renaissance art I'd taken from the school library – these I'd taped to the ceiling above my bed so they were the first things I saw when I opened my eyes in the morning. And there were my own rough sketches on butcher's paper, a pile of them on the desk, the one I was working on when Jack stepped in, quickly turned face-down at the top of the pile.

'So no fighting then?' I asked.

'*They*'ve been at war for fifteen years, and we're stepping right into it. We'll be keeping them apart, keeping them from each other's throats.'

'How are you going to do that?'

'Don't worry about that, Bas. We'll find a way. And it's not just us. There'll be others there too. It's a United Nations mission. We're one of the first countries who've signed up.'

I remembered a black-and-white photo from our grandfather's war: a line of fit, young men queuing to enlist. I tried to imagine how *countries* did it, pictured a line of presidents and prime ministers waiting their turn outside a recruitment office somewhere.

'Why?'

'We're good international citizens,' Jack replied. 'It's what good countries do. We're our brothers' keepers. Remember?'

One of our mother's sayings. *Blessed are the peacemakers* was another.

'So when're you off?'

'Three weeks.'

Cicadas in the dark beyond my bedroom window.

'So, Africa,' I said again.

Jack laughed.

'You got it.'

'Well, don't forget the starving children.'

My turn to call up our mother. The dinnertime refrain from our childhood, so long ago, our mother's gentle reproach if we'd left our peas on the plate. *Think about the starving children in Africa,* she'd say. As if the four of us at our dinner table could eliminate world poverty. As if we had an obligation to. As if it was *our* obligation, one that extended to the other side of the world.

'What about you, Bas?' Jack said, his eyes returning to the photos on the wall. 'What are you up to? What have you been thinking about, Bas?'

That was the question he liked to ask – what have you been thinking? – the one that invited people to share their dreams with him. As often enough they did, allowing Jack to shape them, feeling enlarged by it, Jack's vision. But I was wary by then of my *own* ambition: my hope of joining the pantheon of sculptors up there on the wall. This was a vision I sensed was growing beyond my control.

'You afraid of being shot?' I countered.

'No.'

'What about that girl?'

'Which one?'

'I don't know, the one you brought back here a few months ago.'

'I haven't treated any of them well, Bas. I wasn't serious. They deserved more. No, there'll be no one to miss me. But this, Bas, *this* is serious. Peacekeeping is important. It's a chance to make a difference.'

★

The bus travelled down the coast. When I did look up from my guidebook, the sky was cold, with clouds and stiff winds scudding the blue with grey, and the Atlantic was dark.

There were towns which all looked the same. The half-built structures, the rubbish piling along the streets, the packs of barefoot children running alongside the bus. Petrol stations and tea-houses. The seething bus-stations. Near one I saw a truck with its freight of live cattle standing on a vacant lot of land, the truck jolting from side to side with the movement of the beasts inside. Beneath it, shaded from the sun, the driver slept on the ground, blanket pulled over his body, curved like a crescent moon. A little further along, leaning against a wall, were two youths, one with his wrist draped loosely around the other's neck, their fingers entwined in a quiet gentleness.

The bus stopped at midmorning at a *gare routière* on the fringe of a town my guidebook described as a tourist attraction. I stepped out onto the asphalt, into the eddying humanity of the place, the torrent of passengers and their relatives come to greet them or see them off. All the water-sellers and shoeshine boys and chewing-gum vendors. The touts wanting my business, in my face, demanding to know where I was going. The limbless beggars calling up to me from the ground. And me shaking my head. *Non, non, non.*

I made it halfway to the café to buy some croissants and *millefeuille*, when a woman grasped my arm, her fingernails in my skin, her eyes wide with whatever it was she wanted. At the pitch of her voice I tried to draw away, but she started screeching, her face contorting, flecks of white at the corners of her mouth. I recoiled, but when I looked around for help, I saw that the men had made room and were standing in a loose circle around us, amused. We were a spectacle, I realised, the screeching woman and the cowering westerner, entertainment. But I didn't know how to play my part. I pushed through the crowd and fled back to the bus.

From its sanctuary I waited, my heart pounding, for the bus to fill again. I stared out the window at the sky, not seeing, ignoring the gruff smile of the old man as he resumed his seat beside me, whatever he was offering. Some peace. In time the bus pulled out of the station, drew free of the whirlpool, and set off again through the streets. The movement was a relief.

FOUR

I read the final chapter of my guide, the chapter on Western Sahara. It began: *What the tourist brochures refer to as the 'Saharan provinces' is largely disputed territory.* The peacekeepers were here to resolve that very dispute. When I finished the chapter and thought of Jack, it crossed my mind that I should read the book again, that there was so much I hadn't taken in I might need, that I should reopen it at page one and begin again. I turned to the window instead.

The afternoon was brighter, the clouds had been left behind. We had left the coast. There were hills, and villages on the sides of the hills. There were crop-fields. There were other tea stops. At one, as the bus drew into a village, the old man beside me stood, and reached for a bag in the overhead compartment. He turned and spoke to two women who'd been sitting across the aisle – the first words between them all journey, a gruff direction – and I saw they were together. Without looking at me, the old man led them away, those two swaying folds of cloth following the hooded brown cloak down the aisle.

I hated tea, our stepmother Em's drink, so after stretching my legs I returned to the bus.

Not long after, a young man with close-cropped hair and a serious smile slipped in beside me.

'May?' he asked. A grey woollen hat lay in his lap.

'S . . . sure . . .' I hadn't used my voice all day, and even in that short time it had lost strength.

'May we speak English?'

'OK,' I said too loudly, overcompensating.

'Do you like Bob Marley?'

'I'm sorry?'

I couldn't understand what he'd said for his accent.

'Bob Marley. Do you know Bob Marley?'

I smiled, shrugged, nodded.

'Buffalo soldier?' I said.

He laughed with pleasure.

'English?'

'No. Australian.'

'I want to learn.'

'OK.'

'Can we speak?'

'Where are you from?' I asked.

'*Maroc.*'

'Where in Morocco?'

I didn't understand his answer, heard only a thick guttural sound, as if his tongue had got in the way of the words he wanted to say.

'Where?'

'*Dar El Baida,*' he said it again, slower. 'We say in Arabic. In English: Casablanca.'

The bus pulled away. We talked. He told me he went to university, that he was studying business, that he wanted to go to France. He quoted Bob Marley, shining suns and sweet air and dancing feet, his accent changing to something faintly Jamaican.

We must have been about the same age. He wrote his name down on a piece of paper: *Lhoussine*.

I read it aloud, got it wrong, tried again, this strange name. He tutored me till I'd settled on a close-enough version.

'You have a wife?' Lhoussine asked.

'No. You?'

He shook off my question.

'You have a girlfriend then?'

'No. One day perhaps,' I answered.

'*Inshallah.*' I had never heard this before, but would hear it a thousand times in the weeks ahead.

'If God wills it,' he said.

We were quiet for a moment.

'Where do you go?' Lhoussine asked then.

'Laâyoune,' I said. 'Western Sahara.'

'*Incroyable!*' he said, grasping my hand. '*El-Aaiún! I go to El-Aaiún too!* Why do you go to El-Aaiún?'

'Your dad needs to speak with you,' Em had said, just a fortnight before.

I was down the back, working on my bearded dragon. The monolithic block of pink sandstone had been purchased by the shire council years ago for a sculptor to carve a giant lizard, a gesture of reconciliation to the local Aboriginal people that would stand outside the council chambers. Other sculptors had been commissioned, but had baulked at the piece: the size of the block, the rust lines that ran through it, so unpredictable. But the stone had been cut from our own quarry, and though I was young, though it was my first commission, I was sure I could carve it.

'What is it?' I asked without looking up. The light was almost gone for the day, and I didn't want to lose any of it.

'It's important.'

I didn't detect the weight in her voice.

'What's it about?'

'Bas,' Em's voice sharpened, raw with something. She was not merely my father's emissary in this. I followed her into the house. In the kitchen she went to the sink, her back to me. *Go on*, she seemed to be saying, *you're on your own*.

He was sitting in the sunroom, what had once been a narrow front verandah but was now enclosed. It faced south, with louvers at either end for the sun. The room was filled with orange light. On the piano, which had been taken out there for storage years before, was a vase of hydrangeas, balls of light blue, darkening now. My father was sitting in his old armchair. He was erect in an unusual way, a tension in him I hadn't seen before. He looked at me closely as I stepped from the hallway onto the parched veran-dah floorboards, looking, I guessed, for a sign that Em might have told me already.

'Jack,' my father said before I'd had a chance to sit.

Aah, Jack, I thought. Always Jack.

'He's gone,' my father said.

I didn't understand. Of course he'd gone. Gone with glori-ous fanfare twelve months before. Gone to represent all of us on some foreign shore whether we wanted it or not. Gone to fulfil his destiny and ours.

'What do you mean?'

'He's gone,' my father repeated, his voice sombre. There was a sort of mourning in the room, but it was restrained, incomplete.

'Killed?'

'We don't know,' Em said, following me into the sunroom now, moving towards my father. She pulled up a seat beside him, her hand brushing his shoulder. I sat down too.

'I don't understand.'

'They say he's disappeared.'

'Disappeared?'

'They don't know where he is. The last anyone saw him was at a base, deep in the desert. He had a week's leave but he stayed. Everyone else went to the Canaries, but he stayed down there. In the desert. Now they say he's disappeared.'

'You mean he's gone AWOL?'

Even as I was saying it I knew what it would bring. Still, I couldn't stop the thought turning into the word, couldn't muffle its form as it emerged. When it came out it was hard, like a lash, and my father flinched. My heart was thumping already, racing with the echo of my error. I saw his eyes close, his brow tighten, his whole face grimace. I remembered the stories he used to tell of deserters. Of all his war tales, all his collection of fighting deeds, his deserter stories held special place as warnings to his sons. Men unmanned. Soldiers without rank. Weakness and cowardice and fear and dishonour incarnate. More powerful even than the stories of glory.

He gathered himself slowly, labouring to rise from under the weight of the shameful word. When he eventually lifted his head, and opened his eyes, he was blazing. He raised an index finger to me, shaking with anger, the same index finger that had tenderly stroked the pages of his atlas a year ago and proudly given his paternal assent to Jack's journey. He raised that finger and roared:

'Do . . . not,' each word measured, appalled, 'ever . . . say . . . such . . . a . . . thing.'

How monumental my transgression. The need for him to denounce it. I understood. Oh how I understood.

'He has done *nothing* –' the vehemence of it was shaking him – '*nothing* of the sort. He is *missing*. Got it? . . . Missing! . . . Got it?' It was almost a shriek.

I was nodding before he'd even finished. Nodding feebly, nodding to make him stop. I *got* it.

The way stories begin is important.

The sun continued to fall. In time my father's panting breath slowed, giving over to something else. There was my father and Em and Jack and me. The bonds of our relationships were almost tangible that faltering afternoon, the last rays picking them out. Father and sons and stepmother and brothers – an enclosed verandah full of the living past. A houseful of it, the town outside filled with history, impossible to measure. A late wren tapped its beak sharply against the louvers, a flash of blue. All three of us looked up as it darted away. My mother somewhere in this too, always.

It was left to Em to begin again.

'We know barely anything,' she said. 'We got a call during the week. They told us he'd disappeared. They said it's possible he's been killed, they said it's possible but they just don't know. They've been looking for him. They've sent patrols out to find him, but haven't been able to.'

They'd known this for days, I thought, but they'd kept it from me. Em quickened, her voice rising, a little shrill.

'They say it's possible he's been killed, but there's no evidence. There's no trace, there's –'

'I need you to go, Sebastian.'

The house was suddenly silent. Profoundly quiet.

How seldom my father spoke my name, how momentous when it happened. The power of it. The cruel, unsettling power.

FIVE

The land thinned, shedding its layers, first human, then plant. Finally the landscape itself flattened so much that the only things remaining were bus and road and rock-strewn plain. The nakedness was disorienting. I listened to the roadsong, a lullaby of engine and tyre and wind.

Lhoussine said he wanted to learn about Christian countries.

'What do you mean?' I asked.

'Christian countries,' he repeated. 'Australia, America, England.'

'There are no Christian countries. Only Christians.'

He paused, looked at me, doubtful. But he didn't disagree either.

'We have the Qur'an. You have the Bible,' he said.

These big ideas, and our simple words. I didn't know if it was Lhoussine, or the limitations of language, but I liked it. The directness of it. Perhaps too much language is a bad thing. Perhaps it gets in the way of what we really want to say. But I was callow too: I liked the idea I was representing my country. The thrill of it.

'I don't know anything about the Qur'an.'

'The words of Allah.'

'Like the Bible,' I said.

'The Bible is men's words. The Qur'an – it is Allah speaking.'

I shrugged my shoulders.

'Do you believe the Bible?' he asked.

I became suddenly defensive. There, on that bus, beginning its plunge into evening, on an endless road in North Africa, with someone I didn't know. I shouldn't have cared, but I did.

'The errors,' he continued.

'What errors?'

'Genesis,' he said. 'It is not true, no?'

'No,' I said, thinking of apples and snakes and arks and floods. 'It is a story. A metaphor. It is true in the way metaphors are true.'

I doubted his English was good enough to know what that meant, *metaphor*. I'm not sure I knew.

'And Jesus?'

'Yes.'

'He tells about God, yes?'

'Yes.'

'He is a prophet? A great prophet?'

'Yes.'

'But not God.'

I looked at him.

'If two people have books which describe their God, and one contains errors, how can it be preferred?'

He paused, and because I hadn't answered, said: 'The book without error must be true.'

I had nothing. My Catholic childhood left me ill-equipped for this. I knew about the mass and its rituals, but not the Bible. I knew about the sacraments, and the priests, but could quote no chapter, no verse. There was the profession of faith, the stations of the cross, and what remained of the liturgical calendar. I had the parables, and I had Mary and I had dogma. But I did not have the Bible, let alone the Qur'an. I could not look at Lhoussine then for fear of giving myself away. The possibility this man may have known more about the Bible than I did. And even if that wasn't so, did we, between us, have the language for these subtleties? I trawled through the lyrics of every Bob Marley song I knew for something that might help, but found nothing.

'And what about you?' I asked eventually, remembering, 'why are you going to El-Aaiún?'

'Like you. My brother!'

'Your brother is there?'

'There is nothing to do in Dar El Baida. El-Aaiún is far from home, but there is work. Not big money. Maroc is poor. Not like your country. But money. And work is important, no?'

'What does he do?'

'He is in the army too!' Lhoussine said, laughing.

As the sun fell and the desert softened, the road veered towards the coast again and began to follow it, a thin bitumen seam between land and sea. I looked down to the beach, so different from the soft, warm beaches I knew. It was like a primordial battleground, the front between the immense silent desert and the vast-pounding waves. Great clouds of sea-spray swirled in tumult above. The cliffs were so great, so gouged, so jagged that together they seemed a formidable record of the sea's victories. A few single, desperate huts perched on the cliffs, the hovels of lone fishermen seeking their catch from that utterly inhospitable sea.

The first shipwreck startled me. It was an old carcass, its flesh stripped away by the Atlantic long ago, and what remained was a rusting, ribbed skeleton. It was like seeing an unattended corpse for the first time: the travesty of it having been left alone, abandoned to disintegrate on this distant shore. The first startled me, but I counted eight more before the road turned inland once again, repelled finally by that too-desolate sea.

We travelled through the night, pulled blankets and jackets and jumpers tight, slept.

I woke as the bus slowed – a change in the engine, a subtle fall in its pitch. There was a weight against my right shoulder. I twisted myself from under Lhoussine and wondered how long the two of us had been like that, me his pillow. He stirred, and repositioned himself, his arms folding against the seat in front, head in the woollen hat resting on his own arms, back hunched, face turned towards me. In the dark his eyes opened, seemed to consider me, then closed once more.

I wiped condensation from the window with the bus curtain and peered outside. I could see the beams of our headlights, and the road stretching ahead. The verge, however, was jagged, and in the umbra of the headlights the bitumen fell away to sandy earth, the odd stunted bush, darkness beyond that.

The bus-driver dropped a gear and then a second. When we halted he slid his window open, and muttered into the night. I watched the set of his head, the angle of his neck. The conductor was soon awake and leaning over the driver's seat, his arm draped across the driver's shoulder. I watched the gestures building – hand and head – and the muffled words pushing backwards and forwards, rising without erupting. It seemed like a pantomime. Eventually the conductor stood, swivelled and, adopting the pose of weary messenger, spoke to the bus. One of the passengers responded, some question. The conductor grunted, and slowly a murmuring began to roll up the bus as people shook each other awake. One by one people's heads appeared above their seats as they straightened from sleep.

Through the window I saw a collection of low-set buildings, little more than mudbrick huts. Nearer to the bus and close to the ground, the tiny twin sparkles of some desert mammal's eyes levitated in the dark, before disappearing. Two or three torch beams weaved paths across the dusty ground, thin yellow streaks which, as they neared, leapt onto the bitumen. One of the uni-formed men following the beams reached the bus and grappled with the door handle. The conductor unlocked it and the man's voice was suddenly there with us in the cavity of the bus. He gave some order and we rose from our seats and walked down the aisle, down the steps and out into the winter-dark cold.

The moment my boot-sole hit the ground one of the uni-formed men exclaimed, then jerked torch-light into my eyes. My head turned as if I'd been struck. I was the only westerner on that bus in Western Sahara. The only white, and probably the only non-Muslim.

The soldier with the torch-light followed me as I joined Lhoussine in a huddle of men. He prodded me with his torch and said something.

'*Pardon*,' I replied, '*je ne parle pas Arabique.*' Without knowing if there was such a word as *Arabique*.

'*Où allez-vous?*' he said.

'El-Aaiún.'

'*Quoi?*'

'*Mon frère. Mon frère est là. El-Aaiún.*'

'*Nations Unies?*'

'*Oui.*'

He left and joined the other two soldiers who'd been watch-ing from a few paces, their three torch-beams boring holes of light out of the earth as they talked. They were in uniform, great coats down to their calves, their weapons slung across their shoulders, easy. Jack could have named the gun, listed its features and recounted its history. To me it was just a shooting device.

The soldier returned. In the glow of the bus headlights I could see a blood-red star stitched onto the shoulder of his khaki uniform.

'*Passeport*,' he demanded.

I took it out and handed it to him.

'*Soldat?*'

'*Pardon?*'

'*Militaire?*'

I shook my head furiously.

'*Australien?*' he asked, looking up from my passport.

'*Oui. Australien.*'

He murmured something, then turned, and called this out to his comrades. *Australien.* The entire bus, these passengers I'd been travelling with quietly since Casablanca, all of them suddenly knew my nationality. I felt exhibited. What did it mean to this soldier, stationed out here on the country's frontier, that I was Australian?

'*Venez*,' he said. His hand gripped my wrist, and he led me away from the bus and the road and the crowd, towards the long low-set buildings. I swivelled my head and saw Lhoussine moving towards the remaining soldiers, saw him speak. But the soldier yanked my wrist, swung me around and marched me away. The building ahead seemed somehow humble before the desert, its window gently pulsing with light. The soldier moved in behind me as we neared the door, the point of something pressing against the small of my back.

At the threshold, one of his comrades suddenly yelled out across the dark, and my guard pulled me to a stop and looked back. Through the doorway I could see a wooden table, a lantern set upon it, chairs at angles, a low bunk against a grimy wall, a blanket balled at its foot. I waited as the second soldier joined us, boot-crunch on tufts of grass, and spoke softly to my escort, in case I understood. The solider holding me grunted, then released my wrist.

I started back towards the bus, towards Lhoussine who had broken from the soldiers and was waiting for me, apart.

'They are stupid,' he said. And then, murmuring to himself in Arabic while he looked for the right word, '. . . and hungry.'

'Greedy?'

'Yes! Stupid and greedy.'

The soldiers resumed their search. This time it was meticulous. They swept through us, checking the identity cards of each passenger, all of us shivering in the night. One red-star checked the men, a second the women, the third – the one who'd led me away – searched the bus. In the glare of its ceiling lights his hands clawed the overhead storage compartments, dragging bags out, their contents showering onto the floor and the seats. At the height of his ransack, he stopped and pulled a cheap travel bag from the bus, down the steps and onto the ground. It was the sort you'd find at bus terminals the world over, striped red and white and blue. He lifted it, and waved it to us, his voice agitated. No one spoke. He lifted the bag higher. The night suddenly deepened. He raised the bag one-handed above his head, obscuring stars in his wild shaking. This time, somewhere, feet shuffled. It was a tiny movement, but sharpened by the cold air. It was enough. The soldier turned to the sound, and people parted, offering up whoever had made it. He reached a shaking woman, flung the bag at her feet and yelled, his mouth contorted near her face. The woman bent and slowly unzipped the bag. Its contents spilled out, the top of the bag gaping like a wound, the evidence against her exposed, some contraband.

The soldier led *her* away. No one came forward in protest, no husband, no father, no brother. Once more the soldier stalked towards the hut with his quarry, but this time he crossed the threshold, closed the door, and disappeared. The woman's bag stood on the ground like a thing defeated, hollowing a space from the crowd of people.

The silence was measured in heartbeats.

I watched the building and the glow of light from its window. I willed it to change, to show the movement of bodies in the room – to see and understand, but there was nothing. Eventually the long quiet broke. Someone whispered, then another. The murmuring grew louder until it sounded like a horde of locusts in the night, resistance. The conductor approached the two remaining soldiers, a responsibility cast upon him. I thought I heard a distant muffled cry from the glowing building. The conductor's voice was filled with protest and plea, both, but the soldiers were unmoved. The conductor became more and more shrill until his voice broke, and he stepped away from the soldiers, separating himself. Whether he was released by them or commissioned with some new task, I couldn't tell.

He crossed to where the driver was squatting on the bitumen by the front tyre of the bus. The conductor hissed at him, low and into his ear, before raising his right arm, as if the haunching driver was a dog he might strike. The driver cowered at first, then rose to his feet and followed the conductor, close to his heel.

I was the first they approached because in the dark I was just another body. But when the conductor spoke I didn't understand; I shrugged my shoulders and raised the palms of my hands. Perhaps he thought it impossible to communicate to me what was happening. Or maybe he was embarrassed, even ashamed. That I, the *Australien*, should be witness to this, let alone part of it. He moved on to Lhoussine, who was already reaching into his

36

wallet. Passenger by passenger the conductor moved among us, each without exception.

When it was done and the ransom paid, the woman was returned. Her head was bowed. I looked for some sign of what had happened inside that low-set building, the folds of her cloth disturbed, some unevenness in her step. She bent to her bag, and closed it. A man stepped forward, lifted it to his shoulder and waited for her instructions. The woman made for the stairs of the bus while we stood dumb. Again the crowd parted for her, some right she'd earned. Ultimately, this was something that could not be explained in any language.

I expected this would be the end, that we would all now board the bus and be on our way again. But no.

There may have been a murmur I hadn't heard, or perhaps one of the men had set an example, and the others knew to follow. However it happened, my fellow-passengers began moving as one. Some rolled mats onto the ground. Others simply collected the folds of their gowns and knelt on the earth. Lhoussine joined them, the soldiers too, each of them facing the same direction, back down the highway, back the way we'd come. Together they bowed low, and pressed their foreheads to the ground. They incanted and rose and raised their hands to their heads and bowed again. Whether praying for forgiveness or from fear or habit I couldn't hope to know. Theirs was a quiet fervour, and I felt my separateness.

I stood in the dark, the merest glow of light on the eastern horizon, until their kneeling, and rising was done. Then I stepped back onto the bus with them, the day beginning, finally, to crack open. In those last moments before the bus plunged forward, I wished for something in my hands, some stone to turn in my fingers, some surface to stroke and ease my anxiety.

SIX

El-Aaiún looked to have been swept by the ocean winds into a
shallow trench where once an ancient river had coursed its way
to the sea. Near the low, black tents of nomads on the fringe of
town, foraging goats and camels raised their heads to watch the
bus rumble past. The thread of highway passed beneath a trium-
phal arch of mudbrick. Large chunks of baked clay had fallen
loose from the arch and lay in piles of rubble either side of the
road. As the bus droned out from beneath the arch I saw, off to
the right beyond the town's perimeter, an army base. Inside the
high-security fencing were gleaming modular barracks, and large
military vehicles moved slowly around the compound as if they
were searching for an opening to get out.

Inside the town we passed housing blocks daubed in white,
sheets flapping from their windows. The administration buildings
looked like pieces of pastel Lego, grass grew between the cracks in
the concrete aprons of petrol stations, and a fierce wind blew. The
town's people seemed stilled, as if they'd stopped breathing the
moment the bus entered the city and we were travelling through
a diorama. The body of a shopkeeper standing in a doorway. Two

women facing each other on a street corner. Lone figures with their heads down, faces turned from the wind, eyes averted from the sun. An old man seated on a crate in a patch of shade beside a wall. There were bands of children standing or squatting close, like the trapped citizens of Pompeii. Army trucks idled, their trays filled with soldiers, so many sun-glassed animals, all eyes turned on us.

The bus pulled into the *gare routière* and stopped. The moment the driver cut the engine, we too joined the stillness of the place. A bus company official left his ticket office and walked heavily towards us. Two children bearing trays piled high with small plastic bags of water came in through the gates, disappearing for a moment into the cloud of dust and exhaust which trailed the bus. One by one people emerged from the shade of the terminal building to greet passengers – their stepping into the heat and light startling, an act of magic.

But after the long journey, there was no urgency among the passengers. I followed Lhoussine slowly down the aisle and onto the tarmac. He stopped and looked about. Stepping round him I moved clear of the bus to watch the conductor climb the ladder onto the roof where he loosened the tarpaulin ropes. Lhoussine found his brother and they embraced, kissing once, twice, three times on alternate cheeks, the student and the soldier.

The conductor lowered our luggage to us, and I slung the comforting weight of my duffel bag over my shoulder before stepping away from the bus, into a moment of uncertainty. I didn't want to meet Lhoussine's eyes, didn't want to restart something that had ended, because whatever thread of friendship there'd been between us was broken now. Did we even need to speak again, he and I, this man who'd been my companion these last hours?

But Lhoussine came towards me, his brother a step behind.

I can't recall the brother's name. I remember the uniform with its lone red star and the hat he'd not taken off, and the rifle at his back. He was thin and serious but the grip of his hand was soft.

'My brother has a car,' Lhoussine said. 'May I invite?'

'No,' I said. 'It's OK. Thanks.'

'I would like to invite.'

'Thank you, but no. Go well. Goodbye.'

I turned away. I was hard. Even now I'm not quite sure why.

A few minutes later I saw them again through the glass of the bus-station café, where I was drinking mint tea and circling the names of hotels in my guidebook. Lhoussine and his brother were walking slowly away down the dusty street towards a car, their hands touching. I couldn't help thinking of Jack, and a group of us boys waiting outside the old Art Deco cinema in Margaret Street in Toowoomba.

We'd bought our tickets and were hanging on the footpath, checking things out, Jack the centre of it all. Then suddenly he was beside me, and he was telling the older boys something about me – I can't remember what – and he wrapped his arm around my shoulder as he talked. But even after the conversation shifted and something else attracted their attention, Jack still lounged beside me, the gentle weight of his forearm on the side of my neck a solid thing, more permanent than anything I'd known for ages. For long seconds Jack and I stood there, together, leaning against the wall of the picture theatre, looking out at the world as it moved around us. Then it was over, and there was a movie to watch, stuff to make happen, a gang of boys to rejoin. And me confused for months afterwards, desperately seeking that moment again.

★

The first two hotels were full of peacekeepers, not a room free. As I approached the entrance of the third, the Hotel Lakouara, a convoy of white four-wheel drives was forming in the car park, half a dozen of them, each marked with two enormous black letters – UN – on their sides. Soldiers were opening doors and slamming them shut, engines were coming to life, and one by one the vehicles were pulling out of their bays into the convoy. When all were in place, they passed through the hotel gate onto the street and swept away, each travelling at the same speed, the same distance between them, as if it had all been choreographed.

I almost raised my arm as they went past, nearly stepped forward to wave one of the vehicles down. Because, after all, I'd reached my destination. I was here, in El-Aaiún, and there they were, the peacekeepers, so close, my brother one of them. They probably knew my brother, those men in their sunglasses, and would do what they could, surely, to help. Instead, I stood there on the footpath with my bag slung over my shoulder as the convoy passed, straining to make out the features of each soldier behind his darkened window. And they looked out at me. Wondering, I guess, what a western civilian was doing there, looking as lost as I must have. It was only when the vehicles had disappeared from view at the end of the long street, and the sound of each of their fading engines fell away to nothing, that I went inside.

'Vous avez . . . une . . . chambre?'

My crude French, mere fragments of sound I was trying to pass off as language.

'No. All full,' the man at the desk answered in English.

'Where can I find a room then?'

He shrugged. My predicament was nothing to him.

'The souk,' he said, 'cheaper.' That consolation.

Then, with slow gestures of the back of his hand, he began

motioning me out of his foyer, as if I was dust that needed sweeping away.

I set out again and reached a vast square bordered with avenues of date palms like ancient columns, their ragged fronds harried by the wind. The mosque appeared and a water tower and an array of public monuments. Buildings the colour of the local sand seemed to have risen out of the ground, for some evanescent purpose, as if they might soon crumble and be trodden by goat-hoof back into the soil again. Two boys rode past on a bike, the older pedalling, the younger balancing on the cross-bar, both legs dangling down one side. The arms of the older boy stretched either side of the younger; the one pedalling leaned forward, his chest pressed against the back of his brother like they were one creature, just as Jack and I had ridden the streets of The Springs many years ago. They rolled silently past, interrogating me, their two heads moving, their four dark eyes following me in perfect synchronicity.

The streets narrowed on the other side of the square. The souk had no grand entrance like the medina in Casablanca, nor was it contained by high walls. Its markets spread out organically to fill the many-fingered streets of the district. There were tiled arcades, with food stalls colonising the footpaths, rows of them nestled under low tattered awnings, and plastic chairs scattered when men rose from their tables and knocked them askew with their polished shoes as they left. Even here there were shoeshine boys. A push-cart, handmade from discarded bicycle wheels and the sides fashioned from chicken-wire, languished in the street. Inside a café, a boy was bent before a soft-drink fridge, his body glowing in the fluorescent light. I watched him lift a crate of empty bottles onto his cart, which he tilted then heaved into motion, wheeling it down the middle of the road. I entered and drank a bottle of Coke – a small comfort.

★

I lay on the bed in a room in the Hôtel Atlas, the first hotel I'd found with its name in French as well as Arabic. The grimy shirt stuck to my back and my boots hung over the end of the bed. I looked at the cracked plaster on the ceiling and was exhausted. Already it felt like I'd been travelling for years, and had spent a lot of myself to get here. It seemed impossible that a week earlier I'd been lying on my own bed in The Springs looking up at Michelangelo's slaves, taped near the ceiling. I closed my eyes. I drifted towards sleep before some passing sound from beyond the window – a hushed voice, or a shoe scraping across the ground – startled me and I was overcome by a wave of anxiety, the same feeling as when I first landed.

I got up, showered, changed, and went back downstairs to where the innkeeper sat at the desk, unmoving.

'*Les Australiens*,' I said.

'*Australiens? Oui?*'

'*Je cherche les Australiens.*'

The innkeeper gave me a dull nod, as if what I'd said was some truth taken for granted, utterly unsurprising.

'*Où je peux . . . trouver les Australiens?*' I asked, working hard to assemble the words. Where can I find them?

He made some movement of his head, neck, shoulders. He looked long at me then, trying to understand. I started again.

'*Nations Unies. Les soldats Australiens.*'

'Aah.'

He grew animated, and spoke a torrent of what I assumed were directions, the gestures of his arms like those of a flailing swimmer.

'*Je ne comprends pas*,' I said.

'*Demain*,' he said after considering me again. '*Demain matin. Vous comprenez?*'

I nodded. I was fairly sure I understood. Tomorrow morning.

★

I went to bed that night with French in my head, all those soft words swirling around, each running into the others. Mock conversations. Laboriously laying words one beside the other, I was no more assured than a toddler with building blocks. I could see their shapes, and hear the echoes of the conversation from the day gone. Questions and responses, guessing at meanings I'd missed, I couldn't turn the conversations off, couldn't stop the sentence-building. When finally sleep came, it was because I was exhausted, not my body, but my brain.

In all my time there it never occurred to me to learn Arabic, to learn anything more than the few meagre words that even the laziest travellers pick up as they pass through. The truth, it seems to me now, was that learning Arabic would have meant trying to understand *them*. But French was neutral ground, as if the conversations about hotels and bread and bus tickets were taking place in some safe no-man's land. Perhaps it was the same for them too.

SEVEN

The innkeeper was there again the next morning.

'*Les Australiens?*' I reminded him.

'*Oui, oui.*'

He went to the hotel doorway and, silhouetted, called out into the street. Loud and insistent he called again, agitating the air, as if issuing a threat to the whole town. The buildings reverberated already with the day's rising heat. Eventually a young boy emerged from somewhere across the road. The innkeeper stepped out into the sun, and when the boy reached him, placed a hand around the back of his neck. The man lowered his voice. I recognised just the word *Australien*. Then the boy was off, and as I followed the man back inside the hotel he pointed me to a seat in the lobby.

'*Attends. Attends.*'

And so I waited. The king on the wall. The tiled floor with a mosaic spreading across the room, its geometric pattern broken by the chairs and the low coffee table. I noticed little ridges of sand swept up against the walls by the wind. As I waited a guest came down the stairs, greeted the innkeeper and stepped into the street. I opened my notebook and reread everything my father

45

and Em and I had gathered about Jack and Africa. The key dates and places and people. There again was the name of Andrew Grose, and his rank – Lieutenant-Colonel – the contingent commander, the one I now sought.

It was three hours before the boy returned. He was accompanied by a soldier, tall in the doorway, his head turning to where I sat in the armchair, sizing me up before striding across the foyer with long confident steps. They taught you how to walk in the army. He was dressed in standard army fatigues, those splotches of grassland and forest. His sleeves were neatly folded, a perfect symmetry in the way they sat against each of his biceps. He wore a slouch hat with its leather strap tight at the point of his chin. His face was square, his jaw sharp, his sun-mottled skin and thin red hair shaded by the hat. I read his name – Logan – on the patch stitched above his breast pocket. Had Jack become as hard as this? I wondered.

'Well, what have we got here?' he said, breaking into a grin, wide and mischievous, his eyes glinting with humour. He was in his late twenties. Though it was only days since I'd last heard that accent, it seemed much longer. I smiled back.

'Yeah,' I said, rising to meet him. 'I know.'

'Long way from home.'

I laughed, and took his hand. I barely noticed how vigorously he shook it – his strength, his exuberance – because for the first time since I'd arrived in Africa I was starting to relax. It didn't matter that I'd never met him before, that if I'd come across him back home I would have stayed clear, would have been sceptical of anyone so comfortable in his uniform. After so many days of being on edge, I yielded entirely to his welcome.

'So,' he said, smiling still, 'what's brought you here? Did you take a wrong turn up the road somewhere?'

I laughed again.

'No,' I said. 'I'm looking for someone, Jack Adams.'

How quickly that transformed him. He dropped the smile, stepped back, and folded his arms against his chest. How brief that easy moment between us had been.

I hadn't thought I needed to be careful. Had so wanted to stop thinking for a while, gain a respite from the wariness. But now Logan stared at me, blue-eyed, his jaw set once more. In the long silence I was aware of the boy's voice at the reception desk, heard the innkeeper grunt a reply.

'Who the hell might you be, then?' Logan said.

'His brother. I'm Jack's brother. I've come to find him.'

'You're his *brother*?' As if it was preposterous.

'Yes, I am.'

He must have seen this was true. How could he not recognise our likeness?

'I've come for him,' I said.

'Have you now.'

Was this unexpected tussle simply the sergeant protecting a fellow-soldier against strangers? I took a breath, began again.

'My name is Sebastian Adams. I'm looking for my brother. I've come a long way to find him. Can you help?'

I trailed Logan out of the souk, the Arabs stepping aside to let the peacekeeper through. He ignored the street vendors who called out to him, his eyes straight, head erect. He was easy to follow. When we reached his four-wheel drive he tossed some coins to a group of kids who'd been keeping watch over it.

'Get in.'

I felt like a prisoner being escorted to court. By then I'd realised that of course Logan was a mere errand boy, and it was the Lieutenant-Colonel who'd decide what assistance I'd get. Or whether I'd get any help at all.

EIGHT

I look back now and still don't know what to make of Grose. He barely seems real, claiming too great a place in my memory of those days. He didn't so much fill a room, as encompass it. It wasn't just his physical size – it was the stillness of his voice and his body, the entirety of his being. Rather than shrink with recall he has, if anything, grown larger, more distorted.

His office was bare: a desk and two chairs, a single grey filing cabinet and three or four maps taped to the wall. On the desk was a plastic tray with a single sheet of paper in it, an unsheathed, bone-handled Bowie-knife resting on it as a paperweight. At the top right-hand corner of the desk was an object the size of a man's hand that I didn't recognise: circular with ridges running vertically up its sides, sand-coloured with a disc of dark green on top. Some exotic toy, I guessed. In the centre of the desk was a book, an old hardback with a faded red cloth covering, *Also sprach Zarathustra* in black lettering on its spine. It was open face-down, the pages splayed, as if Grose had just laid it aside, calmly, and only then risen to greet me.

His shirt was open at the neck, the hairless chest bared and glistening with a sheen of sweat. Light skidded off his shaved head, shiny with moisture.

Grose pointed to a seat and lifted his own chair one-handed through the air before placing it beside mine. When he sat, his knee brushed against my own. I flinched. Logan brought in two bottles of Coke, handed them to us, and left, glancing at me over his shoulder as he closed the door. Grose prised the cap off the bottle and it hissed.

'None of the local rubbish,' he said, his deep voice almost a croon.

He raised his drink in a toast.

'The original and the best, for our Australian guest.'

His rhyme amused him, but his smile was not yet something I could hold onto. He put the bottle down without drinking from it and leant back, swivelling his chair and resting his right elbow on the table, his body reclining, the great head still, the cold blue eyes considering me.

'So Sebastian Adams,' he said at last, 'here you are.'

One could wither under that gaze.

'I've come for my brother, sir,' I said.

'Seek and thou shalt find, Sebastian? Do you believe that?'

'Well, yes – you've got to try.'

'I can see him in you.'

He watched me, unblinking. It felt like *he* was trying to pry something out of *me*.

'Sir,' I said, 'can you tell me what you know? Have you had any luck? Have you found him yet?'

'Didn't your father believe me? I told him myself, Sebastian. From this very room I rang him. There is nothing he doesn't know. Not . . . one . . . single . . . thing. You've come a long way for nothing.'

'I wanted to see for myself,' I replied.

Grose laughed – a cackle, high and charged. Then, abrupt as it started, it stopped.

'And what is it, precisely, you want to see?'

I stuttered. 'I . . . I . . . I'm his brother . . . I –'

'You want a wound to thrust your hand into,' Grose said, speaking over me. 'Is that it?'

He paused, waiting, but I'd become entranced.

'Your brother was a soldier, Sebastian. He had a duty to his fellow-soldiers, even when he was on leave. A soldier does not stop being a soldier. He should have gone with them. Instead he stayed down there alone. He went out. He did not come back. He packed his kit one morning, stepped through his door into the desert and has not been seen since.'

'What happened?'

'He failed himself.'

'I don't understand.'

'He failed the army, and he failed me.'

'I don't understand.'

'He failed you, too.'

I looked at him, this giant. I thought of Logan and our little wrestle over Jack, a teaser for this.

'I have no idea what you are talking about. He's one of your men isn't he? But now you don't seem to care.'

'Care? Do you know what it costs to make a man?'

He was mad.

'Because that's what I do, Sebastian, create men. Soldiers. And I protect them too.'

He looked away, seemed to drift, seemed to be talking to himself when he spoke again. 'I care very much about my men.'

He stood up and walked to the filing cabinet in the corner of the room. He returned to the table and placed a document in front of me, two pages with a staple in the top left-hand corner. On it was a list of names.

'My men,' he said.

Then, without looking at it, his eyes on me, he began:

'Abrahams, Samuel. Lieutenant. Twenty-six. Born in Balaclava, Melbourne. Second of three boys. Both his parents are doctors. Received the Commander-in-Chief's Award and a university medal while at ADFA. Quite brilliant. Enjoys military history. This is the best opportunity he'll get for action for a while. If he survives his mother's expectations and marries well he'll be Army Chief one day. Adair, Anthony James. Corporal. Combat engineer. Thirty-four. Born in Maitland. Father is a boilermaker, his mother stayed at home to raise him and his five siblings. One brother, four sisters. Married to Kayla, with three children of his own. Races motorised go-karts on weekends. Likes the security of the army, the regular pay and being able to say he's got a career. Glad to have six months away.'

Without missing a beat, he continued.

'Adams, Jack. Twenty-two. Born in Victoria Springs in the Lockyer Valley. Hides his middle name, Maria, which was given to him by his Catholic mother who died in a house fire when he was nine. Private in Signals. A crack shot. A local hero. The older of two brothers. Joined the army to see the world. Volunteered for this contingent because he wanted to do something serious with his life.'

Grose paused. *Maria*. I'd forgotten about that. Our father had chosen 'Jack' and Mum had selected 'Sebastian', and because I had no middle name, Jack's had disappeared.

'Often intense,' Grose resumed, 'he became increasingly aloof. Was last seen at camp on Tuesday, the twenty-ninth of December 1992 at 2200 hours.'

He leaned back in his chair, and folded his hands across his chest.

51

I took a deep breath.

'You've given up, sir? Is that what you're saying?'

Grose shut his eyes and his nostrils flared. His eyes remained closed as he reached for his Coke and took a deep sip. They remained like that as he lowered the bottle to the table, as it tapped against the wooden surface, and settled. As he lifted his hand and rested its palm against his breast bone. Breathed. And breathed again. I watched his chest rise, and fall. Then suddenly, almost violently, his eyes were open.

That gaze held me for a long time. Then he left his chair and walked around the desk. The thickness of his neck showed, the bones at the back of his skull. He reached up to one of the maps taped to the wall – grasped it, tore it down and turned in one movement and spread it roughly on the desk.

'See the dots, boy. Can you see them? They're not even towns, most of them. They're settlements, handfuls of human beings huddled together in the sand. Refuges against the desert. The rest *is* desert. Know this about your brother: he went out into that desert and he did not come back.'

'You said that. But what happened then?'

'How does a thing happen?' He was soft again. 'How is it the sun burns your skin? How is it your organs collapse without water? How is it the wind here that licks your throat and your temples without pause will drive you mad?'

He was stroking the desk, following its grains with his forefinger.

'How is it our mothers bring us into the world, only to desert us?'

'Is Jack dead or not?' I asked, my heart thumping, unable to comprehend why Grose would play with me like this.

'Is that all you want to know?'

Grose reached for the disc on his desk. His vast hand covered the thing as he drew it towards him, the metal smooth on timber.

His great fingers began spinning it like a top, round and round, faster and faster. Those hands were agile.

'Is Adams dead?' he said to himself, as if considering the idea for the first time. 'Is Adams dead? When he left he accepted whatever dangers the desert presented. I train my men to take risks. But not stupid ones. You want me to tell you he was bitten by a scorpion. Or got lost. Or was captured by bandits. You want me to tell you he stepped on a UXO –'

Then Grose scooped up his toy and tossed it to me in one action. There was no time to think. I caught the thing in my lap, its ribbed sides, my fingers tightening, knuckles stiffening. I looked at the contrasting colours, the smoothness and the roughness of its surfaces, the perfect symmetry of it. I guessed then it was a landmine and placed it carefully back on the table, as far from Grose's reach as I could. When I looked up he was studying me. I was no match for his gaze.

'Well, Sebastian, he may have. Those things are everywhere down here. If *you* wander off the track there's a good chance *you'll* step on one. But that is not the point.'

'Where was he?'

'Here.'

I looked at the map, his index finger against the paper obscuring a name, teasing me, as if to say, Is *this* what you want? He laughed, and slowly lifted his hand, surveying me. But I would give him nothing. I leaned forward and read the name his finger had revealed.

'Tifariti,' I said. To myself, to the contours on the map, to each of the letters which made up the name. It was one of the names in my notebook from the first news my father had heard, but the place was too small for any map I'd seen before then. It looked strange there on Grose's map, *sounded* different now as I pronounced it quietly, as if it was being spoken for the first time.

'You can look yourself in the eye here, Sebastian. You can do that here. There's nowhere else to look. Here's your chance. You either see things straight or you go blind. Eyes that see, Sebastian. Ears that hear. You will wake from your ignorance. You will shed your bliss.'

He laughed, a booming laugh that drew out long until it was almost jolly, rolling in undulation. But when it ended, it stopped cold.

'Is he dead? That's not the question, Sebastian. Why did he leave? *That* is the question. Logan!'

His voice was like a gunshot, and the room was still in echo when Logan entered.

'Adams's brother thinks we haven't done enough. He thinks *we* might be responsible, rather than his brother. Give him a copy of the report.'

Grose turned his back. He moved to the wall and raised the map with his two outstretched arms, pinning it up high like an altar reredos.

NINE

I read the report in one of the souk cafés.

Jack was on leave from midday on Sunday 29 December, 1992. He and Sergeant William Logan had been stationed at Tifariti for six weeks. The two men who relieved them – Corporal Adair, and a Private Duffy – had flown in from El-Aaiún that morning. Their plane had landed at the airstrip at 0900 hours. There'd been a debriefing, after which Jack and Logan were off duty. Logan returned to El-Aaiún on the plane that afternoon, joined a few other soldiers and disappeared to the beaches and bars of the Canary Islands for a week. Jack stayed in Tifariti. Jack disappeared.

Adair and Duffy were the last to see him. Their accounts were in the report, but neither had much to say. They'd eaten together that night in the mess at 1930. They were surprised Jack wasn't returning to El-Aaiún with Logan. Jack told them he wanted to explore, told them there was a rock formation a couple of hundred kilometres away he wanted to see, some ancient archaeological site. When I read that, it pulled at my gut. He told Adair and Duffy he'd be away three or four days, no more, and in the morning he was gone. The army discovered a small Polisario convoy – two vehicles – had left soon after dawn, 0600 hours. No, Jack hadn't told Adair and Duffy exactly where he was going, where precisely the rock site was supposed to be. No, they hadn't asked. Shouldn't they have? No, he was on leave, and anyway he was a different sort of bloke. Wanted to keep to himself. They respected that in a man.

Logan was interviewed too, the transcript attached to the report. What had Jack said to him? Where might he have gone? What was this interest in rock formations? Was it a ruse? What sort of relationship had Jack developed with the Polisario, the independence movement? Did Logan know what might have happened to him?

But Logan knew nothing, couldn't sensibly guess, told the Captain who interviewed him only that something must have 'gone wrong' –

In your opinion, Sergeant Logan, what happened?

There are so many possibilities, sir.

Go on.

I don't know . . . all sorts of things.

What are some examples, Sergeant?

He could have got separated from his lift, sir . . . he could
    have got lost, or been killed, or had an accident, a
    mine . . . it could easily have been a mine, sir . . . or
    taken prisoner . . .

Do you really think so? Seriously, Sergeant Logan. What
    else? Give me something else, something plausible.

Anything's possible, sir. It's the desert, after all.

We would have heard, don't you think? Polisario would
    have given us any information they had.

It's a big desert, sir. With respect, sir. Not even Polisario
    know everything.

I must ask you this for the record, Sergeant Logan. Do you
    know where he is?
No, sir.

I took the report back to my hotel room, and reread it that
night. Again and again, as if it was a poem I meant to get by heart.

I sought courage the next day, clarity. The number of times I
left the Hôtel Atlas to return to Grose's office. But then, usually before I'd even left the souk, I began to doubt myself. I was
a spluttering match against the ferocity of his fire. I'd practise
conversations in my head but find nothing to ask that wouldn't
shrivel before him. Every hole in the report would suddenly fill,
every angle I thought needed exploring would straighten, every
question no longer needed an answer.

I gave up and decided to walk instead, to wander, hoping something tangible might fall out of the report that way, some clue.

The street was more alive in the late afternoon than at any
other time during the day, men playing draughts under awnings,
children running circles in the street, chasing each other or evad-
ing the Peugeots. The wind was up. There was a trace of sea
in it, faint, but it was there, hanging onto the breeze this far,
twenty kilometres in from the ocean. Dogs emerged from their
shade to sniff at the ankles of the old men, and cock their bony
legs against fading walls. I looked for froth at their mouths and
flinched when one approached, dingo-lean, and barked. A boy
struck at it with his foot and the animal whimpered away. I passed
a post-office where the mailbox was being painted over finally,
after so long the Spanish word *correos* disappearing forever beneath
brushstrokes of red.

In time I reached the old cathedral, the tallest building in the city, and stopped before its high wooden doors. I craned my head at the twin white towers, their squared lines sharp against the blue. Flakes of whitewash were coming off its flanks, the white towers, the dome above the apse. It had been fifteen years since the Spanish withdrew, and the doors were long-sealed.

Through the wall of the apse hundreds of shadow-dark Latin crosses had been cut for ventilation, so you could see through the gaps into the belly of the church. The rays of afternoon sun cast delicate crosses onto the tiles of the cathedral floor. Peering through one of the tiny cross-portals, I said a prayer for my mother. And remembered Jack.

We'd bused to Brisbane, the entire school – a hundred uniformed school children for an Ash Wednesday mass by the archbishop. We scattered like marbles out of the bus, the teachers unable to contain us. Jack didn't even bother to run, just calmly disappeared behind the cathedral. I leaned against the cathedral wall, feeling the rough porphyry blocks against my back, gazing at the aerated clouds billowing across the purple sky. A yo-yo came off the string of a boy playing close by and clattered against the apron of stones, and soon the teachers were gathering us to march inside, where we would be trapped for the next hour and a half.

But not Jack. He was twelve, his last year of primary school, and couldn't be found. One of the teachers called me from the pew just before mass started. I didn't know where he was. The teacher then looked each of his classmates in the eye and asked them the same thing. As mass started, two of the teachers left to continue the search in the streets surrounding the cathedral. They even went as far as the river, we heard later. All us kids were distracted those first few minutes of the mass, excited, wondering what he was up to. But soon enough the ritual prevailed, and we were drawn in to the readings, and the gospel and the homily and the prayers of the faithful. The standing and the sitting, and our scabbed knees on the wooden kneelers.

We'd forgotten about Jack entirely when, as the archbishop stood behind the altar to consecrate the bread and the wine, he appeared at the door of the sacristy. Who knows how he'd got inside or for how long he'd been there. He didn't linger in the doorway, but stepped confidently out into the sanctuary. I gasped. We all did, one by one, as we nudged each other and looked up and saw Jack standing behind the oblivious archbishop at just the moment he lifted his arms and raised his eyes to God for the first time. Jack followed. Lifted his face and closed his own eyes and raised his hands.

We were transfixed. The audacity. Though there was nothing furtive or smirking about it. It was imitation, of course, but somehow it was more than that too, more solid. Jack seemed as sure as the archbishop, had taken his place and raised his arms no less confidently. None of us dared move, not even the teachers. We watched as the archbishop lowered the great disc of liturgical bread to the table, knelt, kissed the white altar cloth, then took the silver chalice and raised it up also. Jack followed, his hands lifting his imaginary second chalice to the heavens. We gazed in absolute silence, utterly entranced. If the archbishop had looked out at us he would have seen a sort of terror on our faces. We had somehow become complicit.

The archbishop first realised something out of the ordinary had happened when Jack stepped past him, having finished whatever it was he'd intended, to surrender. One of the attendant priests, who'd been murmuring in prayer near the altar, opened his eyes, stood quickly. As Jack stepped down from the sanctuary the priest grasped him by the back of the arm. The archbishop had paused, and our school principal was already striding down the side aisle — to receive Jack from the priest, to wheel him round and lead him out of the church. Jack was grinning by this time, wide as could be; he winked at one of his mates as he left, gave a thumbs-up to another. But all that was just decoration, trimming.

Jack was suspended for the rest of the term. He would have been expelled but they still had pity on him in the long wake of our mother's death. Our father didn't bother going through the motions of disapproval. Em was embarrassed, then angry that Jack would be around the house more, the difficulties of that. But soon something happened, I don't know what — a thawing. She began smiling at how the town was telling the story of larrikin Jack and the big priest in the big city. She too was under his spell.

TEN

'Oi.'

It was Logan, the door of his landcruiser slamming shut after him.

'There hasn't been a Hail Mary or an Our Father in there for fifteen years.'

'Just checking it out.'

'You want to attract attention, do you?'

'No . . . I . . . it's strange to see it here, that's all.'

Logan stood with legs astride, hands on hips, as if striking a pose for a camera.

'Come on,' he said, 'come for a drink.'

The sun had begun to fall when we drove through a sentried gate and pulled in at the UN bar. Half a dozen white four-wheel drives stood in front, noses to the curb. A group of peacekeepers got out of their vehicle as Logan parked, a looseness about them all, slipping their duties already. They pushed open the door of the building and music escaped briefly, the first familiar stuff I'd heard for days.

I followed Logan. Inside the music was loud enough to feel against my skin. *Our* music, I thought. There were soldiers in groups, drinking. A bartender – also a soldier – stood behind a trestle-table with glasses laid upside down on a bar mat. Behind him were large refrigerators, a mosaic of beer stickers on their doors from all the peacekeeping nationalities. On a wall near the fridges was a large flag of a boxing kangaroo, standing yellow on a green background, its gloved paws shaping up, ready for all comers.

'Look who we've got here,' the bartender called out over the music.

All heads turned to me. The bartender was short, but his shoulders and neck were thick with muscle, and his hairless forearms, swollen in the fluorescent light, glistened with sweat.

'You alright?' he asked, and cocked his head.

'Yeah . . . I'm –'

'We know who you are, mate, Adams's brother. Come from Oz to find him. That's right, isn't it?'

'Yeah.'

'Yeah,' he repeated, some judgement hanging suspended in the air. I was being studied. All the conversations in that small room had paused, their weight pressing the air. Was Jack's story known to the entire peacekeeping force?

'Yeah,' he said again, looking me over, then at Logan. After a moment the bartender nodded, his body easing, satisfied enough, perhaps only that I was no threat. 'Have a beer.'

Logan tipped his head back and downed the first in one, then led the way to a table beside the wall, a second beer in hand, his pale skin glowing, every freckle.

'Wherever we go mate, it's our responsibility, isn't it? Heh?'

I sat facing the door. I'd be the first to see Jack if he happened to walk in off the street.

'What's that?' I said.

'To bring the beer. Run the bar. This'd be a dull old shit-hole without it. Decent piss, that's our job. Always has been.'

'Uh huh,' I said, still looking for something I could grasp.

'You don't look impressed, mate. Well, let me give you a history lesson. Know your history, do you?'

I shook my head, trying to retreat, wondering how much room I had.

'What about your geography?'

I shrugged.

'Let's test you. Where are we?'

'El-Aaiún.'

'More information.'

'The UN bar in El-Aaiún.'

'You're getting colder,' he said, laughing at his joke. 'Try again.'

'Western Sahara.'

'Warmer that time. Keep going.'

I stumbled around, no idea of what he was driving at, enjoying none of it.

'North Africa?' I said eventually.

'Bing-bloody-go,' he said. 'Now, you heard of a bloke called Rommel?'

I nodded, ignoring the sarcasm.

'Well, last time we were here, we showed Rommel the toes of our boots, mate. The toes of our bloody boots. It took some doing – he was good, Rommel – and he had us cornered for a bit, but we sunk the boot into him in the end.'

How strange to hear this account of my grandfather's war. A new teller, the same tale. Both Logan and my father coming at it from the same place: how Rommel needed to be *taught a lesson*. As if we Australians were reluctant teachers, but when we stood up, by God, people listened.

63

'Rats of Tobruk, mate.'

'The Ninth,' I said, without thinking.

That stopped him.

'What?' Logan said.

'The Ninth Division, Second AIF.'

I hadn't looked for it, but there it was.

Logan nodded his head slowly.

'My grandfather,' I added.

He paused, and sized me up, closer now.

'What battalion?'

I gave Logan a number. He grunted, gave me one in return.

We sat there looking at each other, nodding our heads, wondering if our grandfathers had known each other, if *they'd* ever shared a beer in a makeshift desert bar one night.

'Jack didn't tell you?'

'Got a lot to talk about here, mate. Don't need to know every little detail. Who'd want to, anyway.'

'Yeah.'

'Well, you gonna finish the bloody story?'

'I've got no idea what it is.'

He paused.

'Cantoniera thirty-one?'

If I'd heard the name before, I'd lost it. I shook my head.

'The White House?'

I shook my head again.

Logan grunted to himself, then started afresh, but he was no longer giving me a tutorial. Now he was sharing something.

'Cantoniera thirty-one was a road maintenance depot. Thirty-one kilometres out of Tobruk. We had it before Rommel. He took it when we retreated to Tobruk. It was one of them stock-standard, whitewashed buildings you see all over this part of the world. We ran the show from there, it was our headquarters. The

White House . . . get it? . . . Well it *was* white . . . at least until we arrived.'

He laughed.

'Mate, one of our blokes – Doc Dawes was his name, a sapper – gave it a paint-job. They say he'd been a sign-writer. Anyway Dawes climbed onto the back of an old Valentine and painted great big bloody murals all over the outside of the building. Ads they were, for Aussie beer, covering the building. Copied out of magazines. VB and Abbots and a photo-finish of the Melbourne Cup. And they were bloody good. Art, mate, art. That's how good they were. Who else'd create works of art, in the middle of the desert, in the middle of a bloody war? Bloody genius. So what we gave Rommel was a taste of VB, mate. You can have the building, mate – that's what we said to him – but you damn-well won't forget we were here!'

I didn't care if it was bullshit, I was just grateful Logan had shared it. War breeds bullshit, and no one is immune. My father had told a beer story too, a tall tale. Operation Bulimba had taken place between Tobruk and El Alamein, and involved my grandfather's battalion. They named the operation after a home beer, my father said: Bulimba Beer. The beer named after the suburb on the river, the river named after the city. My father loved that. That Rommel's positions were under assault by a Brisbane beer. Anyhow, that was the story my father told, just the basic elements – his grandfather's battalion, the operation to capture a heavily defended German position, the name of the operation. He made it sound glorious, in a larrikin way. So I had this picture of a successful operation in my head, and I could imagine Rommel and his men after their defeat, after their surrender at Operation Bulimba, sitting in some prisoner-of-war compound, drinking tallies of Bulimba Beer under the desert sun, nodding their heads despondently at the first swig.

What really happened I overhead from a conversation one

night at the RSL. It was true the battalion had taken the position, but what my father hadn't told us was that they had to give it up again just a few hours later. By the end of the operation there'd been a sum gain of no ground, fifty-nine men killed, two captured, and one hundred and twenty-nine wounded.

'Rommel, mate,' Logan went on. 'We respected him, the Desert Fox. He was a soldier, not a Nazi. *That* was the difference.'

'*What's* the difference exactly?'

'The soldiers were just doing their job, mate – like us. The Nazis – they were goddamn fanatics. Wanted to take over the world, didn't they? They were bloody evil bastards.'

The door from the street opened and another group of men loudly entered the bar.

'What's Grose's story?' I asked when we could hear each other again.

'He's alright. He's . . .'

'You scared of him?'

'He knows what he's doing. He's been here since the start.'

'So you *are* scared of him.'

'You'd be a fool not to respect him. Did you read the report?'

I nodded.

'Learn anything?'

'That you were with him in Tifariti.'

'So what do you make of that?'

I shrugged my shoulders again, sipped my beer.

'You could tell me what it was like,' I said.

'It's a shit-hole.'

'Why'd Jack stay then? Why didn't he go to the Canaries with you?'

'Two more,' Logan called out to the bartender. He lit a cigarette and looked around the room. 'It's bullshit the way they make us drink in secret.'

'The UN?'

'The Arabs who run this bloody country. Bloody Muslims. Nice way to treat guests. Just makes a hard job harder.'

'Well?' I said, when we had our beers. 'Why did he stay down there?'

'Because he was different, your brother. His own man.'

The room had swelled with off-duty soldiers, so many nationalities and languages, so much thickening smoke.

'Have you heard from him, Logan?'

'Nope.'

'Do you know where he is then?'

'Nope.'

'Could you guess?'

He took a long swig, angling the bottom of the can towards the ceiling fan, looking at me all the while, the can cover for his gaze.

'Mate,' Logan said, 'that's what *I* want to know from *you*.'

'So you think he's alive?'

'Yeah, I think he's alive.'

'What makes you think that?'

'I just think.'

And so we jousted. Trading information, measuring what we were giving, rationing it out. What did I learn? That Logan was from country Victoria. Had got to know Jack from the barracks back in Australia. Was fond of him. Might even have been in awe of him, despite their ranks. Missed him. Didn't understand what had happened. Was trying to make some sense of it. Was hurting.

'Are you protecting him, Logan?'

'From what?'

'I'm his brother.'

'So?'

It's a fair question.

ELEVEN

I was woken by knocking. Loud strikes of knuckle on door, but blurred. The morning's early light smudged the walls of the room when I opened my eyes to the groaning day. Knocking again. Loud and insistent. I rolled from bed, pulled on the jeans I'd slung across the chair, and stepped into my boots without lacing them. There is security in boots, a source of hardness you can draw from if you need to.

I slid the bolt and opened the door – to three gendarmes, yet another uniform in a land of uniforms. The tallest of the three bent his head, hat in hand, calm and full of mannered politeness. As he bowed, the other two peeled around either side of him. By the time he raised his head again, they were behind me in the room. My shoulder blades twitched. I didn't know where to look, front or back.

'Excuse us, Monsieur Adams,' he said. 'It is early, we know. We did not, *comment ça se dit en anglais* . . . want to miss the opportunity.'

I turned my head. One of his men was lifting my bag from the floor onto the bed.

'What opportunity?'

'To invite you.'

The second of the men behind me stepped back into my line of view. He had my Jack book in one hand, the army's report in the other. He handed them to the tall one.

'To invite me?' I said, my eyes on the notebook.

The tall one before me turned the pages of the book, quiet, deliberate movements. His expression was unreadable. He browsed a little, turned to another page, and considered a little more. His nonchalance was absolute, his control of this drama complete.

'To invite you to speak with us.'

Now, slowly, he raised his eyes to me.

'I am the Controller of Foreigners. Come. My colleagues will carry your bags.'

He turned, a graceful pirouette, and left. He had not even entered my room, had remained outside in the corridor the entire time, the demands of courtesy. He moved down the hallway, his footsteps on the tiles the gentlest of sounds, as if he wore slippers, rather than high, black-polished boots.

Their headquarters was set behind white, wrought-iron gates, a sentry box just inside. The façade of the three-level building was also white. The Controller led me through the high entrance doors and down corridors of nodding heads, each bowing to him as we plunged deeper inside, their desks laden with ancient typewriters. Some looked at me as I passed, their faces either curious or indifferent, nothing in between. Towards the rear of the building the Controller descended a flight of stairs. I paused, seeing him reach a basement level, then stepped down to follow. But something clipped the back of my ankle – and I tripped, tumbling hard down the steps. At the bottom I picked myself up and crouched, preparing to be struck again. But nothing. It was like my fall was a performance the Controller was ignoring, while his two men stood silently at the top of the stairs, their eyes sparkling, mouths tight with smiles.

The Controller directed me into a bare room, to a simple wooden chair, which creaked as I lowered myself into it. Its legs were loose, but it held my weight. The two men had followed us in, and one lifted my bag onto a table in the far corner of the room and left it there, in sight but out of reach. Immediately in front of me was another table, small and flimsy like a portable card-table. The only other object in the room was a wooden bench running the length of the wall. It reminded me of the spare pews the priest would ask Jack and me to carry into the back of the church for Christmas and Easter masses. Seating themselves on this bench, however, were the two uniformed men, rifles brought to rest in their laps. On the wall above them was the king on his throne.

'You are not a sculptor.'

Sweat was forming on my skin, rolling down my rib-cage.

'Monsieur Adams, you have not told the truth.'

'Yes . . . yes . . . I –'

He broke across me.

'It is one thing to lie in a hotel guest register, it is quite another thing to deceive me.'

'I –'

'Why are you spying on us, Monsieur Adams?'

Speech caught in my throat as I tried to answer, tripped on itself.

'You are a spy, Monsieur Adams, no?'

I tried a second time, with only a little more control over the sounds.

'No . . . no . . . I am not a spy. I am not a spy. No. No. I am not a spy . . . I am . . . an artist.'

He paused. He smiled. He chuckled.

'An *artiste*?'

'Yes. I am an artist.'

'An *artiste*?'

'Yes. A sculptor.'

The Controller turned and spoke to one of the men, who rose and left. The Controller looked back at me, still smiling. The guard returned with a piece of blank paper. He handed it to the Controller who set it on the table between us. From his pocket he took out a pencil and placed it on the paper.

'Draw for me then, *artiste*.'

'No, I –'

'The king. Draw me a picture of the king.'

My heart and chest and sweat glands and throat and brain – all throbbed. I leaned forward and reached for the pencil. I picked it up in my shaking right hand, and leaned over the page. I placed my left forearm over my right, and leaned hard, trying to still the trembling. A drop of sweat fell from my forehead onto the paper and detonated. I pushed down on my arm. I looked up at the photo on the wall, then at the Controller and his smile. I pressed the pencil to the paper, firm, as if I was looking for footing. Still my hand shook. I leant harder against my forearm and drew a short lead line, from the wrist, on the page. The mark I left was a helplessly jagged contour of lead on paper. It was impossible. I lifted my arm, dropped the pencil on the page, and sat back.

'I'm a sculptor.'

'*Mais oui.*'

The Controller picked up the paper and pencil and handed them back to his man. Then, from his inside coat pocket, he produced my Jack book. I watched its path from his coat to the table.

He placed it carefully in the dead centre, equidistant between us. When I lifted my eyes from the book the Controller was looking at me, hard.

'Why are you spying on us?'

My heart was thumping.

'You must believe me, I'm not a spy.'

The Controller took out the army report and placed it beside my notebook.

'Do you know what will happen if I take you into that room?'

He pointed to a door I hadn't noticed before.

'Do you know what will happen if I take you into that room, and search you?'

I was pouring sweat.

'Do you know what will happen if I take you into that room, and search you, and find something?'

All was still. My interrogator, his men on the benches, the notebook and the report in the centre of the table. Even my thumping heart slowed. I saw the gun balancing in the guard's hands. That gun suddenly became the centre of the room, of the very universe. The Controller's question seemed to withdraw, and instead it was that single rifle in that one guard's hands I fixed upon – so still, the perfect balance of it.

But the guard was not *balancing* his rifle at all – he was cradling it, and that . . . *that* was another thing entirely. He was nursing it, keeping it ready for what was to come, nurturing it so it was ready for *its* work.

'I am a sculptor, not a spy.'

'*Oui*, so you say. Does an *artiste* keep a notebook such as yours, Monsieur Adams?'

'You don't understand.'

'Why are you here, Monsieur Adams?'

'I'm looking for my brother.'

My interrogator did not break stride.

'Where is your brother?'

'I don't know. Missing. Dead. I don't know.'

'Does your brother have a name?'

'Jack . . . Jack Adams.'

'You are looking for him here in El-Aaiún?'

'He was with the UN.'

'And what did he do with the UN, Monsieur Adams?'

'He was a peacekeeper.'

He paused, considering. And when he finally spoke I knew I had broken through, even if it was only a reprieve.

'We can verify that, Monsieur Adams.'

The Controller smiled and left the room. But his two men lingered. They sat, and patiently waited until the sound of the Controller's footsteps had faded into silence. Then, only then, did they rise to follow their leader out of the room, one after the other. They'd done this before, these perfectly orchestrated movements. One of them stopped at the table as he passed, and leant close, his hot breath.

'You,' he sneered. 'You a dead man.'

There's a paradox, one that troubles all carvers eventually, the sculptor's version of the question all artists must face. What does it mean to change the natural beauty of a stone by sculpting it? What is it you have to kill in order to give existence to something else?

At first, when I started, I only wanted to get closer to the stone. After walking through the sandstone ranges as a kid, and collecting rocks, and laying that spectrum of colours out on my bedroom floor – from cream through pink through purple – it felt natural to lift a larger stone in both my hands. To nurse it, feel its weight, its contours, its texture. To see the colour cascading through it. It seemed the most natural thing in the world then, having caressed it into knowledge, to break it open and explore what was inside. To learn if what I'd sensed was there, did in fact exist.

And then, once broken, having felt it give way, I wanted to shape it. Playfully. Furtively. Uncertainly. Purposefully. There are a thousand ways to be with a piece of stone you're about to sculpt. But it did, at some point, begin to trouble me: who was I to change it? Was I seeking to make *more* beautiful that which was already a thing of beauty? Who was I to think such things? To presume. Given all that men did to each other that was so ugly.

It was not the Controller who re-entered the interrogation room two hours later, but Grose alone. He smiled as he opened the door, a smile unhitched from time and circumstance. Nothing about him was reliable. He was a naked smiling head atop a vast body of strength and knowing.

'The authorities seem to think you are a spy.'

'I tried to explain.'

'They've asked me to vouch for you.'

'I explained why I'm here. To find Jack.'

'So you *have* come to spy?'

His glinting eyes. His smile.

'No.'

He sighed.

'What will it take, Sebastian?'

'To do what?'

'What would satisfy you, Sebastian?'

'Satisfy me of what?'

'How many times do you have to be asked, Sebastian?'

'What I'd do to get out of here? Is that what you're asking?'

He looked at me as if discovering an order of ignorance inconceivable to him.

'To find him,' he concluded at last. And sighed again. He seemed almost sad.

'You know where he is?'

He laughed, God alone his laughing-mate.

'What do you think, Sebastian? Do you think *I'm* hiding him from you?'

'Are you?'

'What, Sebastian, would you give to find your brother?'

'You *do* know where he is?'

Again he laughed. I hated him in that moment.

'A hypothetical question, Sebastian, that's all it is. A man who fears a hypothetical question fears himself.'

I remained silent, wanting to strike him, my blood rising.

'I repeat: what would you do to find your brother?'

'Anything,' I choked.

How many traps had I stepped into already? But what else could I say? Any other answer would have been too small.

'Anything?'

'He's my brother.'

Grose nodded.

'Get your bag then.'

At the foot of the stairs I hesitated. Grose took the lead and ascended. I followed. It was so quiet I wondered if night had fallen and the building emptied. But they were all there, the same clustered gendarmes and clerks still at their desks, all of them watching, their eyes trained not on me but on Grose. Those faces I'd seen hours ago – but now one among them stood out. Against a far wall one glanced at me then turned away. This man I'd seen before, sat beside, shared my story with. Who'd called others greedy but had sold what he knew about me for who knows how many *dirham* or what promise of work. As greedy as the soldiers who'd stopped our bus, Lhoussine had betrayed me.

TWELVE

The sun was very high, very bright. I had to blink, but it was a relief to be outside in the open, away from the police and their interrogation chambers and their informants. The air was hot and dry, but still I breathed deep, taking it in through my nostrils as though reacquainting myself with it. Not that I felt free – I was still caught in Grose's mighty wake, and didn't yet know what debt I owed. He strode towards the UN Landcruiser I could see through the compound fence, past the sentry box, and the guards with their steady eyes and the barely perceptible movements of their heads as we passed through the gate. Logan stepped from the driver's seat as we neared, and seeing him was another relief. Yet he greeted me without warmth, no smile, no dry joke. If he wanted to speak, he did not. He merely opened the rear of the vehicle for me to throw my bag in. Grose got into the front passenger's seat, and I slid into the back, where another soldier was already sitting. Logan started the engine and pulled onto the street.

'Where are we going?' I asked.

'I promised them you'd leave immediately.'

'That was not your promise to make,' I said, emboldened by the sun and Logan's presence.

But Grose just yawned.

'It was the only way you were going to leave that building,' he said, looking out the window at children playing soccer with a plastic container, barefoot in the sand. Logan had said he knew what he was doing.

With a shift of gears, the vehicle picked up speed. The crude dwellings at the edge of the city dropped away entirely, and we slipped beneath the arch at the city's outskirts. A young goatherd moving his animals from one side of the highway to the other paused at the side of the road, holding the ear of one of them until we'd passed.

'So, where are we going?' I asked again.

Grose was looking straight ahead.

'You've done well, Sebastian. You've reached Layounne. You've read our report. You know what we think. There's nothing we know that you don't. There's nothing more we can tell you. You can take the report home. You can be satisfied, Sebastian. And I can put you on a plane back to Casablanca this afternoon. Or . . .'

At some sign from Grose, Logan slowed and pulled over to the side of the road. The landscape spread empty and wide beyond the windows: tufts of grass, low rocks, and a few black desert tents in the distance.

'Or I can put you on one to Tifariti.'

'What? Now?'

'Logan's going down today. He could take you. An indulgence, Sebastian.'

Grose got out and stretched his arms to the sky. Logan kept the engine running. Grose tapped my window. I wound it down and he leant in, his hands resting on the roof of the vehicle, his glistening head and his shoulders filling the frame.

'Tell me what you've decided when I get back.'

Grose stepped away from the vehicle and into the desert. I watched him, his broad pitching shoulders, his still head. Logan kept his eyes on the road. A truck appeared over a ridge ahead of us. It slowed as it approached, and I could see the faces of two Arabs in the cab, their scarves flapping in the wind. They too looked at Grose picking his path between the desert grasses. As the truck roared past, the landcruiser shook violently, and Grose moved further and further away. Finally he stopped before the only shrub in sight, set himself, lifted his head to the sun, and began to piss.

'So,' Logan said, turning around to look at me at last, 'what are you going to do?'

Jack had asked me the same question once, years before.

There was a waterhole at the outer limits of our territory, a vast amphitheatre of steep cliffs curving two-hundred and seventy degrees, with a towering waterfall at the centre of the grand arc.

We were summer's leaping boys, climbing the cliff-face and launching ourselves into the air. The excited blood, the fear over-come, the submission, the air against your body as you fall. Then the dark disc of water is pierced and you are immersed, dropping towards the depths, kicking your legs to stop, reversing – and then striking upwards till your head bursts out into the air again and you are finally breathing.

I was still treading water when I heard Jack call down to us. He was on the highest ledge of the highest cliff, supremely confident, utterly capable. All heads turned to him, sleek and glorious, arrow-like as he launched himself and flew, a perfect dive.

'Come on,' he sang out, emerging from the water beside me.

The route up was via a vertical fissure in the rock, wide enough to lodge your foot in, then later your knee. As it widened, you wedged your whole body inside, shimmying higher and higher.

'Don't look back,' Jack said.

Growing from the ledge was a tree, some stunted eucalypt gripping precariously to a shallow bank of soil. I grasped it, the thought occurring: *What if it gives way?*

That grain of anxiety rose with me as I pulled myself up, scrabbling knees and toes gripping the rock face, and swung my right leg over and onto the ledge. I felt Jack's hand on the back of my thigh, felt him pull me up the very last part of the journey, a touch that should have been reassuring, but wasn't: *Wouldn't I have made it without Jack's help?*

Something cold shot through my body as I stood up and looked down at the water. The chill seemed to emanate from the rock beneath my feet, the stone my toes were curling into.

'What are you waiting for?'

I heard Jack through a fog. I'd fallen out of time, and he was speaking to another person, in some other place. Then I sensed him inspecting me, close, intense.

'Oh shit.'

'I can't,' I mumbled.

'You've got to.'

'I can't, Jack.'

He tried to coax me off. There were so many good reasons: there was nothing to fear, people jumped from here all the time, it wasn't that far, it was only water.

'I'm going back.'

'You can't.'

He was calm.

'It's more difficult going down than climbing up. Trying to climb down. *That's* dangerous, Bas. It's easier to jump, much easier.'

The clarity of that logic.

'So, what are you going to do?'

But there *was* another option. I could just stay there.

I didn't say this to Jack. I kept it close as he talked me through the jump, as he said again what it would be like, believing perhaps he'd already convinced me to leap, and that the only thing left was the practicality of doing it.

'Just step forward . . . don't look down . . . there's no need to look down . . . keep your eyes on the ledge and step forward till both your feet . . . I'll hold you . . . then you count . . . and on the count of three you go . . . like this . . . just a practice . . . one, two, three.'

But I was deaf to him, and didn't budge.

So he tried something different.

'Everyone's watching, Bas,' he said.

I become aware of the faces turned up towards us. A summer day's rock pool full of faces, all looking up. And the voices, clear and crisp: *hurry up*, or *don't take all day*, or *we're waiting*.

After a time, the exclamations began to overlap, competing with each other, growing louder. Then they merged completely. At first it was like some acoustic trick, some shape the sound took as it funnelled upwards in the chamber of stone and water. But soon the merged sound sharpened, and it was singing I could make out. A chant, and clapping in time. They were taunting me.

In my own way I responded heroically. I endured. I remained resolute in my petrification, and eventually the mocking lost its intensity and the beat grew ragged, before finally disintegrating. In the calm after that, the silence, I forgot I was afraid.

It was almost tranquil up there on the ledge.

Then Jack pushed me.

The water was like concrete. My shoulder made contact first. Then my whole right side banged against the surface, shuddering,

81

collapsing as the air burst out of my lungs. My body began sinking downwards, heavy and resigned. But I hadn't fallen far when I began to pull myself back, clawing my way through the water to the air. I needed air, was desperate for it. I began sucking it back in even before my mouth was free, even as my scalp and forehead and nose burst from the black.

Jack was treading water quietly, waiting, observing me begin to breathe, and see again. I'd left him on the cliff's ledge, but there he was with me in the water as I gulped for air. For a moment it was a miracle him being there. I felt as safe and secure in that moment as I had ever felt.

But then it all came back, the shameful memory of it, and I fought Jack's hand. I pushed him away and swam – a broken sidestroke – towards the rocks. I felt Jack shadowing me. I was fleeing *him* as much as seeking the safety of the bank. I crawled from the water, stumbling in the shallows, ribs aching, my head bowed to avoid the eyes of all the inflated boys, the preening girls. I reached the rock and my pile of clothes and covered my head with the towel.

Grose returned, the sun itself somehow muted by his dark, exultant shape. The silence inside the vehicle was broken by the click of the door handle, and Grose settled back into his seat like it was a throne. He didn't turn. He looked ahead, surveying the sky and the sand through the windscreen, the road that split the desert in two. There was a hypnotic quality about his breathing. Logan waited in the driver's seat. Breathing. Waiting.

'So?'

'Tifariti,' I answered.

★

The airstrip was surrounded by a high fence with a security post at the gate. We hardly paused as we passed through, some imperceptible acknowledgement occurring between Logan and the guard. Beside the runway a collection of buildings squatted. Logan pulled the landcruiser in behind the largest hangar and got out. The soldier who'd been sitting beside me took Logan's place behind the wheel. Grose stood as I lifted my bag out of the back and Logan set off towards the runway. Before following, I turned to Grose.

'Thanks,' I said.

Grose looked at me.

'You will not find him,' he said. 'You don't have it in you. You don't have what it takes.'

Then he leant forward, his giant head and shoulders looming, the breath from his nostrils on my face.

'You are not your brother,' he whispered.

I pulled away and he laughed. 'Good luck anyway, Sebastian Adams. Logan will look after you.'

I hurried across the shimmering tarmac to where Logan was lowering his head and climbing into the gleaming white Porter Pilatus. The pilot loaded my bag, and closed the doors. The engine started, its sound a guillotine brought down on Grose. Through a small side window I watched the plane's single propeller battle with inertia, its reluctant movement, the first jagged turns, the quickening rotations before it disappeared finally in a blur.

We taxied to the end of the runway. The pilot turned, lifted his dark sunglasses and grinned, letting out the throttle, gathering speed. When there was no tarmac left he pulled back on the joystick and the plane lifted into the air, rising in slow increments until we were banking. It was only then – the vibrations of the engine gentle, and the sky beginning to surround us and me glad to be leaving and not caring yet where I went – that Logan pulled at my wrist. He motioned me to look down. I saw Grose's land-cruiser parked at the end of the airfield, dead-centre and on the verge of sand, its nose facing down the runway. Grose was leaning against it, leaning back with his hands folded behind his gleaming head, looking up at the underbelly of our plane as its shadow swept over him.

THIRTEEN

A line of crescent-shaped dunes appeared from out of the rocky flatness below – sand collected from the gibber plains by the wind and blown into perfect arcs.

'Barchan dunes,' Logan yelled into my ear, above the engine of the plane. 'They creep, those dunes. They're always moving.'

I stared down at the delicacy of that migration.

'The Islamic crescent,' Logan continued, 'always on the march.'

No, I thought, ignoring him, it's like the moon has bent the winds and the sands to her shape. We droned on through the sky. One day, I thought, I'll sculpt crescents.

Later Logan pointed out four parallel lines etched onto the land, each stretching endlessly east and west towards the horizons. Like a cat's claws had swiped the planet.

'The berm,' he yelled.

'The what?' I yelled back.

'The Moroccans built it to keep the Saharawi fighters – Polisario – out. It's their Great Wall.'

I thought of the rabbit-proof fence.

'It's not just one wall,' he said, so close I could feel the warmth of his breath on my cheek. 'Some places it's four, sometimes five, or six, one wall after another. There are trenches as well . . . to stop the tanks. And there's a wall of rocks, a metre and a half wide, one to two high.'

Once we'd passed over, Logan leaned close again.

'We are now flying through Saharawi airspace.'

An airstrip appeared on the earth below, a discoloured ribbon of desert cleared of rocks and lighter than the stone-strewn plains. Laid out on a ridge nearby was a word in large, whitewashed stones: LIBERTAD. A message which greeted all arrivals and fare-welled them as they left, as if it was the name of the settlement itself. LIBERTAD. Whether you cared or not, so you knew.

Beside the airfield was a small mudbrick village, and white and alien next to it was the UN compound, scraps of foreign mat-ter staked to the ground. As the plane descended, half-cylinders formed, white plastic curves one beside the other in a protective arc. Wagons in circles, I thought. This was Tifariti, the last place Jack had been seen.

Logan leaned towards the cockpit and pressed a hand on the shoulder of the pilot, who turned and smiled, seemed to wink.

The plane swung around in a broad sweep, and lined up the airstrip, descending, the strip in front of us, the white buildings to the right. We were so close the ground seemed to be roaring, and for long moments we remained at the same altitude, the rush-ing, howling earth no closer. Then, suddenly, the plane veered towards the UN compound, the white buildings themselves at the plane's nose. I could make out antennae rising from roofs, could see the windows, saw figures emerging from doorways. We were increasing speed and the plane's engine began to screech, and the UN compound was closing – our plane somehow head-ing straight for it.

I closed my eyes and turned my head. Then felt my stomach grab as the plane's nose lifted – and the whole aircraft was pulling out and up, and wresting itself free of gravity.

A new sound joined that of air and engine: a laugh, half-mad, the pilot cackling – head thrown back, all his face tossed open to the light streaming through the windows of the cockpit – as he righted the plane, and swung it in a vast turn over the desert and back around, to line the airstrip up once more.

The pilot gave Logan a thumbs-up and Logan winked back before grabbing my arm roughly, shaking it, then pinching my cheek, long and hard, the side of my face stinging between his thumb and forefinger.

'Get some colour back into you,' he laughed. Was I now an initiate, or just the butt of a joke?

The wind bit our cheeks as we stepped from the plane, full of stinging particles of dust and sand. A UN landcruiser and two soldiers waited by the portable hangar. The building and the landcruiser and the plane looked like pieces of a set, white, clean, powerful and certain. After a round of back-slaps we got into the vehicle. It was midafternoon and we were beyond rank here.

'Cleared the strip. The first thing we did,' Logan said as the landcruiser pulled away. It seemed he expected me to ask and was saving me the trouble.

But I had no idea what he meant.

'Of landmines,' Logan said, shaking his head at me and looking out the window.

'You and Jack?'

Logan laughed at this fresh absurdity.

'Hell, no. *We're* Signals. *That's* sapper work.

Tifariti was a collection of meagre buildings collapsing into the earth. In the heat and the cold the mudbrick had cracked, and chunks of wall had simply fallen out. The whitewashed shells were so marked by tiny pieces of missing wall it appeared they'd been strafed with machine-gun fire. And some must have been – I saw the collapsed ceilings of buildings broken violently apart and angled now sharply towards the earth. Bullets and bombs had accelerated an elemental process, and the wind and the sun and the earth were reclaiming them.

In the middle of the village was the carcass of a Moroccan plane, shot from the sky by the Saharawi. The tangle of metal that was once a fighter had become a public sculpture at the centre of the village-square. Had they dragged it to this inter-section, the body with its metal-and-wire innards spilling onto the ground, or was this where it crashed? Hanging from the fuselage were shirts and underwear drying in the sun and wind, the painted Moroccan flag on its flank obscured by flapping khaki trousers. The wind passing through it all was a kind of music.

After dinner, after he'd polished his boots and buckle on the doorstep of the sleeping quarters, Logan unlocked a metal cabi-net and produced a bottle of scotch. He peeled off his socks, stretched his toes and poured two glasses. He handed me one before closing his eyes and taking the first gulp in the back of his throat.

Did he and Jack relax like this at the end of the day?

'He drank back home,' Logan said.

'And here?'

Logan took another gulp and finished the glass off.

'He went off it when he got over here,' he said, pouring him-self another. 'Not that it mattered.'

The fumes stung my eyes as I raised the glass to my face.

'No?'

'Adams did a lot of things back home he got tired of here. The boys'd go out with him back at Enoggera, follow him, and get up to things they'd never think of themselves. Not really trouble – he wasn't exactly wild – it was more . . . it was as if everything was a horizon to him, and he bloody well wanted to know what was over it. The boys went with him and if they stuck close enough they'd come away with a girl for the night.'

He laughed quietly to himself.

'But something happened . . . He stayed down here while you all went to the Canaries.'

'He grew tired of it.'

'Of what exactly?'

Logan shrugged.

'He started spending more and more time alone. He'd get up early and pick his way through the minefield to a rocky outcrop on the edge of town here. And he'd just sit there by himself and wait for the sun.'

Logan closed his eyes, and started humming the bars of a song. When he spoke again, it was from a different angle.

'In our first few days here at Tifariti, Adams and me set up the radio. We had no proper equipment so we made the fuses out of Alfoil from cigarette packets. Lucky we smoked,' he said.

I watched while he poured a third drink, wondering where he was going.

'Camel,' he continued when I didn't respond. 'If we'd smoked the local shit, we couldn't have done it. No Alfoil, see?'

Still I waited.

'It's the local shit that *should* have been called Camel. Tastes like camel shit, see? Funny, eh?'

The room was quiet for a long time, just the wind hustling around outside. He took another gulp, and turned.

'That was his bed, yeah?' he said, pointing. ' And that locker was his. That was the mat he wiped his boots on when he came in at the end of the day. He stacked his books over there, and that was the sock drawer where he kept his rosary beads –'

'Rosary beads?'

'The boys bring all sorts of mementos with them. All sorts.'

'But . . .'

'Adams is a bloody good bloke, you know that? A *bloody* good bloke.'

As if I didn't know. As if I didn't know better than Logan. But I wanted to find Jack, not be lectured on what sort of person he was.

'What's the point of all this, Logan?'

'What?'

'The peacekeeping. The whole show, the whole operation, you all being down here.'

'The point?'

'Yeah. What's the point. It sounds like it's just somewhere new to drink.'

Logan got up, went to the door, and spat out onto the sand.

'Good,' he said, turning back. 'You're doing good. Yeah?'

'Is that right?'

'You're giving this place a chance. You're making a difference. It's *bloody* important. No one else will. And I'll say it without a hint of sarcasm, mate – you're making the world a better place.'

I raised my eyebrows.

'Go on then, be a cynic. Cynicism's easy. But one thing about cynics, mate –' and here Logan pointed at my chest, challenging me – 'they never do anything. Don't try, don't fail. Never accomplish anything. But not here, mate. Down here you're having a go. A red-hot go. And it's working. Don't bloody knock it.'

'Is it?'

'What?'

'Working?'

'Bloody oath. Your job's to set it up so they can decide them-selves if they want their own country, or if they want to stay part of Morocco.'

'Stay?'

'Become . . . join . . . unite . . . whatever, I don't bloody-well care what word you use, but *they'll* decide. Your job is to set it up for the referendum. That means making the place safe. They've already agreed to stop the fighting. You being here is proof of it.'

He poured himself another glass.

'And you stand for something here. You stand for peace. You don't fool yourself it's more that that. If they started up at each other again – if they *resumed hostilities* – you couldn't do any-thing about it. You'd pull out. You couldn't stop them. And you're not naïve, you know they could turn on you – just look at what that nice young bloke you met on the bus did to *you* – you know all that. But *they* decided they wanted to stop their fighting and have a referendum to work out what to do with themselves. So, you're a symbol of it. Their *will to peace*, that's what the pollies called it. And if you know how to do it . . . and we do . . . Cambodia and everything . . . if you know how to make it happen . . .'

He trailed away.

'And Jack?' I asked.

'Absolutely.'

'You reckon?' I asked. 'Really?'

Logan looked at me.

'What do *you* think?'

I could tell he wasn't certain he knew the answer himself. Perhaps he *should* though. Jack was my brother, but he'd long broken away. He'd spent months here with Logan, close months.

What might Jack have said to him, what might they have shared? What *should* Logan know that I didn't?

'What's in this for you, Logan?'

'What?'

'This trip *now*. Chaperoning me here to Tifariti . . . Looking for clues. I guess that's what we're doing, isn't it. But why?'

'Grose ordered it,' Logan said. 'It's a soldier's duty to follow orders.'

'But you *want* to be here, don't you?'

When he spoke again his voice had softened, all the challenge gone out of it.

'He's a soldier, Sebastian. I want to find him. Make sure he's OK. And he's a friend. OK?'

The next morning I wandered around Tifariti. The wind was still up, perhaps even a little stronger than the day before, a little louder. It was a military base, becalmed by the ceasefire. There were no shops, or mosques, or homes being tended. The women and the children had left for the refugee camps long ago, and the school was deserted. There were only soldiers, a hand-ful of peacekeepers but mainly Saharawi fighters. Men in old fatigues with fraying collars, scuffed boots and crooked teeth. Men who'd pass me in the street and lift their heads from the wind and smile, or raise a hand, or greet me. Invite me inside for a glass of tea.

Who did they think I was? I wondered. A witness to their cause? A sympathiser? Perhaps even a partner in their struggle?

That night Logan and I played chess with them by lantern-light.

'We defend a genuine cause,' one said, confident in his English, strong with this power he had which the others did not. Yet he was not one of their leaders – they were the bigger men with lean cheeks and penetrating stares who talked among themselves against the back wall and had no time for board games. This was his moment, his role, and I wasn't the first he'd formed these words for.

'We are not terrorists, or rebels. We defend our homeland which was colonised by a European country, Spain, then immediately occupied by Morocco.'

The officers against the wall watched me for the effect his speech had.

I moved my piece. He moved his. I moved again.

'We are a country. We defend a just cause. As long as the UN is genuinely involved, we will continue to have faith in the UN. We are not terrorists. We are people who ask for liberty and freedom. We are not terrorists.'

We exchanged our pawns, a bishop for a knight.

'If there is no alternative to war we have to sacrifice ourselves, so our children can have a better life.'

Two of his comrades came over from the back wall and stood behind him, watching.

'But our first choice is peace, not war.'

When it came time for me to ask about Jack – when I could wait no longer – I took out my photos, one of him in his army fatigues, the second at home in a work shirt, his collar upturned, leaning against the back fence, the anthill paddock behind him. They knew him, of course, from when he'd been posted here. Had all probably been quizzed by the army when it did its own investigation. Still, they passed the photos carefully around, hand to hand, as if it was Jack himself they were nursing in their palms.

'You are brothers?'

They'd guessed it before I told them – our likeness – but wanted to hear me say it.

'Yes. We are brothers. The same mother.'

They murmured amongst themselves until one of their officers leant and whispered into the ear of their spokesman, neither taking his eyes off me.

'You must go to the camps,' my chess companion said quietly as he packed the board away.

'Is he there?'

'The camps,' he repeated. They rose then, all of them, leaving Logan and me and our swaying lantern flame.

FOURTEEN

We woke before dawn. The wind had fallen away, and all was quiet. The night itself might still have been dreaming. We pushed open the barracks door and stepped outside. Logan had the torch. The sand was crisscrossed with boot prints and tyre tracks. We piled our bags into the back of the landcruiser. There were more trips back and forth – for food and water, but even when that was all done we lingered. Logan disappeared, and returned fifteen minutes later with an armful of warm bread he'd bought from a bakery somewhere. He opened the front passenger door of the landcruiser, and in the light thrown by the ceiling bulb peeled the wrapping off little triangles of processed soft cheese, each portion stamped with the comic-book image of a red, smiling cow.

'This is great stuff,' he said as he passed me a piece of bread with the cheese smeared roughly over the top. 'Even the Muslims'll eat it.'

I looked at him.

'No rennet,' he said.

A few stars were still holding on against the dawn, but bodies were stirring. There was the sound of boot soles being banged together, a throat being cleared. A call to prayer from someone. From beyond the edge of town a goat cried out.

'You'd swear that was a child, wouldn't you?' Logan said. 'So goddam human. They're *halal* too. If you kill 'em right. Goats, I mean.'

When daylight broke we headed into the east, towards the refugee camps. If the Saharawi fighters told us to go to the camps, Logan had said before we went to sleep the night before, it's because they know something. The camps were on the other side of the border, a day's drive. It was worth a look.

'Congratulations,' Logan said. 'You got more out of them than we did.'

'What do you make of that?'

'Not much. They only ever tell you half the story.'

'But why wouldn't they have told you?'

'Who knows? Some superstitious belief in the power of blood.'

The road was a mere track. All was engine thrum, and rumble of tyres on rough ground. I shifted in my seat after the first big bump.

'*Piste*,' said Logan. 'As in, pissed off I'll be spending the next ten hours giving my kidneys a hammering on this sorry excuse for a road.'

It sounded false, the joke. The flooding light, the vast space, our vibrating bodies.

We followed the track. The land undulated at first, covered by low plants, the odd acacia tree breaking the contours of the earth. We crossed a dried-up watercourse, impossibly wide. There were low ridges on the horizon to the north, an outcrop of rocks rising from the sand at intervals, plateauing, then falling away once more. The colours of the early morning were soft: gentle reds and ochres, soft blues and grey shales. Clouds shuffled across the sky, gathering in knots, unravelling, reforming. In time the day rose

96

and the clouds began to disintegrate, before disappearing entirely. The landscape too began to lose shape. I blinked from the brightening sun.

Logan smoked, cigarette after cigarette, casting butts out the window. I reached for one.

'See that?' he said, as he handed me his pack.

Up ahead, just off the side of the track, was a shape, perhaps two. Trees, I thought at first, sewn as they all seemed to be randomly into the landscape. But is anything really random, or is that an idea we've latched onto for comfort?

As we got closer I saw the shapes were not trees at all. They had more bulk. One, I realised, was a hut and I guessed the second was a vehicle. When we got nearer still, I saw it was a four-wheel drive, and that the hut and vehicle were oddly separated, further apart than they should have been in the vastness of the desert. We slowed as we approached. Logan did not pull off the track as we neared the vehicle, but stopped in the centre of the *piste*.

He cut the engine, wound down his window, and sat there for a long time, alert in a way I could never have been, an animal sniffing the breeze. When eventually he got out, I opened my door and followed him to where he stood, arms folded, in front of the vehicle, staring at it like it was a beast he aimed to subdue. But it was already beaten. The marked lean on it was obvious now, the bonnet and the roof, the whole thing sloping away from left to right, fallen already to its knees. Half the front of the vehicle had been blown away, and the front left tyre was shredded, the metal peeled back with a force that could only have been a landmine.

Logan leant his head through the driver's side window and whistled.

I looked in over his shoulder. The insides had been gutted. The seats were gone, the seatbelts, the gearbox, the dashboard stripped. Even the bulb from the ceiling light. It was hollowed, and burst open. Like the shotgun casings left from when Jack would take me shooting in the scrub behind the house.

I reached for the door handle, but Logan gripped my wrist.

'No,' he said. 'You just can't tell. We'll radio the sappers when we get to the camp. They'll come out for a closer look.'

Instead Logan leaned over the bonnet, and with his right index finger wrote in the layer of sand that had accumulated since the vehicle had been abandoned: *I was here*. Winked and laughed.

We pulled back onto the *piste*.

I still had Logan's cigarettes in my hand.

'Got a match?'

Logan handed me his lighter without turning. I lit a cigarette, and drew back, the first time in years. Since I was at school. Trying, and failing, to keep up with Jack.

The change was imperceptible. At some point we left the sand behind and found ourselves driving on a stone-strewn plain. It was as though the soil had subsided and left only this layer of stones upon this vast, bleak, flat country. The reign of the flat. Not the empty, but the flat. As if the sky above this land was so heavy it pressed all things hard against the ground. I looked for other objects: saw a boundless horizon, an over-full sky, the flat ground pocked by rocks. Then later, a shallow basin of scrub. Some trees, bony and sharpened against the sky. They reminded me of the desiccated scarecrows in the fields of the Lockyer Valley celery farmers during drought, only fiercer.

'They call it the Devil's Garden,' Logan muttered.

'The Sahara?'

Logan glanced into the rear-view mirror. There was nothing to see, no realistic chance there would have been anything back there. It was something subconscious, like a tic.

'We've got just the one word,' he said. 'They have many. They see deserts we are blind to.'

I looked at him, this odd thing he'd just said.

'Who's *they*?'

Logan gestured out the window with the back of his hand, a dismissive flick.

'I don't understand,' I pressed.

'It was something Adams said once.'

'What?'

Logan didn't answer straight away, lit a cigarette instead and sucked it in hard.

'Adams became obsessed with the desert. Talked with whoever he could about it. Not just us, but the locals too: Arabs, Berbers, the Polisario, the Tuareg.'

'Tuareg?'

'The desert nomads. Anyway,' Logan continued, 'Adams also *read* whatever he could. Then he'd practise what he'd learnt, on me. Even got hold of a dictionary some French missionary wrote a hundred years ago, when their language was first written down, the Tuareg's. It was in French, the dictionary. Still –'

Logan sounded a series of words for me, proof of some knowledge Jack had discovered and passed on to him. He told me the word for sand dunes, and the word for newly created dunes, and the one for a plain of gravel. A different word for a rough plain that had a few boulders on it, another for a salt plain, and yet another to describe country with enough scrub for a camel to survive. Evidence of his friendship with Jack.

'There's a story about another missionary,' Logan said. 'An Englishwoman who spent a quarter of a century in the desert translating the Bible for the Tuareg. Though she was advised not to, she added vowels to the written language to make it more intelligible. To make it *better*, yeah? Well, she continued adding vowels over the years, creating, in the end, her own language. A language of one. A Bible no one could read except her! Can you believe it?'

Was that what the UN was doing too, making this all intelligible to no one but itself?

Old car-tyres, half buried in the sand, began to appear beside the *piste*, not distance markers but reminders of where to find the track if one was to lose it.

'What else was Jack interested in?' I asked. 'Besides the desert.'

'It started with the desert. It drew him in. He liked the quiet, the solitude. But if you're a solitary sort of bloke –' Logan shot a look at me to see, I think, if I'd challenge him.

'If you're comfortable with your own company,' he continued, 'the desert's not necessarily the best place for you.'

'How do you mean?'

'It can make you look for things you don't need. Find things that aren't there.'

'Like what?'

Logan lit a cigarette, smoked it, and lit another. I thought he was ignoring my question. The sound of the tyres on the *piste* was a steady murmur. There was something reassuring about it and I'd closed my eyes by the time Logan spoke again.

'So Adams started getting interested in all sorts of things over here. The desert was just the start of it. After the dunes and the winds and the vegetation and the seasons and the whole damn geography of the place, he wanted to learn about the locals, and their *way of life*. Their culture. Their religion. He started talking with them, not to win their hearts and minds, not as part of what we were doing here. Not for curiosity's sake either. It was as if he *needed* to know for himself, yeah?'

'I'm not sure I understand.'

'You can lose yourself out here, Sebastian. In the desert. You can go native, if you're not careful. Can get to the point where you don't know what you stand for. What you believe. Who you are.'

'Is that what happened to Jack?'

Logan smoked.

'It's a question of balance.'

My right forearm – my mallet arm – was larger, more muscular, than my left. But I could balance my favourite chisel across the bridge of my hand, poised between tipping and falling, the handle and blade competing, my hand keeping them apart, holding them together.

There was a border crossing to get to the camps, but as soon as we'd passed through, the experience lost its shape. The crude barrier of piping that had swung down across the *piste*, the cluster of low huts and the goats tethered to the carcass of an old truck, and the two utes with anti-aircraft guns set in their trays – all of it drifted by like a trick of the mind – and perhaps there had, in fact, been nothing there to interrupt our journey across the remorseless hamada.

'Will we get there today?' I asked Logan after hours of silence between us.

'*Inshallah*,' he said, half turning, a hint of mockery, something of a smile.

'You know what the funny thing is?'

I waited for him to tell me.

'The funny thing is the Arabs say *we're* as fatalistic as them.'

'Sorry?'

'Good die. Good die. Good die, mate.'

'What are you talking about?'

'G'day, mate,' Logan said, changing the tone, exaggerating it. 'Get it? G'day. Good die.'

Later, the stones thinned before disappearing entirely. There weren't even any rocks to break the monotony of the land, no object shaped by wind or hand in that absolute barrenness. We seemed to float through the impartial light. The engine's unchanging pitch. The landscape's perfected flatness. The distant blue of the sky. One could drift. Dream. Leave yourself behind.

FIFTEEN

We paused before entering the camp, pulling up on a small rise overlooking the settlement, a discolouration of the land. Late-afternoon and it was still down there, only the shrouded figures passing slowly between nomad goatskin tents or the lighter canvas ones, all pegged wide and lean into the sand. Cluster upon cluster of mudbrick huts the colour of the sand, and their desert-tent annexes, huddled in their thousands against the vast, treeless desert.

The hum of generators was the only sound.

After a while a water truck appeared on the northern approach road, its long white tank pitching hypnotically from side to side on the uneven *piste*. We climbed back into the landcruiser, started up and followed the truck down to the bleak settlement.

In the centre of the camp the water truck stopped at a row of silver tanks, great gleaming metal cubes. We stopped beside it and got out. Logan spoke to the driver while he pumped water from the truck.

As I stood stretching and looking around, a child approached, a girl with crow-black hair.

'One pen?' she said. I reached for my breast pocket, surprised by her English as much as the request. She watched my fingers unhitch the single button of the pocket and disappear for a moment – before producing the pen, suspended in midair between us. Her eyes were so sharp, so intent upon it that she seemed to be willing gravity to slip.

I handed it to her. I expected she would turn and run, or shriek with delight and hold it aloft, her trophy. Instead she did a strange thing. She curtsied. It was stiff – a grasping of the sides of her long skirt with both hands, a step back with one foot, bowing her head, and bending – but the elements were all there.

'Thank you,' she said.

'You're welcome,' I replied.

By then a crowd of children was gathering, jostling against each other, pushing closer.

'Are you America?' a boy asked.

'No. Australia.'

He looked blankly at me, then turned to the others to see if anyone else had understood.

'Kangaroo,' I said, raising my hands together in front of my chest, and cocking my wrists like they were paws.

'Australia!' someone hooted, a distorted echo. And then everyone was laughing and mimicking me, the children turning into kangaroos hopping barefoot all around, muttering 'Australia' as if it was the sound kangaroos make when they jump.

'Do you go to school?' I asked the girl who'd curtsied, not knowing what else to say.

She laughed and spoke to her friends. They broke into a babble of mirth, before turning and running.

She held out her hand. I reached for it, but she pulled away at the last moment. Even though I'd mistaken her gesture, she still waited for me.

'Come on,' I said to Logan, who'd turned back to the vehicle.

'What?'

'Let's follow the kids.'

'There's no shortage of them here, mate.'

'Come on. She wants to show us something.'

'Alright,' he shrugged, and locked the landcruiser.

The girl led us to a simple building not far from the row of water tanks. It was set apart from the huts and the tents all around, and was freshly whitewashed. Above the doorway was a rough sign. One word stencil-burnt onto a piece of timber: *University.* At my shoulder Logan said, not even a whisper:

'You know the Arabic word for "university" is the same for "toilet"?'

'Really?' I turned towards him, to confirm. But he was looking at me hard, pitiless.

'No,' he said, 'not really.'

I swung towards the doorway, angry. If he was closer I could have pushed past him with my shoulder, knocked him off balance. Logan didn't even speak Arabic and couldn't possibly know. But what did he know of *me* that even I didn't know? Enough to feed me, contemptuously, to throw out a lure he suspected I'd lunge towards, as I had.

Bending my head to pass through the low doorway I was distracted by a counter-thought – Hadn't I heard that the first universities were Arabic? That the Arabs had *invented* universities. But was even that true? Or was this hastily formed fact just some guilty consolation for having been fooled, and having allowed the possibility of Logan's suggestion?

The room was empty except for a woman bent over her work at the teacher's desk. She didn't look up. She must have known we were there, yet something about her required silence. Her covered, bowed head seemed vulnerable, yet sure. The yellow, unpatterned material flowed around her, enveloping her. From beneath the folds I saw her hands. One rested still on the desk. The other was tattooed with dark henna, a pencil moving calmly across a sheet of paper.

PART TWO

ONE

Her calm that first moment was absolute. Her veiled hair, the smoothness of her face, the serenity of her bowed head. She was more than a teacher preparing lessons, seemed to hold within her some perfectly clear and timeless vitality.

Yet, when she looked up, her equilibrium faltered. Her eyes widened and her lips parted. She gasped and lifted her hennaed hand to her mouth.

What was it that startled her? I wondered. Not the fact of two men being there – she must have heard our voices outside the door, and been aware of us lowering our heads at the threshold and entering. Perhaps, I thought, it was the surprise at seeing other westerners here on the fringes of the world. Or did she see something in *me* that first moment? That's certainly how it was for me, when she lifted her head and widened her eyes.

But I know now, of course, that she also saw at once my likeness to my brother.

'Hello,' I said, offering him to her with my first words, 'I'm looking for a man by the name of Jack Adams.'

She smiled. She was already composing herself.

'Have you seen him?' I asked, not yet even sure she spoke English.

Her eyes began to glow. I thought she might even laugh, might invite me to laugh with her. I would have.

'Come,' she said, 'see for yourself.'

And with that she rose. She left the exercise book where it was on the desk, her pencil resting across its pages, and crossed the room to where I was standing at the door.

'Come,' she said, her voice low, almost a whisper. There was no excess in her.

I followed. There was no question. I would have followed her anyway, but it seemed she might, that very moment, lead us to Jack . . .

Logan and I bowed our heads and again were outside.

The sun was falling fast. We left the school and crossed an open patch of sand. A boy – barefoot, closely cropped hair, perhaps ten – was balancing on the remains of a bike, stripped of its wheels and chain and cabling. Its blue forks rested on two stones that lifted the pedals from the ground, the stones where the wheels would have been. Hamid – the name she called him as we passed – stood on the pedals, driving one or two rotations, wobbling, then putting a foot on the ground to prevent the bike from toppling. He laughed and waved.

We reached a row of mudbrick rooms. Beside the last of them was a large sand-coloured tent. We stopped outside, anticipation sharpening. She bowed her head at the threshold – we heard her speak to someone inside – then turned back and motioned for us to enter. She slid off her slippers and disappeared. Logan and I looked at each other, then bent to untie our laces, that awkward custom. My heart was beating fast. I almost overbalanced fumbling with my boots, then dropped them outside, to the right of the entrance. I paused and bent again, putting it off, the possibility that Jack might be inside – and tied my boots together. After all our rivalry, Logan put his hand on my shoulderblade, allowing me this entrance. I lowered my head, drew a deep breath of dry air, and stepped into the tent.

She was already seated on the carpet, whispering to three women whose veils loosely covered their hair; perhaps they'd only just been pulled into place. Their faces were open, exposed. A baby lay on its stomach in front of one of the women, playing with the knotted hair of an old Barbie doll that was missing one of its long smooth legs. The women watched us as we entered, taking us in.

A single timber pole, rough-hewn but straight, held the ceiling of the tent three metres above the ground. The inside walls were covered in hanging drapes, the exterior walls sewn tight onto a canvas floor. There were chests in the corners of the tent, and layered mattresses stacked against one of the walls, but the floor of the tent was the most intriguing. It was like a carpet emporium. There must have been twenty or thirty rugs laid end-to-end, overlapping across the floor, a dozen shades of red, so many patterns: stripes and florals and intertwining motifs repeated end-lessly. I sat down and rested my hand on one of them, feeling the texture of it. The particles of sand caught in the weave.

One of the women clapped her hands and called out over her left shoulder through the walls of the tent. Soon a boy appeared in the doorway, followed by a second, both tall and lanky, energy coming off them. They slipped out of their shoes. Seeing us they tightened. I assumed it was Logan's uniform. The woman spoke and the taller boy lifted an arm – an instinctive action – gripping the opposite shoulder with his hand in a diagonal across his torso. He stood in this suddenly defensive poise, looking uncertainly at me.

'There,' said the teacher. 'There's Jack for you.'

I didn't understand. Not her words, nor her smile. I didn't understand why these boys with their too-large shirts and their jeans rolled at the cuffs had been dragged away from their soccer game in the street to be paraded before us.

'You recognise them?'

I looked at her. I'd followed her, trusted her, but what was this? How could I possibly have ever seen these boys before?

But Logan understood.

'Bugger me,' he muttered.

She turned to the boy with his arm across his chest. He was tense, his eyes fixed on Logan. She said something to him in Arabic, her voice low, reassuring. After a while he loosened, and dropped his arm, the khaki shirt no longer obscured. And there, stitched onto the breast, I saw my name, *Adams*.

I began to nod my head, not because I understood yet, but because I was beginning to take it in. I looked then at the yellow t-shirt the other boy was wearing and saw the familiar four red Xs of a local Brisbane beer and the stylised image of the brewery itself.

'Half the boys in the camp are wearing Jack's clothes,' she said.

She spoke to the boys again. They went towards the door of the tent, but then the one bearing my name turned back to face me. He spoke, a few sentences I didn't understand, some formality he felt compelled to undertake. Whatever it was he said, his address seemed to please the women, who murmured and nodded to each other. But I was lost.

'He was here for nearly three weeks,' Sophia Maddison said.

'How long ago?'

She smiled at Logan. A tin kettle came to the boil on a small gas burner. One of the women lifted the lid and dropped in some tea-leaves. Another placed six small glasses onto a silver tray on short legs. The third woman repositioned the child who was squirming out of reach. These distractions. Really there was only Sophe, and what she knew.

Logan did the asking, all the questions he wanted answers to. It was enough for me to listen, and to observe her equanimity. Like a lawyer he examined her, after dates and times, and what – precisely – was said, and what was meant by it. She gave gentle, yet deliberate, responses: when he'd arrived, where he'd stayed, when he'd left. These things she could give. But where he'd gone when he left here nearly a month ago she could not or would not say. The boundaries of what she told us were clear, sharp as a country's borders drawn on a map.

It wasn't that she resisted Logan. Everything she said was freely given, spontaneously, unconditionally. Yet little she said satisfied him. She may have had other duties. Probably to Jack. But there was something else too, and it was only much later I realised she was being faithful to the conversation itself. As if Logan's probing was undignified. That conversations needn't be like this. That they could be subtle and gracious. And, perhaps, she was also cushioning Logan against the consequences of his inquisition.

I accepted a glass of tea. It was becoming second nature now. I sipped my way through it, and the second, and the third. Always three, Sophe would tell me later. The first is bitter like life, she said. The second sweet like love, the third soft like death.

'Death is soft?' I queried.

'It is living that's hard,' she replied.

'But *soft*?'

She just smiled. If I did not understand, I could not be made to understand.

A gust of wind pressed against a wall of the tent, then sucked it out again.

'I must leave,' she said. 'The light will soon be gone and I must prepare for tomorrow's classes.'

'When will you finish?' asked Logan, still unfulfilled, suspicious.

'Will you still be here tomorrow?' she asked, directing the question to me.

I nodded.

'Come again after school.'

TWO

Logan and I prowled the camp the next day, wandering down its alleyways, peering into doorways, asking the women and children what they knew. There were so few men. It had been the same with my own family: when war arrived, it was the women who remained.

We'd seen women greet the aid trucks and take the weight of the wheat sacks stamped with the names of donor countries. Women who lugged plastic containers – old oil or petrol drums filled with water – through the streets. Or who rolled gas canisters along the ground, steering them with two thin pieces of sapling. Women bent over freshly shaped bricks, arranging them in rows to dry. Or walking in pairs across wide patches of sand, infants on hips, their heads leaning into each other in talk.

Those men we did see were old, or broken. Lying in the shade as though hiding, or curved over chess pieces, or hobbling away from us on crutches. Maimed and reclining, reduced by a foot, a leg, sometimes both, their bodies re-sculpted by landmines.

Logan had withdrawn, and was stewing, full of grunts and grinding gears, and cigarette butts flicked towards things rather than away from them. Maybe he'd already found more of Jack than he was comfortable finding. That he was alive. And was a deserter. Meanwhile I felt like a predator, so closely was I looking for traces of Jack: catching people cleaning their teeth with sticks of acacia, interrupting nurses at the corrugated-iron hospital, kicking soccer balls with kids to find out what they knew.

During the morning we passed a doorway and glimpsed a classroom of small boys, five or six years old, rocking in their seats, reciting together. They had wooden tablets like old miniature washboards on the desks in front of them, and their fingers moved rapidly across the boards, as if reading Braille.

'Learning not to think,' Logan muttered as we passed. 'Manufacturing kids who know the Qur'an by heart. By ten years of age they'll be able to recite the whole thing start to finish.'

I raised my eyebrows.

'They even get their women to recite it during pregnancy so their children will have it memorised when they're born.'

I looked at him. He wouldn't meet my eyes.

'Bullshit,' I said, though not with conviction.

Only then did he turn, his glinting smile.

'It's having to learn it at all that's bullshit. Opiate of the masses and all that. Drugging their kids. Yeah, that's what they're doing.'

'You'd know.'

'What do you mean?'

Logan with his army drills. All those reactions trained into him by the military. So *he* wouldn't have to think.

'Nothing.'

We walked the length of the widest thoroughfare after lunch, the camp's main street. In front of one of the huts, on a hessian bag spread on the ground in the shade of an awning, was a camel's head. It drew us, closer and closer, exerting some force greater than mere curiosity. It was only a camel, but an image came to me, a painting I must have seen in one of Mum's books of saints – John the Baptist's head, served up to Bathsheba on a silver platter. It was a proud head, the camel's, the bones of its high forehead, the long snout, and the mouth gently closed, sealed by still-moist lips. A serene head. Through a doorway the rest of the carcass could be seen laid out on the floor. As I squatted before the head, three or four women with tattooed chins entered the hut and leant over the cuts of camel flesh, holding the folds of their dresses close so the hems wouldn't brush the meat.

Beside the butcher's was a provisions store, *Tienda* written above the door. Inside, the stock was eclectic: kitchen utensils, a rack of clothes on hangers, car-tyres, oilcans, a tower of blue plastic buckets. There was food too, but not much: a few cans stacked on one of the shelves, packs of two-minute noodles, processed cheese, sweets in coloured paper wrappers. We bought some packets of dry biscuits.

Outside the shop two boys stood barefoot on the roof of one of the mudbrick houses nearby. A gust of wind blew, and the taller of the two threw the plastic bag he had scrunched in one hand up into the air. The wind caught the plastic, opened it, turned it, and carried it upwards like a ragged orange kite, until it stopped rising and paused for a moment, then tumbled over itself as it dropped. When the boys saw us, they clambered down and ran over to where we'd squatted in the shade, leaning against a wall.

'*Espagnol?*' one said.

I shook my head.

'Speak English?' the boy tried again.

I nodded, consenting to a conversation.

'What is your name? What is your country? What is your job?'

He rattled the questions off, running them together so they sounded like an incantation. Were these boys Sophe's students?

I answered each question. They couldn't understand what I said, but were delighted all the same – perhaps more so, in the simple pleasure of cause and effect: that learning to make sounds in a certain way could cause a westerner to respond. They were learning to exert this power that could shape the world.

I laughed with them and gave them a biscuit each. They scoffed them down, so I offered the whole packet. As they peeled the pack wider I noticed their t-shirts – one featured a matador from Seville in a billowing red cape, and the other was black with KISS emblazoned across the front.

In the camp over the following days I saw Astro Boy, and teddy bears and heart-shapes and cowboys on horses. So much clothing distributed by the international charities. The logos and colours of football teams. Cities and their festivals, the whole of the world in faded t-shirts: *The Big Apple*, and *The Windy City* and *Je t'aime Paris* and the *Calgary Rodeo*. You can get to know someone through what they donate. I wondered what the kids imagined these cities looked like, cities I'd never been to either. What the words meant to them. *Natural Life. Walk Against Want. Go Your Own Way.*

When the time came to meet Sophe after school I feared what Logan might do to the conversation now he was burning out. It was too important, so I started.

'What else can you tell us about Jack?' I said.

My abruptness startled her.

'What would you like to know?'

I sat down in one of the seats in the front row of her classroom.

'Anything,' I said. 'The most important thing.'

She settled back at her desk. Her hair was beneath a new head-scarf, patterned though also yellow. From the few strands pressed against her forehead, and the honey-wax colour of her eyebrows, I guessed her hair was light. There was an elegance in her cheek-bones, and the line of her nose. In the way her cheeks filled and lifted when she smiled. Her eyes were light blue, the colour of some sky I'd once seen.

'It was a surprise when he left,' she said. 'I thought he might stay . . . because of the kids. He spent his three weeks talking with them, wherever he found them, teaching them. He played soccer with them, and when they'd gone to their homes after dark he'd join me here and prepare materials, or lessons, or write out exam papers, one for each child.'

She reached into her desk drawer and produced a piece of paper, holding it out to me. I rose and took it, standing close. It was the alphabet, written in Jack's hand between two sets of ruled lines, both capitals and lower case. Then below Jack's alphabet all fifty-two of his letters had been copied, each crudely, painstakingly imitated by a child. I handed it to Logan to see.

'He spent hours teaching them to write. It was slow work, but I think it calmed him. It was almost a meditation.'

'Well,' I said.

'And the kids loved him. Look.'

She pointed to some drawings taped to the wall. Kids' crayon drawings like you'd find in any classroom anywhere in the world: faces and stick figures and suns in the sky.

'What do you think?'

'What am I looking for?'

She led me to the wall, and pointed to the words *Mr Adams* at the foot of one drawing after another. Twenty-odd portraits of my brother.

'They did them the day before he left . . . they adored him.'

'You realise Adams is a soldier, ma'am?'

Logan's brooding had broken through. She turned to him.

119

'A soldier,' Logan repeated, 'not a child-minder, ma'am.'

She paused, unsure how to meet Logan's challenge, the fragile restraint in the words he'd chosen.

'I understood, from talking with him, that he had – how can I say it? – left the army.'

'Really, ma'am?'

'I may not have described it properly.'

'Use *his* words then. What exactly did Adams say?'

'I can't remember . . . the . . . *exact* words.'

'Give it your best shot,' he snapped. 'What did Adams say?'

'You could show some respect, Sergeant. His name is Jack.'

Logan snorted.

'Is that how people earn respect in your world, ma'am? With little shows of courtesy? What did he say?'

'No,' she replied. 'What he said, he said to me. Not you. But what I can do for you, soldier, is tell you what I think. And you can take it, or you can leave it. How does that sound?'

Logan glared at her.

'What I think is that it dawned on Jack that there was more to life than soldiering. He wanted more. *Needed* more. Urgently. I think the life in him was shrivelling, and that if he'd stayed a moment longer, there'd have been nothing left.'

'Stayed where?' Logan replied. 'With us, or with you?'

He meant to hurt her, but she'd faced that already. She wasn't hiding from it.

'Both,' she said eventually. 'When he first arrived – he hitched in with some of the Saharawi fighters who came for a few days with their families – you could see him coming to life . . . filling with vitality. As if he was recuperating.'

'He wasn't injured, though?' I asked.

'Nothing physical.'

'But . . . ?'

'His need was *like* a wound.'

'And you were his nurse?' Logan snarled, unable to let up.

She rose, and carefully put away the papers left on the desk. Pressing the folds of yellow robes against her hips, she started for the door. There she turned.

'Sergeant Logan,' she said, 'Jack talked about you. He had no regrets about walking away from the army, but he felt sorry about leaving you. He didn't know how else to do it. He didn't want you – I don't know if this is the right word, either – *implicated*. But he was dying inside, and he had the courage to choose another life.'

THREE

'She's wrong, you know,' Logan said as he climbed into his land-cruiser the next morning, the third in a convoy heading back to Tifariti. The other two had already started their engines and Logan had to raise his voice, making it sound more certain than I suspect he was. 'This isn't about me.'

'Don't you want to know where he's gone?' I asked.

'Mate, it's bloody obvious, isn't it? *He* doesn't want *us* to know. He doesn't even want *her* to know. Fair enough then. And good luck to him.'

'Really?'

'Sure. Good luck with his hiding, and his finding, and his turning himself into whatever it is he wants to become. Once a man's gone native . . .'

Logan opened the glove box and pulled his sunglasses from their case.

'So what are you going to say?' I asked.

'You mean to Grose?'

'Yeah.'

'Mate,' he said, 'what she described is no man the army can do anything with.'

'But it might've done things *to* him.'

Logan looked at me.

'I'm in a difficult position here. He's been a friend, yeah? But you can't court-martial someone you can't find. That's how it seems to me.'

So *those* had been his orders.

'And if we'd found him?' I asked. 'If he'd been here and didn't want to go back . . . ?'

'Lucky that didn't happen,' he grimaced.

Logan stepped out of the vehicle, bent and drew a hard black case from beneath the driver's seat. He lifted it onto the seat and snapped the latches open, letting me see inside – a pistol and a pair of handcuffs, some other objects I can't remember. Logan looked up at me, then pressed the lid shut again.

'But he's not here, and I've got to draw the line somewhere.'

'You were hoping I'd lead you to him?'

Logan shrugged. It didn't matter anymore.

'I'll tell him the lead went nowhere. That we couldn't keep looking forever. Caesar and his coins.'

'And if I find him?'

'Then you find him. And if you do . . .'

Logan looked away, sighed.

'. . . say hello. But look, Sebastian. Take care will you? You're a long way from home.' He offered the formality of his hand.

The tinted glass of Logan's window slowly rose and sealed. His silhouette leant forward to turn on the air-conditioning, then the white UN landcruiser followed the other two out of the liaison office compound. He was a soldier. If there was more to Jack's story, he could not chase it. Part of me felt some victory of blood over country and friendship. But I'd miss him, and I was vulnerable all over again.

★

Sophe wasn't surprised to see me return. She found me a bed without asking how long I was staying, a hut rented by one of the Spanish aid agencies. She'd done the same for Jack, she said, the same hut. I slept on a foam mattress on the ground and wondered if it was the one Jack had slept on a month earlier.

So now I wandered alone through the camp each day. After the journey to get there — after the noise of the medinas and souks and bus-stations, after El Ayouune and after the police and the army and all the miles, all the tension, all the frustrations — the camp was a sanctuary. And Sophe was its calm centre.

Along the paths of the camp, the sand between the buildings was patterned by each new day's foot traffic. Some mornings I tracked the imprints of boots, not because I was following anyone, but out of curiosity, taken by the thought it might be possible to trace someone's entire day through the marks they left in the sand. But each path I followed ended in a pile of sandals at the doorway of a hut, or was obliterated by more recent steppings, or by tyre-tracks on the larger paths, or by overnight wind swept down the camp's desolate alleys like a broom. Except for my own footprints, which followed me each day to her classroom.

He'd left without warning, Sophe said, starting again.

'The children presented him with their drawings, and the next day he was gone. Maybe their portraits triggered something . . . like a mirror held up to him.'

With Logan gone Sophe opened up even more, a flower unfolding. She told me she'd found out what she could about Jack's movements on the morning he left — that a social worker from one of the international charities had given him a lift out of the camp to the nearest town. That from there he got another ride, with a truck driver returning to the capital with an empty tanker. But that was where the trail ended.

She couldn't stop wondering, she told me. She'd tried to guess. She had spent nearly a month with Jack, watching the life come back into him.

'So where might a man newly alive go?'

We were sitting together early one evening, just after sunset, when the mosque's loudspeaker crackled and the muezzin's call to prayer reached out above the tents and huts.

Allahu Akbar. Allahu Akbar. Allahu Akbar. Allahu Akbar.

'Jack liked the sound,' Sophe said.

Ash-had al-la ilaha illa Ilah. Ash-had al-la ilaha illa Ilah. Ash-hadu anna Muhammadan rasulullah . . .

'I'm growing used to it now, too.'

'It was more than that for Jack. He found it soothing. He used to stop what he was doing when he heard it, and close his eyes.'

I thought of our national ritual, the scrupulous minute's silence we kept each Armistice Day.

'What do you make of that?' I asked.

'I think he was gathering himself.'

The things she'd observed I wanted to know, anything that might be a clue to where he'd gone. And *she* in turn asked about his childhood, his life before the camp. Sophe was trying to work out not where he'd gone, but where he'd come from.

Some people you understand by stripping layers away, peeling off their false skins. With others it's like working with papier-mache – the layers need to be added. Sophe was like that. There was that moment of beatific serenity at the desk when I'd first glimpsed her. That image would almost have been enough. But now she began to take shape.

Sophe was an only child. She had grown up in the midwest, and then left for New York on a scholarship to Columbia, the university named after the explorer who proved the world wasn't flat —

'For a girl from the flat midwest plains,' Sophe joked, 'New York *was* the world.'

When she got there everything expanded further, kept expanding, the distance from her hometown growing greater by the day . . . yet somehow dissolving at the same time. That's what she said, though I didn't understand it. She decided to study the most foreign of languages on offer. Not exotic, but foreign. At the outer limits, it was Arabic she found.

There was a pamphlet on a student noticeboard calling for volunteers to work in the camps one summer break and she and a girlfriend responded. Afterwards, when her friend returned to study, Sophe stayed.

'Why?' I asked.

'I wanted to help.'

'Why?'

'I've always wanted to help. You can do that here. Among the dispossessed.'

'Dispossessed?'

'The poor.'

The child in the photo on our fridge at home had come from Africa too, the little black girl we were sponsoring out of poverty. Our mother had started this, and Em continued it despite our resistance. The little girl who joined us at the dinner table each evening at grace.

'Like Mother Teresa?'

She smiled but I wouldn't let it go. If we'd been girls our mother would have wanted Jack and me to take the name of the little Albanian nun from the Calcutta slums at our confirmation.

'But you admire her?'

Sophe touched her scarf.

'Don't for a moment think this is a nun's habit, Bas.'

She laughed that unselfconscious laugh of hers. How much she bared of herself. Then her voice dropped and became serious again.

'We've played a role in this, Bas. Our governments. We either had colonial obligations – and not that long ago – or we now have trade ambitions. Often both. So we support independence movements against corrupt old regimes. Or the regimes against the forces of anarchy. We're playing here, Bas. We're responsible.'

'It's atonement then, is it?'

Sophe smiled again, even as I pushed.

'If we didn't have a hand in all this getting to where it is, we still have a responsibility.'

'Responsibility?'

'To do the right thing. To help each other where we can. *Because* we can.'

'And to lecture each other?' I smiled.

Sophe laughed again.

'I'm sorry. The teacher in me.'

Later I accused her of disowning her country.

'Whether you like it or not, it's still your inheritance.'

Her grand response – she said she was a child of all humanity. That nationality is as unimportant as whether one wears one's hair in a ponytail or a bun.

'Or hides it behind a veil?' I challenged, trying to get behind *her.*

'Yes,' she cheerfully agreed, her philosophy large enough for that too.

If I'd known then what I do now I wouldn't have allowed her that easy acceptance, would have fought her.

★

As I waited in the shade of the school building for her one after-noon, I lifted a piece of concrete, which had been lying nearby, onto my thigh. A nail lay discarded on the ground between my legs and I picked it up too. For the first time in weeks I cut a groove into the block, the concrete dust falling onto my jeans. How good it felt. I worked the block as it rested on my leg, changing its shape under the lowering sun, under the eyes of the intrigued school children who stopped to watch when Sophe let them out after class. She brought out a chair too.

'What is it?' she asked.

'I don't know yet.'

'Is that true? You have no idea?'

'A sense. But you never *really* know until it's done.'

The children were as interested in the words passing between us as in the shaping of the block. Their eyes moved back and forth.

'Why *teach*?' I asked Sophe as I worked the concrete.

'Because I'm not a doctor.'

Sophe winked.

'And the children want to learn,' she continued, smiling at some girls, including them. The boys had drifted away. 'Their *parents* want them to learn.'

I turned to the children.

'Why . . . do . . . you . . . want . . . to learn . . . English?'

Sophe translated it and the answers came back through her. Each of the girls had an opinion.

Because it is the international language.

To make money for my family.

For liberation.

'Liberty,' I corrected the girl.

She shook her head fiercely, her face harder than the others, leaner, eyes unafraid. 'Liberation.'

'Yes,' another girl agreed. 'To go to America and tell them about us.'

By then the small block in my lap had become a lizard, head raised and angled to the left, alert, like the one I'd left uncompleted back at The Springs. It wasn't detailed – concrete doesn't allow that, the way it turns to dust – but it held together enough so you could tell it was a bearded dragon. I stood it on my palm, turning and examining it before offering it to the children.

'*Un cadeau,*' I said, before releasing it to the quickest of the little desert hands.

FOUR

We were sitting on the floor of Sophe's tent when a woman entered. She handed Sophe an envelope, unstamped, a letter that had passed through no postal system to get here. I watched as Sophe read her name, and saw the letter grow heavy in her hands. She looked up at me and we shared a moment of uncertainty. I was grateful. Am still. She looked down and then, with a care that seemed almost timid, nicked the seal of the envelope with her thumbnail.

I moved away and sat against a wall of the tent, giving her space. And yet, already I was fearful of looking away.

The wind blew beyond the canvas and Sophe read. Tent ropes vibrated in the wind, a hum coming off them. She read. There were children laughing outside, yet she was oblivious. Trucks unloaded sacks of wheat in the dusty public square, and I listened, and watched her read.

I tried to interpret her face.

When she finished she looked up from the gap in time she'd passed through. Even now I can't properly describe the way she appeared. I'd never seen a woman cry like that, silently. Her bowed head, her hands and the letter in her lap, her tears falling, all her grace. I've dreamt of her like that a thousand times since, almost destroyed myself wanting to capture it, that moment. Then, when she'd stopped crying and there were tracks on her cheeks where her tears had coursed over the fine sand that covered her face, she held it out to me. The letter from my lost brother.

Cross-legged on the floor, I took my turn at what neither of us had imagined. A strange, new, Jack.

Dear Sophia,

Forgive me. I couldn't think how to tell you so I didn't. I couldn't bear your disappointment. I'm not sure I can explain it even now, but I will try and I hope you might understand.

I want to live differently. I need to live differently. I believe I've been *called* to live differently. I've come to realise that until now my life has been without meaning. I've been too much of the world, too concerned with myself and all the million little things that cannot last, and not concerned enough about what is eternal. How the desert has humbled me!

I feel now, Sophia, that everything untrue is being stripped away. It will take time. Leaving the army was not the end. And even before that, leaving my family and leaving Australia were part of that same journey. I understand that now. I didn't when I first arrived – I thought staying with you in the camps, and serving your beautiful children might be it. How I wanted to stay with you! How much I wanted that, Sophia – to work beside you. But that was *your* vocation, not mine (and what you do is extraordinary). It fulfils you, I know that. But it was not enough for me, not *my* way. There is even more stripping away to do.

Now I understand that it's not me, or my family, or the army, or even the children in the camp I must serve. It is God, Sophia. I need to serve God. To be with Him and to offer myself absolutely to Him. To trust Him. Please don't think me mad. I know it is unusual, especially these days, but men and women have dedicated themselves to God for centuries, living lives of prayer and contemplation. How inspiring it was to observe the Muslims and their daily devotion. Their dedication to God. Their simple commitment. For a heart like mine, which is only now beginning to open itself to Him, it is inspiring.

And so, I've joined a monastery. Perhaps you will laugh, but I don't think so. It is tiny but it is perfect. There are just two of us here and it is exactly what my poor heart needs. I read the Bible and I pray all day. And I am getting better at offering myself to God and placing myself in His care and trusting Him. Getting better every day. I am learning to sacrifice, and to suffer and to love. Because God is the source of all beauty and all love, Sophia. I know that now. God is love, Perfect Love. I hope you understand. I pray to God with all my heart that you understand.

May God be with us always.

Jack

FIVE

Sophe arranged a lift out of camp on an aid truck, the two of us crouched on the empty tray which the day before had arrived packed with sacks of rice. It was midmorning but the sun was already high. There was no shade. She tied a headscarf around me, and we sat on our packs for protection from the heat coming up through the metal tray.

Why did we go? Jack hadn't asked for us. Quite the opposite: he wrote as if he was beyond all comings and all goings, all human need. As though he had freed himself from the earth and from Sophe and from me. But neither of us believed it. We each found things in his letter that were, despite his claims, fragile. Things that both of us, for our different reasons, doubted. And we were each separately convinced that Jack needed *us* to mould him back into his proper shape.

Sophe guessed where he might be.

'There is a monastery,' she said, 'a little stone hermitage in the Ahaggar mountains that was built by a French monk a century ago. He called it "Assekrem", which in the language of the Tuareg nomads, means "the end of the earth".'

Which made sense. Or rather *fitted*, like all paradoxes: an inflamed manifesto from a soul who'd lost his centre, written from a monastery, in the middle of a desert, at the ends of the earth.

A cry for help.

Reaching the Ahaggar meant taking a route that on a map resembled a series of descending steps. East from the camps till we hit the Route du Tanzerouf, then south till we reached the town at the end of the road, then east again across the sands until we joined the Route du Hoggar, and south even deeper, to the old oasis town of Tamanrasset and the monastery in the mountains nearby.

The first hours were hard, the sun pounding us, the tray scalding to the touch. We shifted position constantly, sitting on our packs, squatting behind the cab, standing when our legs began to cramp before being forced down again by the torrent of scorching air that rushed over the top of the cabin. I sipped water almost continuously, knowing I was taking more than Sophe. She'd acclimatised and her body didn't need it like mine did. At least that was my feeble justification.

We stopped late-afternoon at the junction with the route south, a handful of low, sand-encrusted buildings scattered around the intersection. Before the driver cut the engine Sophe slipped a plain gold band onto the ring finger of her left hand, winked, and said to me above the motor:

'We're married.'

'What?' I shouted, unsure I'd heard her right.

'If anyone asks,' she shouted back, so close to my ear I could feel the warmth of her breath, 'we're married. *Just* married. It'll make it easier.'

This is it, the drivers said, the Route du Tanzerouf. Are we certain? Sophe nodded, a sureness in her movement as she climbed down which they accepted. They reached up for our packs and lowered them to the ground, an over-helpful gesture, as if, having been unable to persuade us against going, this was one last thing they could do for us, the end of their responsibilities, before they continued on to one of the port cities on the coast.

There were no hotels, and only a single, squat café. At the front an awning hung slack, with tassels limp in the dry air. Three tables were set under the canopy on either side of the doorway. We bought soft-drinks, two bottles each, gulping them down, sickly orange-flavoured soda water, before asking the café-owner about a room for the night.

The room was as desolate as the café, two single beds set against opposite walls, and between them a three-legged bed-side table with a missing drawer. Attached to the remaining wall, pulling away from it, was a sink. Cracks in the stained ceramic resembled lines on a map. I turned the taps, first the cold, then the hot. Nothing. I filled our water bottles from the communal basin at the end of the corridor and Sophe splashed water over her face, washing the day's sand and dirt away. I followed. We dried our faces and hands with sarongs we'd brought with us, and hung them on the door knob.

There was no town to explore, so we returned to the café for a meal. Watching a television in one corner of the room were a dozen men, absorbed in a soccer game, their backs to us. I ordered *pommes frites*, Sophe soup and bread. We ate without talking, watching the men instead, their exasperation and their jubilation, their slumped shoulders, or their bodies leaping into the air.

When we'd finished our meals, we went out into the quiet night and stood in the street looking up. The moon was new, sharp and bright. The café bulbs glowed, and the TV-light pulsed through the doorway. Even so, the net of stars in the sky was bright. Not the thick swathe of light laid out across the heavens above The Springs, but some new chart unfolding.

'Do you know your way around up there?' I asked.

'My Pop used to show me,' she said. 'He'd drive us out of town to look for shooting stars when I was a child. It's not exactly the same sky, but it's close. You?'

'It's totally different. A bit . . . unsettling.'

She looked at me but I kept my eyes on the night.

'The north star?' I asked.

Sophe pointed.

'Really? Is that it?'

'Polaris.'

'That's it?'

'Sure.'

'I'd expected something . . . I don't know . . . bigger.'

We made our way back to the room at the rear of the building. It was dark in the lee, beyond the café lights, the heavens, the north star. We'd forgotten our torches, so had to step cautiously, avoiding the holes which potted the ground. Only when we reached the door, and stood side by side before it, did I realise it was time to sleep, and that I would be sharing the room with her. That her body and mine would be sharing the same small space. I swallowed, my hand fumbling with the room key. Hard-beating heart, and short breath. I stepped aside, then followed her in.

Watched her prepare herself. Take off her shoes and leave them by the door. Watched as she unwrapped her headscarf and shook her hair free. Saw her bend towards her pack on the floor, zip it open, and reach for her nightclothes. Turning away, I could still hear her shuffle out of her jeans behind me. Could hear her unbuttoning her shirt, hear its sleeves sliding down her arms, falling on top of her pack. I began untying my bootlaces, fingers thick. She slipped a nightshirt over her head, and the bed creaked as she climbed in.

'Goodnight, Bas.'

I might have turned but did not.

'Goodnight,' I said.

SIX

We travelled in short trips at first, the distance between towns two or three hundred kilometres at most, the road well-maintained asphalt. Most of the lifts were with local truck drivers, ferrying goods from oasis town to oasis town in their lorries. One or two government drivers gave us lifts they shouldn't have, risking their licences if they were caught. Or businessmen would silently pick us up, study us out of the corner of their eyes for hours and then equally silently drop us off in the next town, not a word passing between us.

I didn't think of Jack much those first few days. Because there was Sophe, and all her beauty. There was also the journey itself to settle into, its practicalities, its rhythms. Finding water, sometimes boiling it, keeping our water-bottles filled. Exchanging American dollars for *dinar* in the first town we came to, the black-market offering better rates than the banks, and me so, *so* ignorant, acquiescing, as with all else, to her experience. Stocking up on food, just in case. Biscuits and bread and preserved jam and tubes of condensed milk and pieces of fruit and chewing gum. Buying sunglasses from a truck driver who insisted on American dollars.

Bartering in markets and in shops, haggling for respect, as she put it, more than a few saved notes – a responsibility Sophe said we had, to all those who came after us.

And the routine of finding a bed in the evening. For even among foreigners there is desert lore. Not the wisdom of the stars and the winds. More like the foot knowledge of hobos and gypsies which I'd learn myself afterwards, elsewhere. Most of the information we've codified in our guidebooks instead of marking the route itself with symbols: the basic matters of food and clothing and shelter. Knowing how to dig a vehicle out of sand and how many iodine drops to add to water. Managing the heat. Avoiding dogs for fear of rabies. In which towns the locals are notorious for cheating travellers and in which they welcome foreigners into their *hammams*. Survival tips in a foreign land.

Every night we'd scout the town for a hotel after consulting my guidebook. We'd inspect the room before taking it, the two of us sharing to save money. Always a twin. We'd check there was running water, that the sheets were clean, and that the room wasn't too close to the communal *toilettes*. Looking for certainty and receiving assurances from the hotel-keeper about the reliability of the electricity. Futile assurances, but ones we'd seek anyway, hopefully. We'd fill in the register as a married couple. Once a hotel-keeper queried our different names and our different passports. Sophe answered in Arabic, feigned offence, and put her arm around my waist as she led me away from the reception desk with the room key. Dropped her arm and laughed when we were out of sight.

Then the task of getting a lift each morning. Someone at the hotel desk the evening before would always know someone heading our way early. We took up the offer the first time, and lingered around the foyer for hours in the morning before realising the promised lift was never more than mere hope, or desire to please, or just to prolong a conversation with a white woman. Instead, after sunrise we'd make our way to the petrol station on the route out of town and strike up conversations with drivers heading south. Or we'd walk to the town's fringe, find some shade, lay down our packs, and wait.

And so we plunged deeper into the desert. At first it was across hamada, the endless flatness, the inexhaustible supply of small stones that lay strewn on the ground either side of the road. The landscape offered nothing to orient ourselves by. It seemed the asphalt road had been laid across that plain of stones according to a compass – south – and that no natural contour shaped its direction.

On the road I still didn't think much about Jack, and Sophe didn't ask about him, not directly. Instead, as we travelled and Sophe asked about our family and life at The Springs, it began to seem it was *me* Sophe wanted to understand.

'Two years at art college,' I answered, 'sucking in what I could about light and shade and texture and perspective. Technique. Memorising the names of those who'd gone before me, those whose work I admired.'

'Why didn't you finish?'

'Because I needed to *start*.'

Sophe looked at me, a raised eyebrow beneath a line of cloth.

'OK,' I said, 'and because I hated being away. *Hated* it. I didn't belong there. I *belonged* at The Springs. I knew what I wanted to do. And I needed to start.'

Sometimes it is an advantage we second sons have, to walk untroubled below our fathers' eyeline. It gives us time to think, time to hone our own visions. How much I wanted to tell Sophe, then, about my vision, its breadth. How much, if I'm honest, I wanted to impress her.

'No one has mastered sandstone,' I said. 'Not like Michelangelo did marble.'

But I would. *I* would. The Master of Sandstone. I would carve. I would sculpt. I would find beauty. And I would elevate my town and its sandstone.

'But your Pop?' she asked.

'At first he wanted me to join him in the quarry.'

'So he was disappointed?'

'In the end he had no illusions about me. And he had Jack, so he let me go. I begged him for stone. And I set up a space in the backyard looking out over the anthills, and began to carve. I told him my carving would do the town proud, that The Springs would celebrate them . . . that . . .'

'Yes?'

'He had no idea what I meant.'

'What about Emma?'

'Her name's not Emma.'

Sophe was confused.

'It's *Em*, isn't it?'

Em was born of resistance, childish and spiteful. It was a year or two after she'd replaced our mother. While I struggled with it, Jack simply consigned her to irrelevance. He had his life to lead. He'd concluded he wasn't the first child to lose his mother, or the first to have a stepmother forced upon him. Nor did it seem to trouble him that our stepmother was our aunt, our mother's sister. *I* knew she was a parasite and a predator, but Jack didn't seem care about any of that.

'She may as well live with us,' Jack said. 'Forget her. Don't let it bother you.'

I took my lead from him in so many things, but ignoring her was not something I could sustain. I was not Jack.

I can't remember the first note to Jack that started it, some child's intrigue. But I do remember that instead of writing her full name – Miriam – I wrote the initial, 'M'. Perhaps I thought it would protect me if she – or worse, my father – found it. And I thought it was clever, a code.

Jack loved it. He didn't just pick it up in his return note. He raised it to another level – that's how he began to address her. To her face! *Good morning, M*, he'd say. *Is dinner ready yet, M?* I watched in silence and wonder, week turning into month. His campaign didn't seem to take anything out of him. This was simply how it would be, the new reality. Our father didn't intervene, his debt to Jack, I guess. And so Jack's will came to pass and the woman who had assumed the place of our mother became known as M. Answered to M. Accepted that she *was*, in that house, M.

As for 'Em', well 'Em' was a softening, years later. A softening born of guilt, replaced in time by a fondness of sorts. One she also accepted.

'And now?' Sophe asked.

'Now what?'

'How do you get on with her now, with . . . Miriam?'

'Take her or leave her.'

'Jack told me . . .'

'What did Jack tell you?'

'That he . . . that he was reconciled with her,' Sophe said.

Easier for him to say. *I* was the one who'd discovered the truth, had learnt about it by chance. She'd wanted me to do something for her, some domestic chore I'd refused, yet another. And this time, rather than give up, she persisted, despite having no maternal authority – only that we ceded, and I was giving none.

'You took Dad even *before* Mum died,' I said, *snarling* it at her, not believing it myself, not even really knowing what it meant, any of its shades. Wanting only to wound her. And expecting, if anything, anger from her. Ready enough for that, ready to make a stand.

Instead she looked at me. I must have been all fury, all hiss and spit. But Em looked at me, cool, slow-blinking, stringing her gaze out so long that I grew uncertain. This was not the woman I'd come to know.

'Yes,' she said. 'You're right. I did.'

Because she'd had enough of my little war against her. *She* wanted to hurt me too.

Jack didn't seem to care when I told him. It's not that he disbelieved me – he listened, and nodded. But when I was done, all he said was 'Is that right?' It wasn't a question, was just a mildly surprised acceptance, that the world is a strange place. It confounded me that Jack wasn't moved. Even in defence of our mother. It unsettled me, because it couldn't be right.

Late one afternoon I walked the streets of the town we'd reached after our last lift of the day, looking for an *atelier*, a mechanic's workshop. Unlike our own towns, where they're hidden away, in the desert mechanics are prominent, their main street shop-signs large and colourful. Being a mechanic is a noble profession in the Sahara. They bring desert-crossing machines back to life. If they don't have a part, or can't source it, they fashion makeshift solutions from the collections in their workshops. They are preservers and creators.

A mechanic lifted his head from the bonnet of a Peugeot 404 to show me an instrument I'd never seen before: a long-necked flat-head screwdriver with rough parallel grooves spiralling up its shaft. Half screwdriver, half rasp. It was perfect. I didn't bother bargaining.

On my way back to the hotel I collected hand-sized rocks which had come away from a building wall, fallen out of the dried mud. I sat on the hotel roof that evening – modified into a terrace

143

so travellers could sit and drink tea under the stars – and worked the pieces of stone, prying small chunks off with the point of the screwdriver, rasping off grains of sand and quartz.

Sophe joined me, followed by a boy from a nearby restaurant carrying a tray with glasses of mint tea. Washed and refreshed, she sat while we drank the tea and gazed up at the stars. I looked at her, the light of the new moon on her face, the softness of her cheekbones. She must have felt my stare and turned.

'May I?' she said, reaching for the carving – a crescent moon cut into the face of the rock.

'I like it.'

'Thanks,' I said.

'And when you're finished with it?'

'I'll leave it here.'

'Why?'

'They're too heavy to carry. And anyway, I'm happy to leave them. You never know what people might do with them.'

'Or is it for you?'

'Huh?'

'Like Hansel?'

'Sorry?'

'From the fairytale. Isn't that what you're doing? Dropping stones like Hansel did as he travelled deeper and deeper into the forest?'

It was gentle enough, but I tensed, and withdrew. I didn't want to have to think – just there, just yet – about the end of the journey, different for each of us. I didn't want to consider what would happen when we reached Assekrem.

'These aren't just stones. They've been transformed.'

And another thing. If Sophe was comparing me to Hansel, I didn't want her just to be my Gretel.

SEVEN

The next morning I'd only just sat down on a large rock at the outskirts of town, when a *camionette* pulled over with its little cabin and its low tray, the first ride of the day. Sophe was adjusting her headcloth in the shade of a nearby palm, so I walked across to the driver's side window. The driver and his companion could have been twins behind their long beards, white hats and flowing white robes.

'*Salaam alaykum*,' I said.

'*Alaykum as-salaam*.'

But the driver wasn't interested in me. His eyes were on Sophe as she gathered up her bag from the ground and turned. How could he not look? Her straight back, her strong shoulders, her confident stride. Green headscarf covering her hair, a fold across her mouth concealing chin and neck. The long street dress she'd slipped over her clothes, the bottoms of her jeans just visible below the hem. What man would not gaze upon her if he had the chance?

Yet he did not speak. Rather he motioned with his head for us to get in the back. We climbed into the tray, its thin raised ridges pressing against our buttocks, our backs to the cabin. We had one arm each on the tray, the other on our bags. After we'd been sitting for a while, and still the vehicle hadn't pulled onto the highway, I bent to look into the cabin. The two men were talking, watching us, the driver with his black-marble eyes in the rear-vision mirror, the second man having swivelled his body around to our window. I gave the thumbs up and a smile that fell dumb before it reached them. In unison, they turned their double gaze ahead, and the truck was soon drawing away from the palm trees, and was out on the asphalt, scything its way through the desert.

Around noon we veered off the road. It was only a matter of degrees, the change in course. But soon the *camionette* was rumbling across the floor of the *oued*, speed unchanged, a cloud of dust billowing behind us and an indistinct purple ridge on the horizon. I peered through the cabin window at the driver. He was intent, hands gripping the wheel. As I watched, the vibrations shook loose a postcard of Mecca that had been wedged into a groove in the dashboard. The man in the passenger seat bent to pick it up, and as he tilted his head back we exchanged glances.

I touched Sophe's leg.

'What's happening?' I mouthed.

'I don't know,' she said.

Before we reached the ridge the vehicle stopped. The men waited for nearly a minute until the dust settled and then got out. They neither acknowledged us nor spoke with each other. They merely moved away from the vehicle and spread out a mat each on a sandy patch of ground, one beside the other, before falling to their knees, cupping sand into their hands and rubbing it over their forearms like water. They even poured sand over their brows and the backs of their ears, then began the synchronised prostration before Allah in the east.

Sophe and I were dry from the dust and drank from our water-bottles, small discreet sips. I wanted to climb down from the *camionette* and stretch my legs but decided this might disturb them. Not so much distract them from their prayer – they seemed too purposeful to be easily diverted – but rather that it might have been disrespectful. I thought of Jack and me at mass in The Springs as children. Prayer's stern demand for silence and stillness, control over even one's breathing.

So I watched. The simple choreography of it, the repetition, the pressing of foreheads against the earth, and their murmuring as if God dwelt there in the ground. There was power in it, Jack was right. The way they wove their devotion into the day, and the sense that without this thread of prayer, the days might unravel and lose their shape, lose their substance. Except perhaps it wasn't the devotion but the *discipline* that was impressive, its touch of ferocity.

After the deviation to pray we returned to the highway. Sand drifted across the bitumen at intervals, the tyres of the *camionette* leaving golden eddies in our wake. We stopped at a roadside tea-house around midday, and the men disappeared – we guessed to perform their rituals once again.

'Tired?' Sophe asked.

'It's the wind as much as the sun,' I replied.

'And the vibrations,' Sophe added, smiling.

'And the noise.'

'And the exhaust fumes.'

'And the dust.'

We were both laughing, giggling like children.

'Come on, let's get something to drink,' I said.

At a small table we drank milky tea. The statuette I'd been

working on rested in the centre of the table, a protean female figure Sophie had watched take shape in the back of the jolting *camionette* over the last hour.

'So who is it?' she asked.

'I'm not sure yet.'

'Is it like Michelangelo said, that there's an angel in there, just waiting to be set free?'

I looked at her, trying to read what she meant, whether Jack had said something to her.

'Did you hear,' Mum exclaimed when we were seated at the dinner table one evening, 'about the *Pieta*?'

I was seven. I thought immediately of the plaster figurine mounted on the sideboard – crucified Jesus taken down from the cross and draped across his mother's lap.

'Someone's tried to destroy her,' she gasped.

The shock of it, that someone – and I knew Mum didn't mean Jack or me – had come into the house to destroy our statue. But then I got confused. Hadn't I seen the statue when I came in after school that day, after I'd dropped my bag and gone into the kitchen for a biscuit?

'But . . .' I began.

'The *original*,' Mum said, realising.

Which was a revelation in itself, though not one I fully grasped that afternoon: that the world was divided into originals and copies. I began to understand *that* later, when a photo of the damaged *Pieta* appeared in the newspaper.

But our father and Jack seemed to know what she meant.

'*Inside* St Peter's,' she continued, shaking her head as if not quite believing herself what she was telling us. 'Inside the basilica itself.'

'So what happened?'

Our father was growing irritated. He didn't share her rever-
ence, wanted to know the hard detail.

'It happened after mass, as everyone was leaving. A man
jumped up with a hammer and . . . and . . .'

She was overcome, shaking her head. It was too much for her.

'It's alright, Mum,' Jack said.

'The *Pieta*'s been injured,' she said at last. 'Damaged. And the
man who did it is *Australian*.'

This is one of the only conversations with my mother I remember with absolute clarity.

We followed the story as it unfolded in the news, charged
with the emotion of mothers and their sons and the desecration
of one of the holiest sites in all Christendom. And through it I
discovered Michelangelo Buonarroti, the greatest of all artists.
The assailant had cried out as he struck the statue with his hammer, that he was, himself, Jesus Christ risen from the dead. God
had commanded him to destroy it because, being eternal, Jesus
could have no mother. Then, at his trial, he accused the judges of
pride, because they wanted to declare him – Christ incarnate –
insane. When he was convicted, he was deported back home to
Australia.

So many revelations. Among them, that a statue could have
such power.

'Michelangelo was a master,' I said carefully.

'Your hero? Your Mother Teresa?'

'He was no saint.'

'He wasn't perfect?'

I laughed.

'His work then?' Sophe asked.

'Almost. Some of it.'

'*David?*'

'*David* is *close*, but no, not perfect.'

'The ankles?'

'Everyone says the ankles, that they're too thin, too weak. That he erred. That his ankles can't hold the block. But David stands. The ankles are fine. So no, not the ankles, but the back. He missed a muscle. Look closely next time. On his right side there's a hollow where there should have been a ridge of muscle.'

'His back is beautiful,' she said.

'But not perfect. His rock would have fallen short, would have landed at Goliath's feet.'

'Though it doesn't matter, does it?'

I paused, the space between us quiet, small.

'Perhaps not,' I said, not caring either way.

'Because it doesn't exist,' she pressed, something she wanted to say to me. 'Perfection, that is.'

'Are you talking about Jack's letter? His *perfect love?*'

'Everything is crooked.'

'Even God?'

'Especially God!' That open smile of hers.

The two drivers joined us at the table. They were awkward, glancing at each other as if for support. Through the pane of glass that morning, I'd observed the religious paraphernalia in the cabin, the cards and the stickers, and the tasselled beads. Sophe had told me what she knew, my first lesson about Islam.

'Where are you from?' the driver asked now. A textbook question, one Sophe had been teaching the camp children just a few days earlier.

We told them. My country then hers.

'What is your name?'

Something made Sophe answer in English, made her keep her Arabic to herself.

'She is your wife?' he asked me, ignoring Sophe.

I nodded.

'What are you doing here?' the second one asked, though with their beards it wasn't easy telling them apart. They all start to look the same, I thought, the old joke, the old lazy joke. The women in the camp, Sophe told me later, called men like that, simply, 'Beards', encapsulating their fanatical attention to every detail of their religious observance.

'What is it?' the first Beard asked, pointing to my rough figurine.

'It is a sculpture,' I answered.

'It is bad,' he said, almost spitting it at me.

'Excuse me?' I said.

'Bad,' he replied angrily. 'You must not. It is forbidden.'

The two of them rose soon after, and turned their backs and returned to their *camionette*. Sophe and I meekly followed, our bags still in the tray. The offer of the lift had not been withdrawn, so we climbed aboard, the vehicle pulling away before we had a chance to settle.

'What on earth was that about?'

Sophe was accepting in the face of their rudeness.

'There are no people in Islamic art. Some Muslims say that to represent the human form is idolatry. That Mohammad forbade it.'

I thought of all those scenes of idyllic waterfalls and perfect, palm-lined, golden-sand beaches with not a human in sight.

'They honour God in pattern.'

Nothing in the world of The Springs had prepared me for this. Suddenly all those Arabesques I'd seen, all those tiled mosaics on the floors of those hotel foyers began to make sense. The fading

151

hennaed patterns on Sophe's hands when she held them out to me. Look, see. Flowers and plants indivisible. An infinite pattern extending beyond the visible world into the eternal.

A part of me had registered the absence but hadn't yet translated it into thought. Just another of the countless things that had disturbed me since I'd been there, unsettling in a way I hadn't even realised. Sometimes the most profound things are the most difficult to see. That to introduce the human into art might be an affront to the perfection of God.

My own nagging thought came back: that carving stone, no matter the image, is an affront to beauty.

A telecommunications tower poked above a ridge on the horizon. After the beauty of dunes and old *ksars*, the oases and the *palmeraie*, and the ancient watercourse we'd followed for so long, this last settlement was miserable at first sight. The town at the end of the line: a single hotel, and a lifeless market and a post-office and a petrol station and a customs depot and a prison. *That* made me smile. Prisoners always, everywhere – the murderers and the rapists and the terrorists – are sent as far away as geography allows, beyond even the fringes of civilisation. The story of my own country, I said to Sophe as we climbed out of the *camionette* at the market.

The Beards would have dropped us off without another word, like roadside waste, their judgement unaltered by the miles since their rebuke. But I refused to let them discard us that way. My little show of resistance. My defence of my art.

'*Besslaama*,' I said, daring them to ignore me. Go in safety, a phrase I'd picked up from Sophe.

'*Besslaama*,' I said again, loud enough for the watchers in the marketplace to hear. Still the Beards refused to reply.

'*Besslaama*,' I said a third time, a direct challenge. Faces in the street were turning, curious.

This was enough to extract a grudging reply from them, twin echoes before the Beards wound up their windows and drove off. My little victory.

EIGHT

The hand on the waterfall-clock above the door had just passed nine when Sophe joined me in the only restaurant in town. I waved the waiter over and we ordered soup – *haricot blanc* – and *une grande bouteille de limonade* that he collected from a crate stacked against a wall. He pried the cap off without looking at either the bottle or us, his eyes fixed on the television mounted in the corner of the room. He swirled two glasses in a tub of water, then lifted them out, shook them, and carried them, dripping still, to our table, where he placed them lightly on the red-and-white checked vinyl tablecloth.

When he was gone Sophe reached into the folds of her dress and produced a strangely shaped object, a stone of some sort, delicately cut – a burst of tiny unfolding petals. She handed it to me. I felt the weight of it in my palm. At first I thought it had been carved, that a master had sculpted this enchanting cluster of florets. But the texture of it was different, a movement no sculptor could achieve.

'*Une Rose du Sable,*' Sophe said. 'A sand rose. They're made of crystallised gypsum. The dew dissolves the gypsum in the sand over many years, leaving these roses just under the surface. No two are the same.'

I was breathless.

'Beautiful, isn't it?'

'Exquisite,' I said, turning it in my fingers.

'See – the whole of nature celebrates sculpture.'

I looked up. Her eyes. This wonderful gesture. I could have wept.

Later, as we ate, the waiter turned up the sound on the television to catch the evening news bulletin. The newsreader with his thick moustache and slick black hair behind his plain news desk – everything in Arabic sounds urgent, I thought. But Sophe turned to watch the television as well, and the waiter increased the volume again.

'What is it?' I asked.

'An attack,' she said, still listening intently to the bulletin.

I watched the images of the capital, agitated crowds of men and the government's security forces in the street, but couldn't tell if they were policemen or soldiers. Still didn't know what the difference was. Knew only that men in uniforms were pointing guns at men with beards in flowing white robes.

'*Fou*,' the waiter said. Crazy. He'd said it in French, so it was meant for us. Sophe asked him what had happened. He gazed at the screen for so long it seemed he might not answer.

'*Les journalistes*,' he said eventually. '*Les chanteurs. Les travailleurs étrangers. Et maintenant les Pères, les sept Pères . . .*'

'Seven priests have been killed,' she whispered to me.

The waiter shook his head sadly, and clicked his tongue. He turned his back on the screen as if to walk away, then cursed and turned around again, muttering at the images of the soldiers struggling to contain the crowd. It was difficult to know whether to watch him or the television.

'*Tout est cassé. Tout est cassé,*' he repeated, again and again. '*Tout.*'

I raised my eyebrows in query.

'He says everything is broken.'

'Everything?'

Sophe shrugged.

'Society.'

'Why?' I asked.

'*Pourquoi?*' he said, turning slowly to me. '*Pourquoi? Vous voulez savoir pourquoi?*'

I nodded.

'*Parce que notre histoire est cassée. Le français nous a cassés, et nous n'avons pas guéri.*'

He reached up to the television and turned it off, then left the restaurant. Sophe and I remained, our meals half-eaten.

'What did he mean?'

'He says they're still wounded from colonisation.'

'I don't follow.'

She moved the palms of her hands across the surface of the vinyl tablecloth with its nicks and stains and burn–holes, as if she were polishing it.

'These stories aren't ours to tell. I don't know *how* to tell it. Not properly, it's so complex.'

'Will you try? Please.'

And so Sophe gave me another lesson. She told me about the war of independence against France and how many were killed back then, an incomprehensible number. About the country's independence heroes and its deteriorating trail of governments since – its generals and its presidents. She told me about the Islamists recently returned home from their holy war in Afghanistan, the political party they'd formed and the elections suspended by the government after they won the first round, the Beards. About France and America's fear of another Islamic state, that they'd do whatever it took to prevent it, that denying the Islamists victory seemed the obvious thing to do. Then the Islamists' retaliation, not just against the government but against non-Muslim foreigners. The threats, the ultimatums, the attacks. Locals too, popular singers and movie stars and journalists who favoured a secular state. The executions, the fear, and inevitably the government's reply. The reprisals. Back and forth, so many killings.

'You can see their frustration,' she said. 'Their anger. The broken commitments by their government. By *our* governments. Broken promises and powerlessness – that they're fed up trying to chisel away at the foundations of their society to make it better. But still –' Sophe pointed to the blank television screen – 'that's no reason. It's beyond understanding.'

These were concepts divorced from any reality I knew. I could sense the drama, a hundred moral lessons somewhere there for the extraction. But it was a maze.

'Come on,' Sophe said. 'Let's walk.'

We left town and made for the dunes, the sand becoming softer beneath our feet, the lights of the town falling behind a ridge. There was more moonlight that night than I'd ever thought possible.

I started up the largest dune ahead of her, my calves stretching and straining, legs driving from the thighs. My boots disappeared below the surface with each footstep, sand creeping at my ankles, beneath my soles, inside my socks and between my toes. Grain by grain filling my boots, as if my feet were swelling inside them.

At the top of the dune I caught my breath, looked around. The lights of the town far below. So much dark land. If I reached for it I might even touch the sky, might feel the texture of it on my fingertips. Instead I stretched out my hand to Sophe a few steps below, panting. She took it, and joined me at the crest of the dune. A fluorescent wisp of cloud passed overhead. I turned full-circle, taking in the panorama of sand, the desert which dwarfed the town. All the dunes were moving, a layer of sand particles blowing and falling and gusting and lifting, the dunes shimmering with movement as far as the eye could see. I was heady with it, swimming in exuberance.

I closed my eyes. Then the sound of the wind changed. It had been different on the dune anyway, less insistent than in the town, gentler. But now there was something else – it was not the wind at all, but a plane's engine, a jet, coming on fast. The faint thrum turning to roar. I opened my eyes and found it, low in the sky. Outstripping itself, in advance of the sound, it was a dark arrowhead and a mighty trail of flame, deafening. There was no time for fear, only awe. Then it was gone, swallowed by the stars and the desert wind.

On some primitive impulse we rolled down the dune. It started slowly, but soon we were careening out of control, losing all shape entirely. Whirling limbs churning the sand into the air, into our clothes, into our hair. That long tumble, pulled out of time, glimpses of Sophe in my spiralling, spinning blood, the pitch of excitement, her laughter in the turning night.

We landed together at the foot of the dune. I leant towards her, a wild exuberance upon me, but she turned away. Gave me her cheek instead, allowed my lips to touch her skin, and my fingers to brush the sand from her forehead.

NINE

Finally, Tuareg, three of them. Tall, indigo-turbaned, sunglassed even in the muted dawn light, they sat together in the front, their bodies close. Sophe and I were in the back. I didn't know enough about the legends that had accumulated around them over the centuries to feel much myself, but Sophe was excited. She knew we were being taken across this next part of our journey, this great ocean of sand, by the real thing. That though they were not on camelback, those three men were the true people of the desert, indivisible from it.

The waiter from the restaurant had arranged the lift for us when we got back from the dunes the night before, and we'd risen early so we could head east across the sand. It was a weak dawn, dust in the air. After just fifteen minutes driving we stopped. Not to pray as I'd first thought, but to reduce the air-pressure in the tyres, a faint hiss against the burr of the engine as the land-cruiser dropped nearer the sand. We started again, built speed, and soon began to float. The sweeping desert, the wind whistling, high and insistent through the landcruiser's partly open windows, the haze that hung in the air that morning – light and distance flattened, and the desert seemed to sigh. There was no need for talk.

There was no road, just tyre-tracks in the sand reaching towards the horizon ahead, and the exhilaration of laying out our own route among them. Every few minutes a *balise* – a darkened concrete marker, sometimes a low cairn of stones – appeared in the grainy distance and grew closer, till we reached it, passed and it was gone. And once more there was nothing but lines in the sand before us.

Sophe offered the men dried biscuits, and in return they passed a bag of sweet dates back to us. We collected the pips in our hands and when we were done tossed them out the window into the throat of the wind.

We slowed as we passed through a village, but didn't stop. On its streets of sand there were women at the well, with its giant arm and fulcrum, and children stopping their play to stare. I wondered if it was the Tuareg or us that interested them. At the edge of the village a clutch of abandoned buildings had fallen to ruin. Nearby was a crude animal enclosure and a handful of hard-headed goats tearing leaves off a branch thrown to them moments before. Beyond the goats, on the outer reaches of that fragile settlement, was a grove of eucalypts, at once both strange and familiar. Such unexpected life. A man harvesting them hacking branches off a trunk, two women bundling them for firewood.

The air began to stir. Particles of dust and sand thickening, a grow-ing orange light. The Tuareg leant forward, looking out through the windscreen. I wondered if their language had a word for a change like this, and whether Jack had collected it as he had their words for dunes during his last months with the army. I pressed the palm of my hand on the window and felt the gusting wind.

We slowed. Then stopped. The world began swirling around, above us, beneath. The rising agitation, the insistence as grains of sand grazed against the glass or lodged momentarily beneath the thin rubber blades of the windscreen wipers, each particle in ecstatic dance . . . Yet the three men in their robes calmly waited for it to pass. There was nothing in the wind's ferocity to trouble us, nothing in all the world to fear, and all that was required of us was stillness.

Then abruptly the swirling winds were gone and what was left was a moaning dust-filled sky. There was visibility enough to see that the tracks in the sand were merely smudged, not erased. We would continue.

An hour later, a small dark mass appeared in the haze. The Tuareg steered for it, three wise men pursuing a star. Nearer, we saw it was a mudbrick hut, now abandoned. The ground was stonier and darker in patches, with a different texture to it, and when the men spoke, their talk was lighter, like chatter. One of them smiled to us, with great white teeth, his veil having fallen from across his nose and mouth. It was only when we opened the doors to get out that we heard a bubbling sound. Not the wind, nor the men, but – an extraordinary thing – the sound of running water. Water! How alien the sound, the gushing of spring water feeding a low concrete trough in the middle of that wilderness, water pouring out of a metal casing at the head of the trough, spouting into a long, low reservoir, filling it, creating in the desert a shimmering pool. This miracle these men were showing us.

They stretched their long legs, as if shaking something from their limbs, like dancers before a performance. The air had thinned of sand and dust, and the sun was cleaner now in the sky. Sophe and I drank from the trough, cupping our hands in the cool water and lifting it to our mouths, the men laughing at us, the youngest splashing water on us with his smooth, dark palms.

While the two older men prepared tea, the one who wanted to play took my wrist and led me to the front of the landcruiser, pointing at patches of paintwork which had been blasted away by the sand storm. He banged his chest with an open palm and threw back his head, laughing, before reaching for my hand and holding it in his long fingers. We all squatted in the lee of the vehicle then, the men hitching the folds of their dress, a fire on the sand, a white enamel teapot filled with dried leaves and fresh spring water and settled in the ashes as the fire died. A row of small glasses pressed into the sand, one for each of us.

'Life, love, death,' I whispered to Sophe, who smiled.

The teapot was lifted out of the ashes, hot, the man gripping the handle with his long sleeve and pouring, raising it into the air as the stream of tea arced into the first of the small glasses, raising the pot thirty, forty centimetres high, the tea frothing from the height, and then, when the glass was nearly full the man flicking his wrist and cutting off the flow. The tea in the glass was then returned to the pot, and the man performed his duties again. And a third time. This virtuosity and his pride in it made me think of our father slicing the roast at Sunday lunch.

We drank our desert tea to the song of running water.

'It's like home,' I whispered to Sophe.

The oldest of the Tuareg asked her what I'd said.

'There is a spring in my village,' I explained. 'Its water was once sweet like this.'

'Once?'

I told them an Aboriginal legend I'd only recently heard, Sophe translating. The story of a tribe camped by the spring, one of the women scratching her head by the fire for lice, collecting them in her hand. Suddenly a gust of wind blows them into the fire, and a celestial vengeance comes down upon the woman's tribe. Her entire people are killed and buried in that place, by clouds. The place becomes known as 'Woo-urra-jim-igh' – place where the clouds fall down – and the water that emerges from the burial place from that day on is clear, and pure . . . According to the legend it had healing powers for those who bathed there – it made the weak strong and the strong even stronger – but it was forbidden to drink the water. That was the legend, the lore.

They didn't understand.

'It is a strange story,' I said. 'I don't really understand it myself.'

'Perhaps it's not yours to tell,' Sophe smiled.

'But you *do* drink the water, yes?' the oldest Tuareg persisted.

'No longer . . . no.'

I recounted how people had once bottled it and sold it and how it had made the town famous: the medals it won at the Melbourne International Exhibition in 1881, and the Franco-British Exhibition in London in 1908, and the Medal of Honour at the Panama Pacific International Exposition in 1915, and then gold in 1925 at the British Empire Exhibition. How we'd built a Spa Park where the sick would come to be healed; people with all sorts of infirmities who'd spend weekends at the spa, *taking the waters*, and who'd leave with their bladders cleansed, their polio-tightened limbs loosened, their gout or their arthritis gone for good. I told them about the recreation camp for soldiers during the Second World War, and how in the 1960s the pool was dug out and concreted to become the largest man-made pool in the entire country. How there was water-skiing, and open-air concerts, and paddle boats and rounds of mini-golf.

Sophe patiently translated it all.

Then, in a slow, painful decline, came the salinity problems that meant the bore had to be redrilled and re-cased. Algal blooms grew on the banks of the open pool, fed on the nitrogen run off from local farmers. Testing lead to fears about radium levels – higher than the government scientists said was acceptable in drinking water. Headline after headline. The Spa Park is deserted now, I told them, a ghost town at the edge of a ghost town.

The oldest of the three stood, and gestured for me to give him my water-bottle. I watched him fill it from the spring, and return it to me.

'He wants you to take it home with you.'

We stopped again at dusk. There was no spring this time, no eucalypts, no date palms. No crumbling buildings. Only sand and falling sun and four men and one woman stopping for the night. The neck of the goatskin – head and hooves severed, the limbs tied off in knots – was loosened, opened, and spring water poured out of the animal's throat into the white enamel teapot. We drank tea again and ate. We laid out mats, and crawled into our sleeping bags or drew blankets over ourselves and nestled into the sand.

At some point in the night I woke. It was the rising moon. When I opened my eyes the dust had been swept away, and above was the night sky in all its nakedness. It was too bright for me to sleep, star upon star. I rolled over and saw Sophe curled like a crescent into the night beside me, her cheek glistening with minute flecks of quartz and moonlight, her day's sweat transformed. She was the stuff of stars and of sand.

TEN

The Tuareg delivered us to the other side of the sand-sea, and dropped us at the edge of an ancient oasis town shadowed by vast red dunes. From here we would turn south again for the final stretch to Tamanrasset and the mountains, the last, long step down to the hermitage at the end of the world. A wisp of sand crept across the road where we waited by an *oued*, seeming to move of its own accord, with a will, patient and determined. As if the progress of the dunes was inevitable, and the road and the collection of habitations, the date palms and the oasis were, when all accounts were settled, doomed.

Beside us was a newly erected road sign, the word for what must be Tamanrasset, 692 kilometres away. Just off the tarmac an older sign lay abandoned on the ground. The same Arabic script, but a different number, 684, as if the distance had increased with the passage of time.

'Why do they use our numbers, but not our letters?'

Sophe laughed.

'The numbers are *theirs*. It is *we* who've adopted *them*.'

I looked at the Arabic on the sign, the grace of the lines, the dancing flow.

'It's a beautiful script,' I said.

That's what I thought back then, the more I was exposed to it, the more time I spent with Sophe. And though for a long, long time since, a thought like that would have provoked something in me I couldn't control, I'm beginning to think that way again.

Sophe pointed to a stop sign not far from where we stood, the universal red octagon with the Arabic word for 'stop'.

'It *is* wonderful isn't it? The simplicity of the calligraphy.'

'It looks like two people on a toboggan,' I said. And I told her about a caravanning holiday Jack and I had at the beach when we were kids, a week of doubling down dunes on a sled like that.

'Do you miss him?' Sophe asked softly.

It was not a question I was ready for.

'I've never thought about it like that.'

'How then?'

'He left a long time ago, Sophe.'

'What do you mean?'

'He left home to join the army a year before he left Australia to come here.'

'Did you miss him *then*?'

'Did I miss him then?' I looked at the ground and pushed sand over the toe of one boot with the other. 'I . . . I felt he'd . . . left me behind. Even though he was always his own man. Even though I always knew that . . . that he wasn't bound to us, that he was always going to leave. In some ways was never really with us. But still. . . . Still, when he left home, things did change.'

'How?'

The gentleness of the question. I would have answered it if I could.

'I was the only one there to deal with Em . . . with Dad. It fell on me. I was angry. Even though Jack and I never . . . Anyway,

166

they missed him. And, well . . . I was a very, very different person. I was not Jack.'

I bent to retie my bootlaces, which had come loose – but a man appeared suddenly beside us.

I straightened, startled. His eyes swung wildly.

He began burying me with sound – not English, not French, and not, I could tell from Sophe's face, Arabic.

I shook my head. *Je ne comprends pas.* I don't understand.

He grew more frantic, as if I'd sided against him. He pressed closer, his arms beginning to thrash around, the long, crooked fingers of his hands scratching at the air, closer and closer to my face, as if trying to claw understanding out of me.

I had raised my arms to ward him off, when a woman joined us. She too was distraught, yet there was something compelling about the movement of her hands, the intensity with which she pressed her fingers against Sophe's forearm, woman to woman.

Sophe followed her gestures and we saw, some distance off the road, a clump of half-stripped gums. There was more sun than shade beneath the ragged branches, and under the tree we could see some bags, and a sleeping body. Somehow through the woman's pleadings Sophe apprehended that a fever had taken hold of her daughter. Could we give them medicine?

I placed the palm of my hand on my chest, a gesture of regret I'd observed. I thought I understood its courtesy, its reasonableness. I shook my head.

'No,' I said, gentle as I could. '*Non.*'

It was neither the man nor the woman who responded to me, but Sophe, the look on her face an immense incomprehension of the soul. Her lips opened, but then she shook her head, appalled. She turned her back on me and left – crossed the dirt towards the trees and the body of the girl, the man and the woman hurrying after her. I remained beside my bag. Though I watched.

Sophe knelt. The man and woman hovered either side, allowing her to lean close to their daughter, giving her space, freedom,
trust. Tenderly, Sophe placed a palm on the girl's forehead. After
a while she rose and turned, stepped away from the weathered
three and returned to me.

'She is very sick.'

I nodded.

'We need to give her something.'

'We don't have anything.'

'What have you got in your bag?'

'Not much. Aspirin, Panadol.'

'Nothing else?'

'Well, amoxicillin, but there's just the one course of it,' I said
uncertainly.

'Antibiotics! Excellent.'

'It's all we've got.'

'It's all we've got to give then.'

'No.'

'No?'

'We don't know when we'll need it, Sophe.' Not explanation,
not even plea. 'If one of us were to fall ill –'

'We're strong. We're healthy,' she said. 'We *don't* need it.'

'But tomorrow? The next day? The day after?'

'There is only today. We are healthy. She is sick.'

But I couldn't retreat.

'No,' I said.

Sophe folded her arms and looked at me. She swept the scarf
from her head, and refolded her arms. Her hair was wild from
the sand and the sun and the camping in the dunes. She breathed
through flared nostrils, once, twice, then seemed to harden before
my eyes, or rather, to withdraw. A process that might take a life-
time seemed to happen in moments.

'Give me the biscuits then.'

She'd stripped herself clean, and only words were left. I opened my duffel bag and handed her one of the packets. She looked at it, and then looked at me and said:

'And the bread. And the cheese.'

I did not resist. I took out the loaf we'd bought that morning for our journey and the packet of *La Vache Qui Rit.*

'A bottle of water.'

A third time I reached into my bag.

'Thank you,' she said, the politeness of a stranger.

She walked the food and water across the dust and squatted, as if shielding the girl from me.

When eventually a semitrailer stopped I was relieved. Something to break the awful silence that shrouded us. I was quicker to my feet than Sophe and called up to the two drivers high in the cab of their truck, repeating the name of our destination, Tamanrasset, over and over until they understood me. They talked between themselves for almost a minute before motioning us – reluctantly it seemed, as if they had no real choice – to climb into the back of their truck with its cargo of commercial-size refrigerators. We squatted low in the tray as the truck pulled away from the red town. Behind us, light sand swirled on the dark surface of the asphalt road, patterning and settling in the truck's wake.

For the first hundred kilometres the road held. Then, as the distance from the red town grew, it began to break up. Cracks appeared, then holes where chunks had come loose. Finally the road became rubble, and the truck pulled off the ruins of the asphalt, and joined the *piste*, a more flexible, more durable route running parallel to the collapsed bitumen. Eventually small cairns of broken asphalt appeared as markers every few kilometres, the remains of the road itself lost beneath the sand.

The truck pounded southwards.

We entered a long narrow valley, granite ranges close on either side of us, parallel ridges of darkness. Suddenly we turned off the *piste* and headed west, following tyre-tracks across the valley floor. Ahead of us, at the foot of the black range, a building appeared, squat and whitewashed. Its roof was rimmed with small, stepped turrets, and flags hanging limp at each corner. The building seemed small, humbled by the towering wall of rock behind it. Within its orbit was the distinct shape of a Kombi van. Even from a distance we could see the van was slumped broken upon the earth, a carcass discarded to the sun.

The ground grew rougher as we approached, the truck swaying and banging its way across the stony pan of the ancient valley floor. My kidneys jarred. It seemed there was not a rock missed, or furrow avoided as we lurched forward, each jolt transmitted directly into our wretched bodies.

With the building upon us we slowed, and were glad of the respite. It had a rectangular base, and rose three metres high. There were two doors, blue-painted wooden frames set into the mudbrick. One of the men wound down his window, leant out and back towards us, said something brusquely, then withdrew.

'It's the tomb of a famous *marabout*,' Sophe said, 'one of their saints. He says we should pray.'

The truck began circling the shrine: it was blinding beneath the overhead sun, each of the four walls flat and white and compelling. Nothing broke the light, nothing varied the texture. Through the window I could see the driver fingering prayer beads with his right hand. His left remained on the steering wheel, holding it to a steady turn as the truck bumped slowly round the mausoleum. Once, twice, three times, the voices of the drivers and their incantations louder than the truck's engine.

When the rite was completed, the truck straightened, and lumbered away. Passing the Kombi, it stopped. The driver leant out his window once more, pointing with his hand at the charred remains of the van.

I didn't try reading his face, but looked to Sophe instead. Watched as she leant forward to receive the message, then pulled back as her brow knitted.

'What did he say? Sophe?'

She tried waving me away.

'No, Sophe. What did he just say?'

She looked ahead, out over the cab of the truck, a reluctant witness.

'He says it was an infidel's vehicle,' she sighed. 'He says Allah set it alight because the infidels didn't circle the shrine correctly. He said Allah punishes the wicked.'

I wanted to laugh. I wanted to draw Sophe in so the two of us could laugh together at their ignorance and the dark cave of their unreason, the comedy of it. But after what had happened that morning, I didn't risk it. I looked back at the mausoleum, small against the mountainside, and the rocks and the scree, and the rounded boulders resting so precariously on layered platforms high above the fragile mud construction, no breeze to stir its limp flags.

When the truck stopped suddenly on the easterly side of a heavy-bouldered ridge it came as a surprise. We were dazed from its violent lurching along the rutted road, the slamming of our bodies against the cabin with every new pothole, the constant hammering of our kidneys, the ache in our fingers from gripping the rails so tight. It had become a condition of existence. The sick girl and her parents and Sophe's nobleness and my smallness seemed such a long time ago.

As I climbed down the semitrailer was letting off waves of heat. I joined the drivers at the rear wheel. One of them crawled under the truck before rolling over so he was lying on his back, looking up at its workings. A glob of oil hit the ground beside his head. I squatted for a better look, but the second man placed a restraining hand on my shoulder.

'*Non,*' he said sharply. This was theirs.

So I withdrew, and Sophe joined me on a large rock nearby. The sun cast soft shadows on everything it couldn't reach, deepening all things.

'Can it be fixed?' she said.

'A hole, that's all.'

Eventually the two men stepped back to consider the truck, to gesture at it with open palms, to look across at us, back to the truck, and at us once more, their voices growing increasingly agitated until one of them strode over to where we were sitting, armed with some accusation.

'What?' I said when he'd returned to the truck.

Sophe shrugged her shoulders.

'They want someone to blame.'

'It's *our* fault?'

'We've brought bad luck. Infidels, you see.'

'Of course.'

And so we waited as the men went about the repair. I left the road and climbed among the boulders, higher and higher. There was stone and there was dry air, and there was the hazy ridgeline and the buzzing sun.

In the shimmering light I saw what appeared to be a figure on the ridge. I stopped and blinked, but the apparition was gone. I climbed higher, feeling the mountain in my hands, boulder by boulder. Mountains have character. Even as kids we wanted to divine the spirit of our own mountain, Table Top. Her crest is scythe-clean and flat, and only grasses grow there – not a single tree or boulder mars that flatness. Yet even as kids we'd seen her different faces, and on nights when lightning jagged earth-wards, our mountain illuminated in fierce shards as if to reveal her true self.

In that name 'Table Top' we knew our own inadequacy: we'd been told none of the Aboriginal myths as kids, nothing of the Dreaming. Our parents and theirs, and theirs before them had heard none of the stories either, or judged them not important enough to remember. But while we didn't know the creation story of our own mountain, we knew about rock gods and river gods. Barefoot on her slopes we became Aborigines climbing towards corrobo-ree. Jack on a rock, poised, still as death on one thin leg, the other raised, his arms out to either side, some solitary bird on the verge of flight. Hand over foot we scaled the rock-slides, our palms pressed into sharp scree, our hands filled with mountain imaginings.

I stopped, a hundred metres or so above the truck, and looked down. The men must have finished and were lying, resting. A child appeared, moving along the road towards the two men and Sophe. A small, stiff-haired girl in shreds of cloth that might once have been an ankle-length dress, skipping barefoot between potholes, moving lightly across the earth. She was carrying some-thing in her skirt, both hands lifting the hem. As she danced towards Sophe, I began scrambling down the slope, then leap-ing from boulder to boulder. I saw Sophe raise her head from her journal – she was surprised by the desert urchin padding her quiet way past the sleeping drivers, and moving tentatively down the side of the truck. Sophe smiled to her. It was then I tripped and fell, dislodging a small cascade of stones and landing on my shoulder, a rock-edge tearing my shirt and skin.

When I regained my feet, both Sophe and the girl were look-ing up at me.

I picked my way more cautiously down the last of the slope. At the bottom Sophe held out her hand to guide me over the final rock. I sat in the shade where a moment earlier she'd been sitting herself. From my duffel bag Sophe took the first aid kit. She had me remove my shirt, and then knelt before me. With the blade of her own pocketknife she scraped pieces of gravel from my hands and shoulder before splashing water on the wounds. She squeezed antiseptic cream over the grazes, and unpeeled some band-aids, the child watching all the while, fascinated.

When Sophe was done the girl came forward. She approached Sophe and knelt before her, as she'd observed Sophe kneeling before me, lifting her tattered skirt as she bent. Her knees, and the skin of her shins, and the top of her feet pressed against the stones of the earth. She lifted the apron of her skirt for Sophe to see, unfolding it like a petal. In it were pieces of flint. Sophe leaned forward to look, and, encouraged, the girl began picking them out, one by one, and laying them in two neat rows on top of a flat stone, her prehistoric arrowheads, her treasures.

The little desert girl spoke no Arabic or French but spread her arms instead, a gesture encompassing the rocks and the boulders, the granite range, the entirety of the desert. It was a prologue to a pantomime, for the girl then began to act out how she'd found the arrowheads, crawling on her hands and knees and turning over loose stones with her fingers, inspecting the fragments of rock. Next she picked up one of the pointed shards of flint, and fitted it to the end of an imaginary spear, her eyes darting towards Sophe constantly, making sure she hadn't lost her. She returned to the ground then, and with the edge of a stone drew the outline of an elephant or a wildebeest or a lion, so crude the sketch, it seemed not to matter. When Sophe nodded that she understood the girl rose for the final act of her story, the child now become a hunter, a Diana in miniature, stalking the land for prey, bringing her quarry down with her prehistoric weapon.

When she was done Sophe motioned for her to come closer. I thought she might embrace her. But as the little girl inched forward, the driver came round from the other side of the truck, his boots hard against the ground. He yelled a scornful rebuke at the girl, and waved the back of his hand at her while keeping his distance as if she were a rabid dog. The second man joined the first, these two men and their great vehicle and this tiny ragged girl.

And so Sophe stood, and stepped between the drivers and the cowering girl, and faced the two men.

Their surprise that a woman would oppose them was momentary, and soon they'd turned their snarls on her. But Sophe responded and she was no less vehement than they. The argument escalated into a contest, more at stake than merely whether the girl would stay or go. It was as if every belief they held dear was in jeopardy. And all the while the rock-girl watched – more fascinated than frightened – as the Arab truck drivers and the white woman argued in that vast chamber of desert stone. Finally Sophe prevailed, her determination stronger than the men's custom and their pride. She outlasted them and they withdrew. *Folle*, they muttered. She was mad, as if therefore different laws of human behaviour, and authority, applied. They retreated.

Sophe gestured to the girl again and nodded as she stepped forward. She bade her kneel once more and began producing gifts from her daypack: shoelaces, a pen, half a dozen sheets of blank paper which she tore from her journal, all the remaining sweets she'd bought from a street vendor a week ago, three hundred *dinar* in notes. Then she scooped the arrowheads from their display-stone, and carefully lowered them into the skirt of the transfixed girl, her black eyes full of wonder.

I rose. The desert child looked up as I neared, uncertain, but Sophe nodded and patted her arm. Without looking, without it mattering, I emptied my medical kit into the girl's skirt. Sophe pressed her palm against the little girl's cheek then, and the girl turned, and began her climb back into the rocks.

Night fell and with it the cold. The truck roared relentlessly on, tunnelling its way through the darkness. We were wearing all of our warm clothes, but still they were not enough. Dry skin in the fierce air, we sheltered behind the cabin with our shoulders pressed against each other, but the bitter, curling wind reached us there too, prying beneath collars and sleeves and robes and the cuffs of our trousers.

Near midnight we slowed to pass through a gorge – the mountains momentarily smothering the stars – so narrow I leant out to touch the sheer granite walls, but the cliff-face was just out of reach. We followed the fissure as it carved its way through the rocks, till we spilled out of the earth at the other end of the gorge and were bared to the stars once more.

We began shaking with cold, first Sophe, then me, our teeth chattering. Shuddering hard, I remembered the huge fridges stretched along the length of the tray behind us, the truck's cargo. I reached for the handle of one. Though my fingers were numb, I managed to release the latch, and lift the door open. Long, cavernous, and empty, the metal box was cold, but inside there was no wind. I wrapped the latch of the door with a sock so it couldn't shut and motioned for Sophe. She peered inside then nodded and swung her legs over, lowering herself down. I followed, and suddenly all was quiet, all the night's roaring above us as we lay there on our backs, the metal biting against our shoulder blades and our buttocks and the smalls of our backs, but the stars out there somehow brighter. The aluminium was cold but Sophe's arm and the outside of her thigh where she pressed against me were warm, the vibrating truck forcing our bodies against each other, absorbing the jolts, a careful, heart-filled trembling.

I blew against my hands, the breath stinging my frozen fingers. Then, when they'd thawed, I pressed my warm palms first against my cheek, then Sophe's. And Sophe nestled her cheek into my hand in reply, almost imperceptible, perhaps just a bump in the road. The heat returning.

Then another jolt, and the backs of our heads knocked against the metal, both of us gasping – the surprise and the momentary pain of it. 'Here,' I said, sliding my arm beneath her head. Not thinking. Risking everything. And for a long time of stillness, neither of us breathed. I could count the stars.

Then Sophe's body shifted, turning, an eternity in her rolling to face me. Her eyes and my thumping heart, and then Sophe reached her hand around my back, pulling herself closer. Her hips. Her head on my shoulder. Her breasts beneath her clothes, against my chest. I slipped the scarf off her head, bared her forehead to the starlight, felt the fall of her waist, tasted the salt of her lips.

Sophe sat to lift her robes from her legs and waist, and over her shoulders. My fingers followed her shirt-buttons, and her hollowed neck drew me down, and my palms met the flat of her stomach and there was a precipice, and we were over it, falling through the night.

ELEVEN

When we booked into the hotel in Tamanrasset we followed the routine we'd perfected on our journey south: room inspection, assurances about electricity and water, our passport details entered into the hotel register, checking in as a couple, just married. But everything was altered, everything. Sophe was changed beside me, and I was new, somehow undiscovered.

And I could also feel Jack now. His presence up there in the Ahaggar, so close. These streets he must have walked, the vendors he would have bought bread from, the blue-veiled Tuareg men he might have exchanged greetings with, perhaps even in their own language.

I asked the hotel-keeper whether he'd heard about an Australian staying in the hermitage in the mountains, Assekrem.

'*L'ermitage chrétien?*' The Christian hermitage?

He was another of those Arabs in white, the beard and the flowing gown and the white Islamic hat.

'*Oui,*' I answered.

He paused, considering me closely. I'd assumed it was my accent, or that I'd asked the wrong question, or something about me had given Sophe away. He narrowed his eyes and shook his head slightly, wanting more, some motion of his wrist.

I took out my two photos of Jack. He looked at them both and reached for the one of Jack in uniform.

'*Qui est-il?*'

'*Mon frère.*'

'*C'est un . . . soldat?*'

A slow question. Filled now with suspicion. Perhaps even more.

'*Non, non,*' I said quickly. '*Je crois qu'il est dans les montagnes. Ahaggar.*'

'*Le soldat est dans les montagnes?*'

The conversation was deteriorating.

'*Non. Il n'est pas soldat.*'

His eyes were hardening, some lurking danger.

'*Il n'est pas soldat?*'

'*Non, non,*' I persisted. '*C'est un . . .*' I was floundering, not knowing the right thing to say, the right description '. . . *un père.*'

But that word – father – wrong too.

'Can you explain, Sophe?'

The hotel-keeper listened carefully to Sophe. His concentrated eyes, the questions which followed, Sophe's answers. The sound of her voice alone was reassuring. So calm. I understood nothing of it, of course, the Arabic.

In the end he placed our room key on the desk and turned away as if he didn't want to know us.

I had to call home. Though I hadn't yet found Jack, I'd collected enough to share – things I *needed* to give to my father. Thanks to Sophe and to the journey itself, I was confident enough at least to do that now.

I left Sophe at the entrance to the women's hammam, her wrist pulling away from my fingers. Past the mosque with its minaret was the post-office. At the telephone counter I wrote down the number on a piece of paper in overlarge letters, and handed it to the operator. He read it back.

'*Oui,*' I said.

'*Australie?*'

'*Oui.*'

He nodded, and pointed me to a booth. After a few moments the phone shook, with that old bell sound, and I picked up the handpiece. Down the line came ringing, sad and plaintive, so far away. The voice, when it answered, was Em's, off-balance. It was not yet dawn.

'Em, it's me, Bas.'

A little groan, followed quickly by a burst of pleasure.

'Bas!'

'Sorry to wake you, Em.'

'Don't be silly!'

A swelling within my chest. A familiar voice. Even Em's. So, so, so distant. So much forgotten, momentarily at least.

'How are things, Em?'

'Oh Bas.'

I could picture her standing in the kitchen, having fumbled the light on, blinking in the hardness of its fluorescent blast. Her hair would be pressed out of shape by her pillow, her nightdress hanging loose, falling around her knees. She'd be barefoot, the floorboards warm still from the day. She would have stumbled from her bedroom down the hall, the sound of her footsteps dulled by the long scarlet runner. My father must be lying awake, trying to work out who it was.

'How's Dad?'

'Yes, he's fine.' He's awake listening, I thought, the tone of her voice. 'He'll be glad you've called. Where are you?'

'I'm in the desert.'

'The desert?'

'A desert town.'

I named it, and the town before this one – the red town – and said the name of the country too, just in case. Where I was going next, the mountains. I was leaving my own trail.

'Have you found him?' she asked.

In the end it came to that. And to think I'd believed the information I'd gathered so far might have been *worth* something.

'No, but nearly. I've learnt a lot –'

'We were wondering when you were going to call. We got a letter.'

'My postcard?'

'No, Bas,' she answered carefully, not wanting to hurt me. 'From Jack. A letter from Jack.'

Even *this* – Jack had beaten me to them! So it was *me* ringing *them* for information. I could have laughed out loud, black and bitter.

Then I heard my father's voice in the background, could sense his bulk in the corridor, heard that hiss of his – *for Chrissake* – and the vehemence he could get into it, knew he'd be grasping the phone from Em's hand.

'Bas,' he bellowed, 'is that you?'

I breathed in, held it, let the air out again slowly.

'Hello, Dad.'

What was I resigning myself to?

'For Chrissake, Bas, you've got to bring him back. Em'll read you the letter. You've got to bring him back. Poor bastard. He's not *right*, Bas. Understand? He's not thinking right. It could happen to any of us, Bas. You've got to find him. Got to bring him back. Are you there? Bas? Bas!'

How easy it would have been to walk away.

181

'I'm here, Dad. What's happened?'

'He's not right *in the head*, Bas. There's no shame in it, Bas, absolutely no shame. War can do that. There's no shame. Understand? Something happens and you crack. There's no shame in it . . . understand?'

'I understand.'

'Good, son. Here's Em. She'll read it to you. Here. Listen to this –'

And Em read out Jack's letter of God. Like his letter to Sophe, Jack's evangelism had arrived straight from the mountains of the desert: He is alone and face to face with all that is Eternal. Jesus is Lord and Jack is daily cleansed so he might live and die at Jesus' feet, the feet of his Beloved. Jesus calls him to that which is simple. And he has found it here, among the Muslims. There is nothing to fear. He is happy, and he prays for them. For peace. They are not to worry. They are bathed in Christ's love.

There'd been so many Jacks. Powerful Jack. Ironic Jack. Sceptical Jack. Jack of escapades. Playful; neglectful; laughing; dark. Jack the soldier. Jack who was destined for greatness. All true. I'd seen it. But not this. Not this. Of all the Jacks, this was the odd one out.

'He wants to be alone,' I said to Em.

'Oh Bas,' she sighed. Resignation or despair.

In the background I could hear my father. *Make sure he brings him home. Make sure he understands to bring him home.*

TWELVE

Sophe was already seated when I got to the restaurant that evening, her head turned to the waiter at her table, listening to him. She was glowing after her bath – her clean skin, the henna rubbed from her hands – and I wished I'd been brave enough to try the hammam, rather than having a short, cold shower in the hotel. She was wearing a new headscarf, one she'd probably bought from the markets that afternoon. She saw me coming and smiled, before turning back to the waiter and whatever he was telling her.

I sat down. Their conversation washed over me, Arabic with the odd word in French, something serious the waiter wanted to say to her. But they are all serious, these Arabs, I thought, so unreadable. I studied Sophe's raised face, the strength of her chin, her stretching neck – so intent, so alert, beautiful. The waiter turned, including me in what he was saying.

'Pardon,' I said, '*je ne comprends pas.*'

'He says we're safe down here,' Sophe interpreted. She thanked him and he turned away to serve the table beside us.

'Safe?'

'There was another killing up north yesterday. A French journalist in Eucalyptus.'

'Eucalyptus?'

'It's the name of one of the suburbs in the capital.'

'I don't believe you.'

'There's nothing to worry about. We're a long way away.'

'I mean about the suburb. There's not really one named "Eucalyptus", is there?'

'Sure is, Bas,' Sophe said. 'Sure is. And it's where a lot of the trouble is.'

The thought landed on me there in the restaurant, detonating in my lap. Had she slept with Jack?

'Jack . . .'

Sophe leant forward.

'Yes?'

'Did . . . ?'

'Yes?'

But I didn't really want to know, not then. Not now.

'I need to go up there alone,' I said.

Suddenly I had this vivid image of what might happen if we went up together. I pictured both of us walking towards him, calling out his name, Jack turning, recognising us, and stepping towards us. But then having to choose. And what I saw was Jack greeting her first. Or worse, embracing her but not me, instead merely shaking my hand. Or Jack falling at Sophe's feet weeping. I could not bear that, could not face the possibility that all I might ultimately achieve was to deliver *her* to *him*.

So I said, the promise bulging in my throat, my heart:

'I will bring him down.'

'What do you mean?' she said, each word weighted, tangible, as clear as everything she ever did.

I would make my way up into the mountains, find him at his monastery, and . . . And what? *Bring him down.* What did I mean? Bring him back to earth? From out of the clouds he'd ascended, back to reality. Or did I mean bring him to his knees? Did a part of me want that?

'I will find him and bring him back.'

I remember her eyes, so true, so sharp, laying me open. But not to contest this, because Sophe refused to be my rival. Her eyes were unforgiving in their penetration – *What is it that you want?* – demanding I understand myself, challenging me to. But I was flailing around again. Do I flail any less today, after all these years? Who knows. I've no wish to chase shadows now, I know that. I prefer to let them be.

'I will find a lift up the mountain. I will be gone three days, no more. I will bring him down.'

She looked and she looked. How thin I felt under her gaze. Whatever solidity I thought I had dissolved before her. How insubstantial and small my heart must have appeared to her.

'OK,' Sophe said. The same calm as the first day I saw her, all equanimity residing in her breast. 'I trust you.'

THIRTEEN

When I first glimpsed the Ahaggar, the distant mountains looked to be a series of mounds rising from the desert, like the abandoned anthills in the back paddock at home. Slowly they metamorphosed, the entire landscape rising, swelling, enveloping us as we drove onwards, inwards. I've since heard travellers marvel at their beauty, read their breathless descriptions of wonder and of majesty. It was nothing of the sort. The creative drama of the place was dark.

Everywhere were the scars of gods and demons. The land was what was left over after their warring. Or their play, who could tell? But it was desolate. All the miles of desert I'd passed through till then were fertile when set against this heartless landscape. No blade of grass, no tree, had *ever* lived here, no memory, even, of life. No ancient trace of it. In the wind that whistled and howled and screeched all the hours of the climb, there was no longing. There was nothing mournful or nostalgic. This place had been created by darkness and unto darkness it had been eternally delivered.

It was earth, but set in a turbulence of volcanic movement so great it seemed the mountains were still shifting. How many volcanoes? An expanse of them, like a never-ending field of mines, bursting and blowing, spitting and exploding – the cores were what remained now, ramparts and pinnacles, peaks and broken spires and towers, all cracked or crumbling. And the lava, splattered and piled. Nothing – anywhere – smooth. Everything was damaged, every surface scoured like an overworked piece of stone.

Up the jagged track we went, the vehicle jolting and shuddering, my shoulders bruising against the insides of the cabin. That a track existed at all among these upward-rising slopes brought a sense of foreboding: that this undertaking was folly, that I was being lured towards some disaster. But I was beyond any decision to continue or to return. Wide-eyed and anxious, I huddled close to the car while each puncture was repaired. Though these pauses were respite from the violence of the climb, outside the vehicle we were exposed to these canyons and whatever spirits dwelt among them.

Eventually, I became numb. The unrelenting jarring of my body, the continuing barrenness. The hardness of it all. The total victory of the forces of lifelessness.

It was late-afternoon when we reached the end of the track and stopped. My Dutch companions hoped to sell photos of the Ahaggar sunrise the next morning to *National Geographic*, and were soon busy making camp for the evening. The cold was bitter, chiselling out shadows all around.

'You're sure you know what you're doing?' one of the photographers asked.

'If I need a lift down again, I'll be back here by midday tomorrow.' I answered. 'And thanks.'

A narrow footpath led from the road's terminus, pushing even higher. For me there was only onwards so I leant, alone, into the path. The way passed between boulders, deep in shade. My bag across my shoulder, filled with emergency rations, was a comfort. I moved steadily upwards, scuffing the dark path with the toes of my boots, checking it without tripping.

Night fell, the awful weight of it dousing the sun. The boulders at each side seemed to grow larger, became walls of rock, till the darkness was so complete I imagined the stones might grow over me.

And only then – at the prospect of absolute envelopment – did I see, in the sky, light. It was the stars, breaking through into immensity.

I stopped to put on my last jumper; not even the steep hike was enough to warm me. When I looked up, to draw breath before pressing on, there was a rock ahead darker than the rest. I climbed closer and it seemed to glow – despite its darkness – from deep within. Then, when I was almost upon it, the glow became a pulse of soft yellow light and I realised the rock was a hut. Slabs of wood had been set into stone, as walls, and in the gaps between stone and timber I could see the small flickering of a candle or a lamp. The door was small and the night was vast.

I knocked. I was ready to wrap my arms around my brother, and to weep, or laugh.

The door opened and a tall figure appeared, but it was not Jack. The man's face was in shadow, his body shrouded by a long white cloak.

'Je m'excuse,' I said, 'je cherche un homme qui s'appelle Jack Adams.'

There was a sound behind the monk, the smallest of movements from deep in the room's interior.

The monk slowly turned his head, then lowered his eyes and stepped aside for my brother.

'Bas.'

'Jack.'

He too was cloaked, a blanket also wrapped around his shoulders. He stepped forward, across the threshold and into the cold night where still I stood, my bag fallen beside me on the stony earth.

'Bas,' he said again, and as he embraced me the blanket fell from his shoulders to the ground.

FOURTEEN

He'd always been larger than me. But now, chest pressed against chest, something had changed. He had thinned, turned into bone and sinew. Not frail, but lean, and there was power in it.

His hands pressed my shoulderblades, firmly at first, and when my arms still hung by my sides, Jack drew me to him a second time. I felt his fingers in my back gently prompting me, my older brother guiding me even here. Not only how I should act, but how I should feel. And I did follow. I raised my arms and wrapped them around him and held him. And wept.

Inside we sat at a simple wooden table, facing each other. The monk had disappeared into a back room. Jack and I studied one another in the flickering light of a lantern.

So much was unrecognisable. Jack was darkly bearded, and the tops of his cheeks were tanned and leathery. His forehead appeared broader, though that must have been because of the beard and the leanness of his face. Then there were his eyes – a new intensity in them, as if their youthful green had been polished and sharpened by the sun until they might do damage. He looked so strange in the white robe, its hood drawn back and resting on his shoulders. Stitched onto the front of the loose garment were a crude red heart and a rough cross, and hanging from the leather belt around his waist was a large set of rosary beads. On his feet, handmade sandals.

Then Jack smiled, and there was something I recognised.

Here was my brother. *Here*, after so much time. Lean, bearded, robed, Jack. A stone hut at night in the desert. The cold. Time and distance stretching then contracting. The giddiness of it. I wished the occasion would guide me, but it remained immense.

Jack spoke first.

'You've come a long way, Bas.'

His voice was a little quieter perhaps, but as compelling as ever.

'We didn't know . . . whether . . . you were dead or alive,' I stumbled. 'We thought dead . . .'

'Bas, I've never been more alive.'

I let the words go. Barely heard them. They didn't belong to my quest. The lantern's flame swayed then leapt, as if it might rise through the opening in the glass. Again and again it leapt, stretched, thinned, peaked and paused, and some luminescent gravity would draw the tongue of flame back into itself. It would settle, and glow once more, solid.

'You're a long way from home, Jack,' I said.

The word fell awkwardly. Home. Jack laughed.

'I *am* home.'

Again, he waited for me. As if allowing me time to understand what he was saying.

'How are you, Jack?' I tried a third time, aware I was failing, falling back to formula.

'I'm alive, Bas. Gloriously and gratefully alive,' he said.

Only minutes before I'd been hugging him and crying. But

how great was the distance between us? They seemed false, his words, as if they were practised. A mantra. Perhaps he'd expected me, and this was how he'd readied himself: I'm alive, he'd say in prayer. The ecstasy of performance, fragile and untrue.

'But come,' he said, 'let us eat.'

At which he rose and was busy. He lit a gas burner and put a small pot of water on it. Even these movements appeared awkward. But here was my brother! That simple fact should have closed the distance. Was he not filled with the wonder of it too?

'We save the tea for guests,' he said.

I felt a pang. I was a mere guest, undifferentiated from anyone else.

'How are Dad and Em?' he asked from the safety of his task. Was this formula too? As predictable as the withdrawal of his fellow-monk to pray?

'Worried,' I said. 'Confused. Angry.'

'Both of them?'

'Dad, at least.'

'So, Em?'

'Just worried.'

'I wrote to them.'

'They told me. It made them more worried . . . *Both* of them.'

'I tried to explain.'

'You failed, I'm afraid, big brother.'

'It's difficult to explain.'

Of course, it wasn't just about our father and Em, and it wasn't just about escorting him back to The Springs. There were things to know, too.

'Come on, Jack –' and I waited until I had his attention. 'What's happened?'

Jack sighed. He turned off the boiling water but did not pour the tea. He returned to the table and sat down once more. He seemed suddenly small. For a long time he didn't look at me. Then, drawing breath, he began.

'This I know, Bas —' each word was mouthed with care – 'I must embrace humility . . . poverty . . . detachment . . .'

Finding the words, weighing them, then with each pause it seemed he was *sealing* the word he'd just uttered. This was a new language, one I'd never heard him speak before, almost as foreign as the Arabic that had been swirling around me.

'. . . abjection,' he continued, '. . . solitude.'

Each word so full of sorrow and loneliness. An inventory of suffering.

'I must seek the lowest of the low places, and arrange my life so that I may be the last among men. I will rejoice not in what I have, but in what I lack – in lack of success, and in penury – for then I have the cross and poverty, the most precious possessions the earth can give.'

A manifesto.

'When I am sad, or angry, Bas, I must think of Jesus in his glory, sitting on the right hand of the Father forever, and rejoice.'

These words from childhood liturgies – 'Jesus in his glory', 'the cross', 'the right hand of the Father' – the shock of them now, spoken by this man who resembled my brother less with each passing moment. The words quickening, Jack absorbing the energy of them, growing stronger, word by word.

'Little by little he is sweeping me clean. He is cleansing the filth from my soul. He is entrusting it to his angels.'

Jack looked at me then, his eyes wider than when he'd begun, almost pleading:

'Bas, he plans to re-enter my soul himself.'

Where had he gone, my brother? From where had this other man emerged? Who was it my father wanted brought home?

'Jesus sweeps me clean, Bas. Clean.'

His eyes were shining.

'I long for Jesus' embrace. I long for death.'

I didn't know what to say. I wasn't prepared for Jesus, or for death, or for religious ecstasy, or for the God of my childhood intensified a thousand-fold. I had not prepared myself to meet a brother I did not recognise.

I fixed on the lantern and its dancing flame. Its rising and falling. The shadows on the stone walls.

'I'm getting hungry.'

If Jack was disappointed, he didn't show it. He just nodded and returned to his pot and his burner.

We ate in silence, except for our breathing and our jaws munching on the stale bread and the clattering of our teacups against the table as we lowered them after each sip. The night grew colder and the lantern flame seemed to shrink. We drank a second cup of tea, for warmth. Even so I began to shiver, and nursed the mug in the palms of my hands, leaning over it to feel the rising steam on my neck and face.

I noticed Jack's lips were moving. I was startled, confused – I'd heard nothing. I was about to ask him to repeat himself when I realised he was praying, and below the table, in his lap, he was turning his rosary – all the while humming like an insect.

'Jack . . .'

He turned his face to me and smiled.

'Come, Bas. It is time for sleep.'

FIFTEEN

A rough square of morning framed the wooden door when I woke. I'd slept in my clothes, covered by three blankets, a fourth folded beneath me as insulation from the cold stone floor. Jack had offered me his mattress and slats but I'd refused. My pride. Now my shoulders ached, my back, my neck. I was stiff from the stone and the night's shivering. I stood and stretched.

I was still stretching, arms raised above my head, fingertips brushing the low ceiling, when the door swung open and brightness sprayed in. I had to turn my eyes away.

'Good morning!'

'Morning,' I replied, unable to match his energy, not willing to try.

'Have you eaten yet?'

I shook my head.

'Come,' he said. This new language of his.

I folded the blankets and laid them in a corner while Jack and the monk prepared breakfast. It didn't take long: tea and bread, this time with jam.

At the table Jack and the monk bowed their heads and pressed their palms together for Latin grace. With closed eyes and the angle of their heads the same, their voices joined in low-murmured harmony. I was still inspecting the monk's face when he opened his eyes and looked at me. They were dark eyes, hooded and unmoving. After this moment of silent regard, he reached over the table, placed a hand on my forearm, and nodded. I didn't understand, but smiled – out of habit, or nervousness. He smiled too, patted my arm once or twice, then straightened a crucifix he'd positioned at the end of the table before we'd sat down.

As we ate Jack talked quietly about the mountains, and the seasons, and the priest who'd first lived here at the turn of the century, Charles de Foucauld, a refugee from the French Foreign Legion who'd been called by God to live among the Muslims in the desert. He was the first to translate their language into French. He was a humble man, a man of service, a man of God. The church had already beatified him, Jack said. Sainthood could not be far away. He'd built the hut with his own hands. *This hut was built by a saint* – that's what Jack said. And that it was an honour to be there. To replace a stone when it cracks from the cold and falls out. He studied his hands, in thrall to the wonder of it, that privilege.

'We're going out,' Jack said when the table was cleared and he and the monk had returned from a tiny chapel where they'd spent half an hour praying. 'Make yourself at home.'

And he grinned, then winked. A joke. Home.

'We'll be back before sunset. Is there anything you need?'

I shook my head, more in amazement than in answer. That he was leaving. Just like that. That he and I – brothers – had been reunited in the mountains of the desert, after trials yet unknown to each other, and he would leave me alone in his stone hut for the day.

'See you soon, then, little brother.'

And with that the two men passed through the door, and let it swing back into place on its own weight. I followed them to the threshold and watched their white robes disappear down a track between two dark boulders.

With a cup of tea I sat on the doorstep. The hut faced east and sunlight fell on my cheeks. The stone step was slowly warming under the sun and my body. I opened my palms to the warm light.

Later I wandered the small plateau above the broken landscape of volcanoes, less fearsome in the brightness of the day though still strange and powerful. I explored but kept the hut in view, tethering myself to it. Still later I propped the hut door open to let the light in, and sat at the table and sketched, then moved again to the front step and resumed carving a piece of rock I'd laid aside for a few days. Eventually I tired of that too, set down the rock and tool, and moved inside to examine the hut.

Behind the living space was a tiny chapel with cross and shrine and kneelers. Beyond it, in the back of the stone shelter, was a bedroom each for Jack and the monk, both furnished with a simple wooden bed, a set of drawers, icons hanging from the walls, sacred hearts. On the floor beside Jack's bed was a pile of books: meditations and lives of saints and spiritual exercises and daily prayer books. A Bible with a dried gum leaf as a marker.

There were also notebooks. I picked one up, a diary of sorts. I'd never known Jack to keep a diary. I opened it without any sense of guilt; this Jack was so different from the brother I grew up with. Sitting on his bunk I read passage after passage in his hand. Prayers, and half-formed philosophies, aphorisms and confessions of failings I didn't recognise in him. Jack's declarations of the night before were there, his ideas reworked with subtle

197

variations. Was he trying to perfect his thinking, to better capture what he believed? Or *wanted* to believe – Was he writing himself into being?

Jesus says, 'Never worry about small things. Break away from all that is small and mean, and try to live on the heights. You must break with all that is not Me,' Jesus says.

There was much like that: things I might have read in a thousand of my mother's prayer books, but could never have imagined Jack writing.

I turned the pages trying to imagine Jack composing by lantern-light, trying to picture the expression on his face, what labour it must have taken to lay out this new life for himself. How long had this been going on, I wondered? Not long, surely, I thought. He was a novice, wasn't he, fired by a novice's fervour? Or a zealot's.

At some point the voice in the notebook changed.

It is through detachment you will attain all this, by driving out all mean thoughts, all littlenesses which are not evil in themselves, but which succeed in scattering your mind far from Me, when you should be contemplating Me from morning to night.

I had to reread it to make sure I'd seen it right. *You should be contemplating Me from morning to night.* He'd adopted nothing less than the voice of God.

Make to yourself a desert where you will be as much alone with Me as Mary Magdalene was alone in the desert with Me.

He repeated it, repeated himself practising being Jesus, being God. Like Sophe's schoolchildren making the shapes of the letters of the alphabet, again and again, to become literate.

Make to yourself a desert. Make to yourself a desert. Make to yourself a desert.

Or was it a punishment, a hundred lines, for some wrong he'd committed?

Make to yourself a desert.

On some pages these were the only words, set in the middle of an otherwise blank sheet. My brother, the desert ascetic.

So Jack had become one of those for whom the body and the mind were things to be conquered and he was determined to defeat them. We'd been taught about those desert saints and their feats of endurance, their lives of fasting and solitude and nakedness and battles with demons and nights of endless prayer. John the Baptist, and his diet of desert locusts. Others had been even more bizarre and fascinating. The saint who lived for thirty-seven years on a tiny platform at the top of a pillar set among the ruins of a deserted town. The one who tied his hair to a chain hanging from the ceiling so he would pray standing throughout the night. The ascetic who, before retreating to his desert cave, lowered himself into a tomb overnight to confront his soul. So many desert caves.

So it was this form of man, *this* tradition my brother had joined.

Towards the end of the notebook, though not quite the last entry, he'd written just once:

Lord, I pray that I die as a martyr, stripped of everything, stretched naked on the ground, unrecognisable, covered with wounds and blood, killed violently and painfully. How beautiful such a gift would be. I desire this today, Lord. That I may grant You this infinite grace, watch loyally, carry Your Cross faithfully.

The perfect logic of it. The inevitable conclusion of his radical belief.

SIXTEEN

Jack and the monk returned the hour before nightfall. It was impossible to tell how far they'd travelled, where they'd been, what tasks had occupied them. Had I found enough to do? Jack asked on the step of the hut. Yes, I said, and showed him the miniature I'd finished carving just moments before.

'Eve?' he asked, looking at Sophe's nakedness, some wildness of her hair I'd managed to capture, perhaps what he thought was a piece of fruit in her hand but was just rock I hadn't been able to pry from her fingers. He couldn't have known it was her. That having reeled away from his notebooks it was Sophe I needed.

'Mary,' I said, expressionless. 'Though I don't know which one – whether it's the sinner, or the mother of God.'

I paused before looking up at him and smiling, releasing him, turning it into a joke.

He smiled too, though uneasily.

'Just mucking around,' I said, to make peace. 'Maybe it *is* Eve. I don't know. It's just a woman, any woman. Any woman you want it to be.'

A lie to keep Sophe to myself.

'We don't get many of them around here.'

There was still humour, but it seemed morbid, a relic of that easy charm he once had.

After dinner the monk disappeared to the chapel to pray.

'Do you want to go with him?'

Jack hesitated.

'I don't mind talking,' he said, as if keeping me company was a chore.

'So, you want to die.'

'That's a strange thing to say, Bas.'

'You don't need to feel like that,' I went on. 'Because it wasn't you who was responsible for her death.'

Jack stiffened. He pulled his hands from the table to his lap as his shoulders straightened and he sat back in the chair. He stopped breathing for long seconds – then his first breath caught, and he looked at me with eyes wide, nostrils flared.

This conversation had been so many years in coming. And now that it had finally arrived, how could he not fear it? I was anxious too, my heart racing, but I'd started it and there is a strength that comes from beginning things, a momentum. Jack waited. He would not venture out, my brave brother. He was waiting for me now.

'You weren't responsible,' I said again.

That winter night so long ago, cold from the early-set sun, the valley preparing itself for frost. The sky was clear: stars and broken moon low on the horizon and pyres of chimney smoke rising from the town, house after house. Our fireplace was lit too. I remember Jack, nine years old, tossing a log in, old enough that our parents let him. I remember the burst of embers as the fresh log hit the burning wood, rolled along it, and settled cross-ways on top, the flame rising and wrapping itself round them both.

Our father had come in, and he had gone up. It was Mum putting us to bed. We had separate rooms by then. I remember Mum's hand on my forehead after I finished the glass of warm milk she brought in, her thumb wiping drops of milk off my chin. Then everyone I knew was called forth in prayer, asking the Lord to keep them safe. Then Mum leaning over me and kissing my hair. I remember too, sitting up in bed to watch as she retreated from the room. I remember the door of the bedroom ajar, and the thin band of light between frame and door turning on its axis as I laid my head back down on the pillow. That ruler of light glowing like sunset on the horizon when I closed my eyes to sleep.

I can't remember waking. I can't remember climbing out the window. I remember only that I was standing on the footpath in pyjamas and bare feet and that I was not cold. Jack was beside me, and there were neighbours running, our father running, and the house a tower of flame, and beyond the terrible sound of the inferno – inside it – was Mum's voice calling my name. Screaming it. Screaming my name over and over and over and over until it was gone.

'You couldn't have done anything,' I said. 'You couldn't have saved her.'

These were the right words to say to my frightened brother. I believed that. They were the things I *should* say, because from where else could his death wish have come than from the burden of an older brother's failed responsibility?

Yet Jack looked blankly at me, as though not comprehending what I'd said, not even listening. And in that blankness, his breathing calmed and his body began to loosen.

'She got you out, Jack,' I continued. 'You were asleep, and she got you out. That was *her* responsibility. *She* went back in. There was nothing you could do about that.'

So, I uttered the words I thought might rescue him, might allow me to put my arm round his shoulder and lead him home. But in truth I didn't believe them. It was just another arid formula.

This was what it was like to reassure one's brother, something I'd never done, something that had never been necessary with Jack. But when I uttered those words – *you weren't responsible* – I did it without conviction. Because Jack *was* responsible. That's how I'd seen it for years, something I'd repeated to myself so often I needed it in order to survive. It had become a foundation myth.

Because Jack *was* older, more *was* expected of him. He *was* bigger, he was stronger, he had been privileged. And it had been *Jack* who'd taught me to leave the window open, so that some nights when our parents were asleep we could put our day clothes back on and climb out our windows to our bikes at the back of the house.

And yet. And yet. This flipping. That one event can carry two truths, bear two extremes. I'd come so far. I would bring Jack back whatever it took. Whatever he needed, whatever truth or duty.

'She went in for me, and I wasn't there,' I said, 'I'd already climbed out. If I'd been there, she would have saved me, as well as you. If I'd been there, there would have been enough time for all of us . . .'

This was *also* something I believed, contradictory but no less true. Perhaps it was even truer. I'd carried it close, lived with it, wrestled with it. I'd won, and I'd lost. I kept winning, and kept losing. Some eternal damnation in the variations.

'If I hadn't escaped,' I continued, saying the words aloud for the first time, 'Mum would have found me.'

The thought struck me for the first time that Jack might think that too, that I was responsible. Had he, in fact, always thought that?

'If I'd been there . . .'

I wanted to weep, out of pity. It was me. It was Jack. These two beliefs had been night and day, each true, each overcoming and in turn being subdued by the other. Now the options were starker than they ever had been. Me. Him. Both. Neither.

'It wasn't your fault.' As I spoke the words of ritual relief it struck me: perhaps *both* of us had reeled away from that childhood night, perhaps each of us had been flung out onto our different trajectories, chaotic and monstrous – but destined to meet here, this night. Suddenly I felt, in that hut in the mountains, the sun having set and the cold falling fast, *solidarity*. That Jack and I were united in something we'd carried silently through childhood, something neither of us deserved to carry. That it didn't matter what we'd thought until now. That there was only now.

When our father left for work at the quarry each morning, the last thing he would say before closing the door behind him was *look after your mother, boys*. What did that mean? What did it mean to a kid? What did our father mean by it? Perhaps he was saying it for Mum's benefit, not ours. But a kid doesn't know that. I didn't, couldn't. To a kid, everything is true. And sons *want* to care for their mothers. I think we do, all of us. A primal instinct, for which we cannot be blamed.

'We were kids, Jack. We couldn't have been responsible. We weren't responsible for our mother's death.'

Our mother's death. There, I'd said the words. Thirteen years of loss suddenly coiled around my heart and pulled tight, constricting me. I closed my eyes hard. It didn't matter. I wept, scalding tears of release.

Then finally, through my tears, Jack spoke.

'It is God's will,' he said.

I blinked.

'What is?' I said.

'What happened that night. It cannot be changed. I've accepted it, Bas.'

'God's will that Mum die?'

Wasn't he going to reassure me as I'd been trying to reassure him? Weren't we in solidarity?

'It is a mystery.'

'God *willed* Mum to die? *Wanted* it?'

'Allowed it.'

'No you don't. If it's God we're talking about it's the same difference.'

'God gave her life. He takes it too. It is the same for all of us. Only the time and the circumstances differ. Death is not to be feared. It is to be welcomed.'

'Can you hear yourself?'

'It is a mystery.'

A cold and heartless mystery.

I think I wanted to kill him. For his distance, and his coolness, and his heartlessness. His disloyalty. He'd left her. He'd turned his back on our mother, buried her with theology.

'She was burnt to death, Jack.' I said it as coolly as I could. Each word deliberate and fierce, each an effort to pierce him. 'Have you forgotten that, Jack? Have you forgotten her screams?'

That quietened him.

'Have you forgotten her screams of agony, Jack, as the flames melted her flesh, set alight her hair, burnt her alive? Burnt . . . her . . . *alive*. Have you forgotten that? Her terror?'

He was still.

'You forget *that*, Jack, and you forget her. She's our mother, Jack. You can't forget your *mother*.'

He'd stopped looking at me. He was looking over me, through me.

'*Have* you forgotten her, Jack?' I asked, and then, when he didn't answer: 'Oh, Jack. You can't forget your mother.'

For a long time he was silent, then, slowly at first, he began to weep.

'I know,' he rasped as he began crying uncontrollably. 'I know.'

SEVENTEEN

Never had I slept like that. A sleep stronger than cold and hardness and distance. Jack's tears and mine, and our long embrace, had delivered justice and forgiveness.

'Let me show you something,' Jack whispered, close to my ear, waking me.

It was still dark. By the light of the single candle Jack had set on the table, I pulled one of the blankets tight around my shoulders and laced my boots. He opened the door onto the stars, fierce against the night sky, so bright I blinked.

We left the sanctuary of the hut. It was cold outside and I was happy for Jack to lead me. He traced a way through the chill night to a ledge, a natural platform where we stopped and looked out at the world. The twisted volcanoes and the towers of unsheathed stone below were barely visible. Instead, everywhere were stars, in front and above and below us too, sharp, prickling needlepoints of white. Holes in the firmament, bright as the belief that this would last between us.

Then, from the midst of that absolute silence, there was a crack so loud and clear I thought it was a rifle shot. I dropped to the ground, flattening against the rock. It had come from somewhere below, but where exactly I couldn't tell. My heart thumped as that almighty sound still resonated – yet Jack remained unmoved on the ledge, as if he would accept a sniper's bullet should it come.

'Jack,' I hissed, and he turned and saw me on the ground, and laughed.

'It was just a rock cracking in the cold, Bas. There is nothing to fear. Come, get up. Let us pray.'

I was too surprised to answer. Rising, I listened silently as Jack began to intone.

I can't remember at what point I realised that, while I'd slept, Jack's bleak vision had reclaimed him. I know he offered thanks, made petitions on my behalf as well as his own, though he had no authority. I cannot even say to whom his prayers were directed, what god he spoke to. None I recognised. Not the god of our shared childhood, nor the god of wrath. Not the god I'd encountered walking the seams of sandstone back home. Perhaps it was simply the god of that one night, raised up from those mountains to overwhelm Jack. The vanquisher abroad.

'Lord . . .'

I listened in the deathly cold. And have forgotten his prayer.

Because in that desert night I could not believe Jack's medicated hymn to freedom, his plea for escape, for liberation. Rage welled in me, that it was not enough we were two brothers united, that he insisted God interpose. That he insisted on God despite everything. That he *preferred* God. I listened as day shook itself free of night, and could not believe him. *Bullshit*, I thought, with vehemence. *Bullshit* to Jack's account of his life, *bullshit* to his grand philosophy of abnegation, *bullshit* that Jack had embraced it, *bullshit* to his myth of Jesus. A rising, sweeping bullshit-fuelled fury.

The extremes Jack was prepared to go to, to escape, and I had been made to follow him – my weakness, his coldness. And now Jack would prefer this coldness to me. He left me utterly alone, and, ignorantly, instead chose to pray.

Finally the east loomed, and Jack's long incantation faded. The new day began to form, flushing the sky and its stars into oblivion.

Jack stepped forward into this. He stepped to the very edge of the rock platform, his feet over it. I saw him as a boy readying himself to dive from a cliff into a rock pool. He raised his arms from his side, and lifted them out to form a cross. He flung his head back. I sensed him closing his eyes. I heard his intake of breath, guessed the shape of the ecstatic smile on his face. The transportation. He stood there – a statue – his chest filled with breath, his arms flung wide, his head facing the heavens.

'The beauty,' he whispered, 'the beauty!'

I saw myself at the edge of that boyhood cliff too, trembling with fear, not so many years before. I'd asked for mercy. Instead Jack had pushed me. Knew what was needed, what was right. Now Jack sought death there in the mountains of the desert. The two of us on that cliff: there he was, his back to me, his arms outstretched to greet death, the thing he sang his lullaby to. I could do it, I could. The compass-light of the east. The direction of the sun, of light, of clear-sightedness.

I might have stepped forward. I don't know, today, if I did. I might have. Might've inched closer to Jack and his back, and his Messianic embrace of the dark and silence and nothingness and the god of nothingness. I might have moved closer in my rage, and my blindedness. My breathing might have quickened. I might even have spoken. But I cannot be sure. Blood had overpowered me –

Perhaps it was the panting of my breath that interrupted Jack's reverie, caused him to turn. Did he turn? The blood that pumped in my chest thumped a rhythm. Was my blood leading me, bit by bit, closer to Jack at the cliff's edge? Blood pounded the image before me, an image I see to this day – it comes to me both dreaming and waking, it causes me to break into sweat – the image of my hands on Jack, my open palms on the blades of his shoulders, of me gathering myself into a moment, and of Jack teetering off the edge, falling into the abyss.

This solution.

The end Jack was praying for, that surely he was praying *to me* for. Wasn't that, *really*, what he was seeking?

'I am ready.'

Did he whisper that too?

I think he turned. At some point he looked at me, as if I was his confessor. That's how I remember it. Perhaps I conjured it from desire, mine or his or both. I don't really know. Neither whether he said it, nor, if he did, whether it was true. Whether anything was true, or ever could be, ever again.

'What about Sophia?'

Because there was nothing but her left.

'Sophia?'

Dawn had risen. Jack's voice, in that great wash of first light, was small and uncertain.

'How do you know about Sophia?'

His arms had fallen and he was stepping towards me.

'She's in Tamanrasset,' I answered. 'Waiting. I told her I'd bring you down.'

Jack looked at me hard, as hard as at any time those three days. His eyes narrowed. He was, I think, weighing me up. Judging whether what I'd said was true, whether he should believe me or whether he should respond – as airily as he did as a kid, so confident in what he knew was true there was no need to persuade anyone else – that what I was saying was rubbish.

'Mmm,' he said, pulling away. 'So you thought you could deliver that, did you, Bas? Taking *me* to *her*?'

Everything was brightening now. It was difficult to remember what night looked like, how it felt, whether there was any substance in it, cowering as it now was behind the rocks. It had become mere shadow and everywhere I looked was brokenness. The gentle curve of the earth destroyed by the uneasy monoliths which towered and toppled onto the land in oblivious showers of rock and dust and debris. The scree itself, so much crushed ground, sharp-edged and forbidden, like tiny warriors massed on the slopes.

'She wanted to come up too. She wanted to see you.'

A whisper. Or was it a groan?

'She's waiting for you.'

EIGHTEEN

Tamanrasset appeared, low and unpresupposing on the horizon. I'd resigned myself to losing Jack when we got there. There was nothing I could do to change anything, I thought, as we descended out of the Ahaggar. We had hiked to a dig-site the monks knew of, where each week they rode down for supplies on the archaeologists' truck. Now we were bouncing and jerking over a thousand rocks, a thousand holes, a thousand jagged hairpin bends. Jack and I clung, face-down, spread-eagled on the roof rack for hours, our backs to the sun as if in some medieval punishment. Either he'd go with Sophe, I guessed, or he'd return to the mountain.

The buildings began to thicken, and we slowed. There were lean trees, and loose-robed Tuareg, and camels tethered to stakes in the ground, their heads bent to piles of dried grass, their lips quivering, even from that distance. We slowed even further when a group of boys emerged from behind a mudbrick wall, running towards us. It was not the running that startled us, but the angle of their approach. They did not swerve, nor did they hesitate. They ran straight at us, hard, three or four from either side – ran and propped and threw, with the purity of their adolescent courage.

Jack and I ducked, pressing our bodies flat, our arms over our heads. The rocks missed. They either flew over us, or thudded into the vehicle's flanks. One of them shattered the driver's side window into a map of glass tributaries. I lifted my head when the barrage was over and saw the boys disappearing behind houses, down alleyways, out of history. There was no lolling around after battle like Michelangelo's *David*, no fallen giant at their feet.

We sped away, pulling over only when we reached the centre of town. The driver got out and stood beside the truck, hands on hips, inspecting his broken window and the dents in the panelling. He cursed, and looked up as we slid off the roof.

'What the hell do you make of that?' he said, not needing an answer, wanting us only to join in, to share the experience, its shock.

Instead, Jack said:

'I'm sorry. Please forgive them.'

'What are you talking about?' The archaeologist looked at him curiously.

'They don't know what they're doing,' Jack said.

The archaeologist screwed up his face, but Jack kept talking, a rambling mix of gratitude and apology that sounded like *he* was taking the broken window upon himself, that it might somehow have been his responsibility, his *fault*. Eventually, the driver raised his hand to stop this speech. When Jack continued, he shrugged and turned his back on both of us, began consulting the rest of his party who by then were squeezing out of the vehicle and inspecting the damage, knotting together around the shattered window.

We didn't go straight to the hotel; instead, we made our way to the market. They didn't know what they were doing, Jack kept mumbling, they just didn't know. Did the refrain have some

213

power in itself, like prayer is supposed to if offered in the right way?

When we reached the fruit stalls people began calling out to him, and Jack greeted the vendors with handshakes, and *salaam alaykums*, his agitation slipping away. He'd been down here no more than a month, but already he'd made a name.

We stopped before a young orange-seller Jack knew, his crates of oranges laid out on a blanket on the ground. The two of them kissed each other on the cheek, once, twice, perhaps even a third time. Jack introduced me, but I wasn't interested in his name, just shook his hand and stood back. Jack and his friend laughed, and put their arms around each another, and pointed at the oranges, selecting pieces of fruit, inspecting them, smelling them, joking all the while, Jack as at ease here as on the streets of The Springs. Eventually the vendor filled a plastic bag, which he hung lightly from Jack's arm.

'We need to get going,' I said, irritated, wanting to get back, fearing more greetings like this.

'Sophe likes oranges too.'

'Too?'

Jack looked at me, confused, almost hurt.

'Like us,' he said.

Then I remembered the orange trees in the back garden at home. They grew as well as anything in that sandy soil. As kids we'd collect the fruit for weeks, in Mum's cane laundry-basket, and empty it onto the kitchen table, the fresh citrus smell sharpening the house. We'd eat our fill – juiced at breakfast, or packed for school lunch – but there were always more than enough and Mum would offer oranges as gifts: to visitors or neighbours, or on trips to hospital to visit people we knew. I'd be sent out on orange-giving errands all over town. 'Here comes the orange-boy,' some of the older kids would yell out as I cycled past their houses or the cricket oval, or the Railway Store where they'd sometimes hang out. But the teasing didn't bother me because there was something pure and good and right in what I was doing which lifted me above their joking.

Now I offered to pay, but the vendor waved me away, smiling, patting Jack on the shoulder and saying for my benefit, 'Friend, friend.' But Jack insisted, and took some notes from my wallet, too many, and tucked them into the pocket of the young man's trousers, then stepped away, waving.

'Now,' Jack said. 'Which hotel is she staying at?'

I could have kept the name to myself, and been the one to lead *him* there. But I told him, and Jack set off – striding out of the market and through the streets, his blue plastic bag of oranges swinging from his hand like a manic pendulum, and me in his wake.

Jack hadn't exactly forgotten me, but it was now Sophe he sought. He turned around from time to time to see if I was following, but barely slowed to let me catch up. At one place Jack paused beside a wind-harried eucalyptus, and pulled a dusty leaf off a thin branch. He handed it to me when I reached him, panting. For me to crush in the palms of my hands and raise to my nose. Then hand back to him. The little ritual Jack had created so long ago, me never knowing quite what it meant. And certainly not knowing how to read it now. If there was anything to read into it at all.

We reached the hotel. In the lobby Jack greeted the bearded man behind the desk, the same one I'd shown Jack's photo to, three days before.

'*Salaam alaykum*,' Jack said.

The man looked startled, eyes wide beneath his white hat.

'*Mon frère*,' I said to him, showing my brother off. Proof that he *had* been in the mountains, just as I'd said, and that I'd found him.

'*Vous voyez,*' I continued, pointing to Jack's robes, '*il n'est pas soldat.*'

He reached for my room key then, having recovered himself, and placed it on the desk once again before turning away to make a phone call. Dismissing us like that.

Only then did Jack step aside for me to lead. I began the climb up the single set of stairs to our first-floor room, number 119. It's strange what one remembers, what one forgets. I remember too that Sophe's room key had been on its hook on the key board at reception, which meant she was in. Jack and I moved down the corridor, past the communal bathroom. I remember the light blue of the corridor's paint – the colour of ducks' eggs I'd once found in the bush behind the house – and the white ceiling. The line of lights, hanging equidistant along the length of the ceiling like inverted stepping stones, or warning flares. I remember knocking. I remember the door swinging open, as if of its own accord. Or, as I've thought a thousand times since, as if it was Fate itself who opened the door for Jack and me that day.

Sophe was sitting quietly on the bed, her back against the wall, her body moving, though oddly slumped, her feet pulled up, knees bent, her arms grasping her legs to her chest. But something was wrong. It was an eternity before I realised it was a pillowcase over her head and not her headscarf. And that her wrists and ankles were bound.

This image, of Sophe on the bed, helpless, silent as death, shrouded like it, framed by the widening door of the hotel room. This image stays. Sophe and the pillowcase tight on her head, one of the corners upright, like a small triangle of cat's ear. This image of her.

Then came a blackness, hard as concrete, perfect as night.

★

When I came to, hours later, there was no victory of light in it. Death had merely withdrawn, the slowest of tides, to return at the appointed time.

I was in a different room. It was askew, the lines of its geometry – where walls met floor and ceiling and each other – at odd angles. Human bodies, the shape of them, filled the space, close then distant with each new pulse of blood. The pumping blood swelled the ache in my head from dull to sharp, dull to sharp, dull to sharp. The ferocity of it was so excruciating it seemed to catch in my throat. Another pain – it was difficult to isolate them – came from my side, the gasping crash of a boot into my ribs.

Jack and Sophe were already conscious, both of them propped against a wall as if waiting for me to arrive. When the Beards saw me open my eyes, the one who'd been kicking me dragged me across the floor to join Jack and Sophe, all of us lined up in a row, one two three. Our arms were pinned behind our backs, our ankles tied with cloth. I turned my head to look at Jack and Sophe and was struck in the face by the butt of a rifle.

There were four Beards in the room. They may have had different physiques, different faces, different eyes. They each may have had different lives. May have been different men, may have *been* men, joined to humanity in all the usual ways. I can admit the possibility of this, the *theoretical* possibility of it. But they were just Beards then. That's how I've thought about it until now, that's how I've come *at* it. Thinking wouldn't have been possible otherwise.

What came next? Next came next – an eternal loop back and back and over again, destroying time. Next are Beards, and rooms, and bindings, and sweat and fear, and the movement of Beards around the room. In and out. Our attempts to whisper to each other are met with rifle-butts and strips of cloth wrapped hard around our mouths, pressing against our tongues and cutting into our cheeks. Next is learning to breathe despite the fear. Next is listening to what the men are saying through the expressions on Sophe's face.

That is what next is. Reading the loss of what is precious through her eyes. There is no next.

That night, I prayed. The prayer of our childhood. The prayer we were told to pray. The one I learnt by heart.

Our Father. Who art in heaven. Hallowed be thy name. Thy kingdom come. Thy will be done. On earth. As it is. In heaven. Give us this day. Our daily bread. And forgive us our trespasses. As we forgive those. Who trespass against us. And lead us not. Into temptation. But deliver us. From evil. Amen.

But whose evil? I used to wonder that as a kid. I wonder still. I don't believe I could have prayed any more fervently, that I could have been more earnest. Unless fear intervened. Unless terror somehow got in the way.

It was three days, truncated into nothing. The details I've lost. Did they give us water? Something to eat? I don't know. Did we cramp? Did they loosen our binds so we could stand or walk around the room? Escort us ever to a squat toilet in another room? I can't remember. What I *do* remember, is that when the gags came off, they were replaced by the torment of blindfolds. Denying us even the fleeting solace that we were in this together. In that enforced dark I strained for signs that Jack and Sophe were still there in the room: a change of breathing, the heel of Sophe's boot scraping across the concrete floor, Jack humming a hymn we both knew, an involuntary cry from shallow sleep.

One of them spoke some English, a few words, a clutch of fevered commands, all verbs. I wonder if he'd learned them for this. *Come. Go. Wait.* Each command accompanied by a prod, or a push in the back, or a kick.

But I can never forget this.

At the end they took off our blindfolds. We looked desperately for each other, blinking the light away until our eyes met, while the Beards crouched beside us, covering our mouths with duct tape.

The Beard with the English said, pointing to *me*, 'You remember.' An injunction. These days there'd be cameras and video footage posted to news stations or the internet, but not then. Back then the Beard with the English merely stood above me, behind me, grabbed my hair and turned my head, forcing me to look. '*You* remember,' he said. 'You *tell*.' My head being shaken from side to side, a marionette's head forced one way then the other from above. 'Don't forget. You tell your people. You tell your country.'

Then the scream. No words I could recognise. The scream was not mine. Not Jack's nor Sophe's. The three of us were denied that, staring, our mouths taped mute, our own screams gurgling in our throats. This injustice, that even our fear was trapped. Nothing human allowed, no matter how primal. No words. No final wishes, no conversations, no discussions. No scream, even, allowed. We were mere animals, mere beasts in that bleak room.

But there *was* scream, and it was theirs. Sound, pitch, fever, a room-filling war cry. A frenzy. A cry to transport the crier. The Beard and the scream. But the room could not hold it, that war cry, that cry of the knife. The cry of the head pulled back, the cry of the slit throat. The wail of blood, heavenwards. First one throat, then the other. My head jerking too, my eyes neither open nor closed, the broken voice above me all the while, some dull backing to the wailing Beard: *Look*. I, too, am transported. *Look*. *Don't forget*. The room, the scream. Jack's throat, then Sophe's. Their wide eyes. *Death to America!*

PART THREE

ONE

I see his shape as he enters the room, the cut of his hat against the doorway so different from the silhouettes of the man and his wife who've come and gone, day upon day, with tea and bread and damp cloths for my forehead. I touch my forearm under the shirtsleeve as the shape enters, and dig my fingernails into my skin to feel I'm still here.

He squats before me where I sit on the floor, my back wedged in the corner of two walls. I see curious heads in the door, haloed in the sun – the woman who's been tending me, and two or three of her children.

'Oi,' he says softly, his hand on my shoulder.

'Oi.'

And so Logan has come, not knowing if it was Jack or me he'd find.

I hold onto Sophe. The statuette of her I sculpted from desert stone those last days in the mountains. Someone tells me I was gripping it when I reached the guesthouse, mute, fingers clenched hard around it, palm cut from holding it so tight. Only when I fall into something resembling sleep is it prised from my hand.

There's too much to remember.

They feed me, water me, wash me – these people whose names I'll never know, kindnesses I'm told about later. They find my passport in the pouch slung round my neck, tucked under my shirt. Not just mine, but Jack's and Sophe's too, shifted there by the Beards because I am their messenger. *You. Go. Tell.* The faux wedding band Sophe wore is also in there, caked dark with blood. The guesthouse keepers give over their living room to me, the floor with its thick carpets and stacked cushions. I wear the man's grey trousers and his collared shirt. His jumper is tight against the desert chill. I do not stop shaking. I cannot understand the simplest of gestures, queries that would overwhelm me even in my own language. It is all I can do to respond to their hands, and lay my head on the pillow they set out for me. But it is not rest.

The Beards had dumped me at the edge of town after nightfall, a new emptiness. In the morning, a boy and a goat, the animal chewing my bootlaces as I hunched rocking in the sand. The flare of locals that followed. The men who lifted me the short distance to the guesthouse. The swirling faces: the police and the army and the embassies and that question – *who are you?* Until Jack and Sophe were discovered a few days later in a nearby *oued*.

TWO

The army arranges for Jack's body to return home, the honourable thing to do. Sophe's people have already taken hers. I follow Jack. I am no more than a body myself.

He is lowered next to Mum in the cemetery at The Springs. The whole town comes out for it, the autumn sky retreating with each passing minute, each late fly that buzzes at the corner of our mouths, each word of requiem. But Jack and Mum: the two of them there, side by side. The weight of my responsibility. The crushing, suffocating weight of it. *Both* of them.

Logan drives me back to the house after the funeral.

'You going to be alright?'

'You going to be alright yourself?' I parrot, beyond even wondering what the words mean.

He looks at me and sighs.

'So this is where he grew up?' He peers past me through the car window, over the hedge of roses to the timber cottage.

Em's car, with my father in the passenger seat, stops just beyond us at the top of the driveway. Em's head turns to my father's momentarily before she gets out and comes across to us.

'It was good of you to come, Sergeant,' she says through Logan's window.

He shakes his head.

'It was good of the army to let me, ma'am. By rights Lieutenant-Colonel Grose shouldn't have approved my leave. And I owed it to Jack, ma'am.'

'Do you want . . . ?'

'No,' he says. 'I've got to get back.'

Tears well in his eyes.

I open the door and swing my foot down onto the road.

'He *was* a good soldier,' I hear Logan say to Em. 'It may not have been right for him, but he was a good soldier. Make sure Mr Adams understands that.'

'Why don't you tell him, Sergeant?'

'I told him at the cemetery.'

'Tell him again, will you? Please.'

In the sunroom Em pours tea from her best china teapot. First Logan because he is the visitor, then Dad, then me, Em last of all. I watch the milk jug as it hovers above each teacup before moving on to the next, avalanches of sugar crystals sliding off silver teaspoons. I see four wisps of steam, like the corner-posts of some ghostly edifice rising in the afternoon light.

I watch their lips move. The sound has been switched off. What is Logan saying? Dad and Em nod. She looks grateful. But where has the sound gone? What's the low buzzing in my ear? I lift the teacup to my mouth. My tongue curls and I splutter. My thigh knocks against the coffee table as I rise and turn, and stumble, retching, for the bathroom.

★

The afternoons shorten.

Em asks me to stay, *begs* me to, but my father is silent. I stand at the back stairs looking out at that giant block of carved sandstone, quiescent now beneath a flapping tarpaulin. Just a few weeks ago I'd resented having to leave it, but now it is huge and my chisels are blunt or too heavy to lift. I've become someone else's message.

My ancient creature is a stranger to me, lost like everything else in those blinding flashes of Sophe's opened neck and Jack's, and the loved bodies hunched and blood spilt and *Allahu Akbar* screeching through all waking and sleeping. The smell of blood in my nostrils at night, the feel of it in my throat. I choke in my sleep from the mask of blood that covers my face and I wake in terror and I gasp for breath, for the very rudiments of life, and I vomit until I am dry and exhausted.

Pursued by blood. That's how it feels. Jack's and Sophe's – whatever it is I carried with me of Jack and Sophe on my shirt, on my trousers, on my boots. What part of her fell on my skin, and seeped into my open pores, *entering me*. How much sprayed onto the hairs of my forearms to dry in the desert wind.

I am not coherent, and the great vital dragon is buried in the stone. That man who cut it has gone. Only my father and Em are left.

THREE

A second time I leave The Springs, with as little choice as when my father sent me away to Africa. Less. But this time I have my statuette of Sophe, tangible and intact. There are some things that cannot be held tight enough, some things one clings to for life itself. Things without which we would fall away.

I track down her parents in a quiet midwest home near one of the great lakes. It is summer, and strange insects buzz above the hedges, their loud wings beating in my ears. I climb five enormous steps from the front path to the porch and the white door and the ornate bronze knocker are warm from the sun. I breathe.

Like a soldier keeping his promise, I've phoned. So they are waiting for me, Sophe's broken parents. Both of them come to the door. I think from the way their eyes widen as it swings open, the way their shoulders straighten and their heads lift, that they hope Sophia herself will be standing out here on the porch, her spirit returned to them. It is like watching the earth's last spark go out.

The emptiness in that house as they lead me inside feels absolute.

I sit on a chair with a floral print and tell them about the camp and Sophe's *vocation*. About the children she taught, the women she befriended, the honour they gave her of hennaing her hands. That her students loved her. The generosity of her spirit. I tell them about the rituals of tea under canvas roofs, and the long days we spent hitching towards the mountains. That with my antibiotics she'd saved a girl who was dying at the side of the road. I know it's not true but that's what I tell them. Because if I'd listened to her that's what *would* have happened.

'She's a better person than me.'

Sophe's father's eyes don't leave mine, but her mother gazes only at the wall, her hair pulled back tight from her forehead.

'What does that matter?' he says.

When I don't answer, her father takes out an atlas and lays it on the coffee table between us, moving a bowl of rose petals to make room.

'Show me the route you took,' he says, Sophe's mother still sitting upright in her armchair, looking away, her perfume, her pale makeup on her pale skin.

I lean over the atlas and catch my breath. It's the first time I've seen a map of Africa since I left. The shock of its shape in that wallpapered sitting room. Seeing for the first time – Sophe's story fresh in my throat – that Africa is a disembodied head stripped of its flesh. Bone and skull, the profile was laid out there on the page, coloured in with the pastels of nation-states, the borders between the cranium and the frontal and parietal bones, the mandible. With an elongated jaw and long chin, a little devil's horn where the blunt nose bone would normally be, and the island off the coast a loose bone-chip – Africa is clearly, unmistakeably, the skull of some primitive hominid, some time-blasted ancestor of ours, gazing off to the east, blank and emotionless.

I baulk.

'We know the camp is here,' her father insists, pointing. 'Where did you go after that?'

My hand is shaking, but I show him, tracing the line of our route. East, south, east, south. Down, down, down.

'The girl she saved,' her father says, 'where was that?'

I swallow and show him a place.

'And then?'

And then. This is what the Beards left me with, their directive. *Don't forget. You tell your people. Tell.* It is what the Beards want.

'I can't remember everything, Mr Maddison,' I say, pulling away. 'I can't remember what happened . . . at the end. I've blanked it out, I'm sorry.'

Not just because I won't give the Beards their victory. But because it is the merciful thing to do, surely, a responsibility I have to her parents. Though there is more to it than that: I also just don't have the words. And the story can neither soothe her parents' anguish, nor atone for my guilt.

'What about your brother?'

I point out where the hermitage is, name it for them.

'He'd become a monk,' I say.

'It didn't save him, though.'

'Save him?'

'He was in the army before, wasn't he? Confronting death every day?'

I nod, but let it pass. I've come for Sophe, not to defend Jack.

'I'm going to go,' her father says, raising his voice, a growing vehemence in it. 'The government says it'd be suicide to go now, but when things settle down I want to see it with my own two eyes. I'll go to her camp myself, Sebastian. I'll go to that hotel too.'

He is staring at me, boring into me, a fever in him.

'I'll stay in that same goddamn room. Just see if I don't.'

I rise to leave. Sophe's mother looks at me for the first time since I've been in their sitting room.

'Was there . . . something . . . between you?' she asks.

I go to speak but there is nothing there, just my gaping mouth, and their eyes. I turn away, and go down the hallway, not knowing what else to do. I will not deny her.

Her parents follow silently.

'May I visit her grave?' I ask at the door.

'We cremated her,' her father says. Then, as if to ward me off for good, 'And we spread her ashes.'

The responsibility he takes for it. There are so few decisions left for them. I think about Sophe's scattered ashes, set upon the breezes that blow across this town she was born in, this country which raised her. How desperately I'd hoped there'd be a headstone I could touch, an inscription I could read with my hands, a delicate limestone angel. A conversation of some sort I might begin.

I reach for the door handle. Her mother leans round and grips my wrist.

'But why?' she says, a horror in her eyes I cannot meet. 'Why Sophia?'

FOUR

Why? The blood-smeared question that curves back again, and again. It has a new shape each time. It refuses all dealing, can neither be looked at straight, nor ignored. It fragments under its own weight – Why Jack? Why me? Why Sophe? – It divides, like a cell, again and again. Magnitudes of complexity, a different why in everything.

I am a drowner in a sea of question.

I go east to where Sophe lived, New York. Take a room at a YMCA on West 34th Street – a creaking lift rising through fourteen floors of long, dark corridors and small, cramped rooms.

I wander Sophe's university and the city streets in widening loops, avoiding the lawyers and bankers and traders in their suits, the certainty of their stride. Stepping back from all the dizzying men and women, from the smell of blood.

One day there's a wilted rose on the ground. I look up, at a wall of opaque glass. At first I don't realise that it is a memorial, because *our* war memorials are obelisks, set in parks, or at the end of avenues of honour – towers reaching for heaven.

People are leaning forward, their faces close to the glass tiles, reading the words cut into the wall. A hundred letters from Vietnam, our father's war. Letters home from soldiers, from parents to their boys, from sweethearts in Kentucky and Connecticut and Phoenix:

I feel different now after seeing some horrible things and I'll never forget them. To kill somebody, turn your head and walk away isn't hard, it's watching him die that's hard, and even harder when it's one of your own men.

Might my own father have written a letter like this to *his* parents, I think? I read to the end of the wall, and discover another behind it, a second layer of letters, more pleas.

By the time this arrives I will have told all my hairy war stories and shown you my scar. One thing that worries me . . . will people believe me?

There are a thousand letters to be lost in, a thousand clear voices.

Several times a week we visit the hospital. We see fellows with their arms and legs blown off, their heads smashed in and pieced together, eyes lost and hearts completely broken. The biggest gift we can give them is a human female hand and some cheerful words. Like 'Hi, how are you doing?' We're not in the business of giving sympathy. We have to treat them as if nothing is wrong at all. Absolutely nothing. . . .

Finally I look up, gasping for breath. But everything is still unutterably wrong.

An Arab family is standing beside me: a tall man in white robes with a black cord around his white-scarved head, and polished shoes. And the beard. His wife is standing behind him, and his two daughters in their pretty dresses, ten or twelve years old, bobby clips with pink plastic flowers keeping their straight dark hair out of their polite dark eyes.

That fucking beard.

He peers hard, his nose close to the glass, to all those lives etched there. His neck stretches forward; the wife standing, waiting. He

233

shakes his head, his face just inches away from the last words of a nineteen-year-old soldier from Idaho. He couldn't have read them, he isn't there long enough. He steps along, glancing at letter after letter. Begins stroking his beard with his hand, one of his daughters looking at him, watching as he mumbles to himself. I can tell there is no feeling in his straight, haughty back, no respect. He turns and says something, not looking at any of them, his disdain for what is in front of him, for everything. His ignorance. I see the prayer beads he's looped around his wrist slide from under the sleeve of his robe and catch on the flesh of his palm.

'What are you doing here?'

He gives me a blank look. As if he doesn't know what I mean.

'You right, mate?'

But I don't want him to understand me.

'I said, you bloody-well *right*, mate?'

There is no question in it. I am yelling, and all the pilgrims at the wall turn away from it to look at me instead.

'So what does it say, mate? How much of *that* do you understand?'

I poke my finger into his chest. Then begin hissing at him – *Allahu Akbar! Allahu Akbar! Allahu Akbar!* – forcing him back against the glass, one of his daughters crying and tugging at my shirt.

Two policemen appear. They pull me off him. Their hard peaked hats and golden badges. Their dark blue uniforms, almost black, a cold hard baton pressed against my throat.

'Are you alright, sir?' one of them says when we are separated.

I think he is talking to me.

I try telling my story in the lock-up, squatting on the hard floor surrounded by sleeping men with cracks in the soles of their feet and pieces of string for belts. One of the policemen on night shift encourages me, curious about my accent.

'You're saying he killed your brother?'

'Yes.'

'That man this afternoon?'

'Him. His brothers. His fellow-believers. *That's the whole point!* It's the same thing. It doesn't matter.'

He shakes his head, mutters, bends his head again to the magazine in his lap.

'Want my advice?' he says. 'Give it up. That's my advice to you. Give it up.'

But it is impossible.

FIVE

I lean against a wall for a second day. Across the street is a mosque. The street vendors ignore me and I count the Beards as they come and go, the whole teeming nest of them.

It is midafternoon when one of them steps out the door of the mosque alone, pauses on the sidewalk and looks straight across at me. He has a fitted skullcap and wears a black suit with a white shirt beneath his coat. There is no tie, and I can't tell if he has buttoned his collar – his beard is too thick, wiry like a bushranger's. He steps onto the road in a break in traffic and comes closer. I see a streak of white in his dark beard. My throat constricts. I swallow to breathe. I would turn and run if I could, but am rooted to the ground as once I was on a cliff-face not so many years before. My eyes swim, and the Beard loses focus as he steps up onto the sidewalk in front of me and I ready myself. *You. Go. Tell.* I expect him to lean close, his foul breath on my cheeks, and scream. I close my eyes and turn my head.

'Can I help you?' he asks.

But it does not register.

'Can I help you, sir?'

He tries again, his perfect English and his American accent adding to my confusion.

I open my eyes and look at him. His black, shining eyes, his full glossy lips.

'Sir, you have been sitting here watching now for many hours. Are you interested in us, sir? Won't you come in. Perhaps we can talk. Would you like to talk? Sir, would you like to learn about Islam?'

A muscle in my face pulls involuntarily, and my left eyelid begins to twitch. He mistakes my agitation for embarrassment.

'Ah! You want to learn about Islam! We have lessons. You can come to a lesson in our teaching hall.'

I shake my head urgently, my eyes widening. Can he not see my horror?

He pauses, considering, then turns and steps back onto the road, holding up his hand to the traffic as he crosses. When he returns a few minutes later he is bearing a book.

'We have lessons every Sunday. You are welcome. But . . .' and he pauses to see if I have reconsidered while he was away, 'if you don't want to join us for a lesson, you may have this. It is the Holy Qur'an.'

I feel sick.

'If you can't read it in Arabic, read this. It is not a translation, because the Qur'an cannot be translated, but it contains the teachings of Almighty Allah. It is by Marmaduke Pickthall, an Englishman. The Qur'an should be read in Arabic, but, this . . .'

The imam holds the book out but doesn't give it to me yet, as if he is weighing the two wrongs: the risk of my misinterpretation against my ongoing ignorance of Allah.

'. . . this is the next best thing for Americans.'

★

Allahu Akbar. The altar-cry of the Beard with the knife. God is Great. One can say God is Great while opening a throat – and presume to know the nature of God. Does it not instead end all argument?

So I shut myself away in my room at the Y and read the Qur'an, surah after surah, night after night. A month of reading passes, a month of shuddering pipes and voices outside in the corridor at all hours, my fingers stained by nicotine and printer's ink, so many surahs coming away so easily beneath my thumb. I find passage after passage, underlining them. Opening my Pickthall every time with the promise of finding even more to corroborate what I'd experienced.

I read to accumulate evidence against them. When I go out I take my Pickthall with me. I sit in a booth at a diner and read, or spill Starbuck's on it as I rest on a park-bench, memorising passages, mumbling them to myself till I've got them off.

'. . . *whoso fighteth in the way of Allah, be he slain or victorious, on him We shall bestow a vast reward.*'

The verses burn their way into my brain.

'. . . *slay the idolaters wherever you find them, and take them captive, and besiege them, and prepare for them each ambush. But if they repent and establish worship, and pay the poor-due, then leave their way free. Lo! Allah is Forgiving, Merciful.*'

'What's happening, brother?'

I look up from the bench I've settled into in Washington Square these last afternoons, as around me men in long coats pass small Alfoil packages to students and receive greenbacks in return, their eyes never meeting, these people glancing off each other, and me no threat to any of it. A black man stands in front of me, his jeans hanging loose off his hips. His hair is beaded, his short beard shaved low and sharp on his cheeks, a glittering cross swaying across his chest.

'Hey brother,' he says. 'What's that you're reading?'

'Slay the idolaters,' I answer.

'Say what?'

'Are you a Christian?' I ask, pointing to his cross, knowing of course.

'Are you a religious nut?'

'Make those who believe stand firm. I will throw fear into the hearts of those who disbelieve. Then smite the necks and smite of them each finger.'

'Fucking religious nut,' he says, turning away.

'No, no.' I reach for his arm. 'Hang on. That's one thing I'm not . . . that's the last thing. No, no . . . all I'm doing is quoting the religious fanatics . . . *smite their necks*. That's what the fanatics say.'

'What's it supposed to mean then?'

'Cut off their heads, cut off their fingers.'

'Huh?'

'It's from in here. The Muslims' holy book, their Holy Qur'an. That's what this book is. Allah is kind and merciful they say, but did you hear that? Cut off their heads. Their God wants them to cut off our heads.'

'That's shit, man.'

'It's in here.'

I point at the passage, and shove the book towards him. I watch eagerly as he reads, his whole head moving from side to side. He finishes the paragraph, then flicks forward some pages, reads, and flicks forward some more, his brow creased, before closing it and handing it back.

'That's like reading fucking Shakespeare, that is, brother,' he says eventually. '*Smite of them each a finger*? Who knows what that shit's supposed to mean.'

★

The waitresses, their hair in buns and their hands hardened by dishwater, whisper to each other when two veiled women sit down in a booth and order milkshakes.

'Primitive, isn't it?' I say to them when the doorbell tinkles and the Muslims leave.

'Glad I wasn't born one of them,' the younger waitress replies, wiping her hands on her apron.

'If they get their way, they'll make you one,' I say.

And when she cocks an eyebrow, I know I have her.

Like this I start conversations on the slightest pretext, sometimes for no reason at all. Some people are already haters and we feed each other. Others are ignorant of Muslims and terrorists, and I set myself to educate them. But sometimes it irritates me that people could be apathetic, that they can't see all the pieces coming together. The kidnapping in Tehran, those fifty-two Americans holed up in their consulate for years when I was a kid, held captive by terrorists. The honour killings and the veils and the clitorectomies. The harems and the seventy-two virgins waiting in paradise for their martyrs. The novelist with the fatwa on his head. The entire stuffed-up Middle East.

I'd shaken God off when I began holding rock in my hand, began moving through the bush like a tracker, stoop-shouldered, my senses closer to the ground than the air. Left God behind as I sought out thin fissures in great seams of rock, as I cut slabs of sandstone out of mother rock, shouldering it away to work on in the backyard. And then, when I began to stay out there, in the bush, carving figures into the rock-faces themselves – God disappeared entirely then. All those Hail Marys, all those ecstatic saints, those feast days. Gone. Not a grain of evidence God was ever there.

But God returned in Africa, and now there is no escaping. *Allahu Akbar.*

I lie in bed and read, the counterweights too. That there is *no compulsion in religion.* That he who kills a man who hasn't killed another is guilty of having killed all mankind. It's a Qur'anic dance! – verses setting themselves up against each other, two warring selves accommodated, jihadist and peacemaker. I spin off, and away, dizzy, the ceiling blank above me. There is no God but Allah. There is no God at all.

Everything is contested, *everything.* There is a counter to all things.

Even in my sleep I reel:

They are criminals. They are freedom fighters.

They are murderers. They are soldiers of God.

They are evil. They are guaranteed a place in heaven.

They are Muslims. They do not speak for Islam. Their deeds are abhorrent to true Muslims. Muslims condemn what they have done.

They *say* they are Muslims. They are mistaken. They are not true Muslims.

They are Islamists then. That word is an invention of the West.

I read the counterweights – and do not believe them.

When I open my eyes the room whirls. There is the sound of guitars through the wall and voices singing *No Woman, No Cry* and *Buffalo Soldier* and *Redemption Song,* moving through the Bob Marley songbook. But the tunes are dead in my ear: I am on a bus to Western Sahara, shivering in the dark.

I get up giddy, and walk down the corridor to the communal bathroom where I sit in a cubicle with my head in my hands. *Whoso fighteth in the way of Allah, be he slain or victorious, on him We shall bestow a vast reward.* The bathroom door swings open and I hear the voices of cleaners, and the sound of their metal buckets clattering against the tiled floor. There is splashing water and mop-swish, then banging on the cubicle door.

'Is someone in there?'

'Yeah, yeah,' I answer.

'You gonna be long?'

'Probably.'

There is a grunt and the mop moves on.

Graffiti covers the cubicle walls. Names and phone numbers, drawings of body parts, the names of things people do to each other. There are slogans too, *No War* and *Death to Capitalism* competing with *America: Love it or leave it* on the toilet door. So, how much of it was politics? How much had Jack and Sophe become prizes, trophies for the Beards?

While Sophe and I were stepping down through the desert towards Jack, there were communiqués delivered to governments and statements issued to newspapers in Paris and Algiers. I know that now. That the Beards had returned home from Afghanistan, and gathered round their imams, and stockpiled their cachets of arms, and sought power through politics and were rebuffed, and were rebuffed again – that they warned foreigners to get out and set deadlines and that on the other side was apocalypse. *Allahu Akbar!*

Allahu Akbar! Death to America! No Freedom Without Justice. Give Peace a Chance. Not In Our Name. Mere marketing, absurd in its simplicity. Is that what Sophe and Jack are reduced to? The priest and the American. The Christian and the aid worker. Is that it? Symbols from which all that was real and true and difficult have already leeched away, the eternal torment of a few distant relatives all that remains.

'You done *yet*, mister?'

The sound of his fist on the door splits my head.

'Friend or foe?' I say to him, opening the door.

My face is burning.

'What?'

'So what are you? Idolater or Muslim? One or the other?'

'Mister, I'm just here to clean. You done?'

But I don't let him go.

'You've got to choose. You're either one of us or one of them.'

'You've been drinking.'

'They're everywhere.'

'You're not allowed to drink here, mister. What room are you in, mister?'

SIX

I give up on New York after I'm kicked out of the hostel, six months of scratching away, nothing to show. I move on, a week here, a year there, into a whole continent's buffeting winds. My ragged self, so light, so much lost and stolen by the Beards.

Dish-hand, breakfast cook, mower of lawns, and fixer of gutters; fruit-picker and landscaper and hole-digger and production line worker – I crawl along the surface of things, desperate not to blow away or fall through. It is enough to keep me going. I have seen a neck bared and opened.

There are things I avoid now, so deep I barely know they're there. I look away when passing butcher-shop windows, or barbers. I've taken to using electric razors. My hair grows long. Could my own hand trim it, or sharpen pencils, or slice bread?

All the while carrying her in the inside pocket of my great coat, wrapping her in a jumper at night when I sleep rough, as my pillow. Careful she's safe during the day if I'm working in a field, or that my locker is secure when I'm on a factory floor. I'm alert to anyone getting too close, am ready to shield her.

I write to Em sometime in my second year, hung-over, angry, turning on them all, the words bursting onto the page in fits, a ferocity time will not suppress.

Jack wanted it, Em. He WANTED it! He brought it on himself, Em. It's ALL HIS FAULT. He WILLED it to happen. If he hadn't prayed his little heart out to die like that, none of this would have happened. You know what he wanted? 'Lord, I pray that I die covered with wounds and blood, killed violently and painfully. I desire this today, Lord.' I saw it, Em. THAT's what he wanted. Jack's responsible, Em. Tell that to my father. That Jack CURSED us – stop bloody well thinking he could do no wrong. But you know what? The worst thing? He took someone else with him. HE's responsible for Sophe. I didn't tell her parents that, but I should have. Tell my father that. His golden bloody son.

The girls in our country town had their books of saints: virgin after virgin who preferred death to defilement by God's enemies, who greeted death joyfully and yearned for its perfection. It was no different for me at The Springs – at least before the fire, before Mum died. Isn't every boy at some point willing to die for what he believes? How strange it seems now. I was purer then. I yearned to be tested, that year before our mother died, longed for a chance to prove myself to God, *before* God. It was a simple choice. But then faith began to blur into adolescence, and stretch out formidably, long and confusing.

★

Em doesn't bite, is just pleased to receive the contact after so long. Will I come back home? she asks. *We'll look after you*, she says. *This is where you belong. Everything will be OK.* Of course not. There can never be contentment, I will never be the same again, and if I am to live like this then Sophe's country is good enough, big enough, after Africa.

We write. I've shed so much in my American purgatory I could just as easily shed my wicked stepmother. But I don't. I've come to think it's something of a miracle. I don't resent her.

Usually she writes news of The Springs, the businesses that have closed and the new ones come to town, the local elections, the dirt roads being sealed, where the police put their speed traps, the latest scheme to do up the Spa. She writes about a conwoman who's arrived from the south with visitations from Mary and plans for a six-thousand-seat basilica in town. How she and her followers carry a giant crucifix up Table Top for a dawn service each Sunday.

Sometimes Em includes happenings at the hospital – a new type of needle they're trying, the outbreak of a virulent winter flu, patients she's come to know, their courage. But mostly she just describes her days. She writes what time the sun rises, how cold it is in the kitchen in the morning when she puts on the kettle, what the quote of the day is from the wisdom calendar beside the phone, how many oranges she's picked, the colour of the previous day's sunset, whether there's been a frost, if it has rained overnight, or how much water is left in the tank. I picture the thermometer, see the rain gauge on the front fence, imagine the palings my father painted warping in the sun.

My replies are mostly short geographical pieces: that I am in this or that city and can receive mail at a certain address. A few times, when my mood darkens, I spew out my ideas about Muslims. I keep Sophe to myself after that first letter, in turn too precious or too dangerous. Only once does Em respond to my philosophy on Islam. *We got a letter,* she says, *from Tamanrasset. It was in Arabic. It might be the only Arabic letter ever to arrive at The Springs! Your father and I thought about taking it to the police, but decided in the end to ask a family of refugees at the hospital (their teenage daughter contracted appendicitis, and her family was always up there visiting — her mother and I got on, even though she didn't speak English). Their son is in grade 11 at school and translated it. This is what it said, Bas:*

Monsieur,

It is disgraceful, it is truly shameful. The teachings of Islam are clear about the sacredness of life, love of one's neighbour, hospitality towards strangers, whatever their religion. These are the true teachings of Islam, which sadly have been trampled upon by this handful of fanatics who every day ruin our reputation as a welcoming and hospitable people. We pray you will accept this message of fraternity and friendship.

Yours truly,
An Algerian family,
just like so many others affected by this event.

There is no signature, no Mohammed, or Hussein, or Ibrahim. Rather it ends like that, with those words. *An Algerian family.* It might well help *Em*, I think, a nice letter like that. But she's never been bloodied by *Allahu Akbar*. And her reconciliation instinct blinds her to truth.

Eventually, though, there is the letter about my father that I retrieve from the Washington *poste-restante* where I find myself

247

washed up at the end of the millennial summer, my seventh in America. I sit on the hard post-office steps, the sound of the city surrounding me, and open it.

29 August 2000

Dear Bas,

Your father died on the 3rd of July following a stroke. He is buried in the cemetery beside your mother and your brother. It was a fine funeral. I'm sending you a photo of the grave, just in case. I intend to sell the quarry. If you have any objections, please let me know within the month.

Yours
Em

SEVEN

There are angels carved into the limestone of the cathedral on the highest of Washington's hills. The Archangel Michael with bared chest and sword high in the south transept. A host of angels amongst the gargoyles on the central tower, their eyes closed and their palms pressed together in prayer. There are forty-four voussoir angels – I count them before crossing myself and entering – in the cathedral's south portal, and too many to count on the high altar.

I choose a pew away from a tour group with their bulbs flashing in the high chamber. I cannot bring myself to kneel, but sit instead with my face in my hands. My father. My brother. The family quarry that could have been sold years ago, *should* have been. I see my father futilely hanging onto it, year after year. So much reduced to so little. To a transaction. My blameless father. I cannot pray, but wish, fervently, I could weep.

As I leave the cathedral I see a small wooden hut across the road under the shade of an old cypress. The tree and the shed look almost forlorn beside the cathedral towers. Through a window I see a ghostly figure standing at a bench, his legs splayed, his shoulders set, a cap pulled low on his forehead. The dust is so thick on the inside of the pane it is difficult to make out clearly what he is doing. But as I watch the movement of his arms and sense their power, see the stillness of his head, I know. Pressing my nose against the glass to examine the other end of the room, I make out a series of bas-relief carvings arranged on joists. There is a wall of hanging tools, and I peer closer to identify them: the mallets and hammers and callipers and rasps and squares and levels.

'Eh!'

I step back from the window in surprise, like a thief caught in some act he doesn't yet understand himself.

The carver is a short man in his early sixties, his neck and shoulders thick with muscle, chips of stone lodged in the hairs of his forearms. The plain short-sleeved shirt and dark trousers are faded with dust and wear. He stands there inspecting me, his forehead high and his eyes steady behind dark-rimmed glasses.

'You look for someone?'

I have a dozen responses to that sort of question by now, answers that usually allay the fears of shopkeepers or landowners or mothers with prams, but my mind has seized up. The old stone-carver has me transfixed.

'You got no tongue?'

His cap is like those I once saw in a nineteenth-century photo of an old craftsman's school in Italy. It is cream-coloured, and pulled halfway down the back of his head, with a rounded peak reaching out over his large nose. His point chisel nestles comfortably in his left palm as if it might be an extension of his hand.

He shakes his head and turns his shoulder, preparing to move away.

'I used to carve!'

He stops and looks at me with eyes that have been so sharp for so long, eyes practised in detecting error and rooting it out, but which have now softened. After what seems a long time he grunts.

'You want something to eat? Drink?'

He sits me at a lunch-table covered in checked cloth. Around it is an assortment of old chairs with names carved into the wooden backs, or engraved into the metal ones: Roger, Vincent, Frank, CS, Roberto.

'Milk? Sugar?'

I nod.

'Two.'

He places the cup in front of me with his large, gentle hands. Then he sits down. I barely notice, looking around the room, taking it in: the high ceiling, the exposed wooden beams, the skylight with the northern sun flooding the space, softened by the filter of dust. What seemed like carvings from outside are actually plaster models: keystones and capitals, bishops and saints. A plaster version of one of the angels inside the cathedral stands on a high ledge at the end of the room, looking down on us. I think of Sophe, can't help but see a resemblance in the tilt of the angel's head, the line of its mouth.

We sit in silence for some time. Eventually he pushes his chair back and moves across to the workbench where there is a block he is beginning to rough out.

'Limestone?' I ask.

'Indiana limestone,' he says, and then laughs. 'This whole cathedral comes from Indiana!'

'It's soft?'

'When he come out of the ground, my friend, he has a lot of water. The water makes him soft. But in the sun the water evaporates and he hardens. He has a compact grain, and holds the cut. He is sweet to work. And you? What is your stone?'

'Sandstone. Though some people call it freestone because it doesn't weather like most sandstone. It holds its grain.'

'You from Australia?'

'How did you know?'

'We had carvers from all over the world here not so long ago. More countries than the League of Nations. Now it's just me.'

He seems to sigh.

'You have a family?' he asks.

Such a simple question. I almost say no. A day earlier and I would have. A day earlier, though, I wouldn't have visited the cathedral.

'My mother died when I was a child. My older brother was killed. I just learnt my father has died. That's why –'

I choke.

He waits.

'We had a quarry,' I finish.

Before dawn the next day I've set up a little tower of coins on the shelf of a phone box. I dial the number and hear the phone ringing fourteen hours away.

'Em. It's me, Bas.'

'Bas. Oh, Bas. Bas! How are you, Bas?'

Her voice surprises me, is different from how I remember it. Somehow, despite the years of letters and her voice in those little domestic stories, her accent seems to have seeped away. She will have finished dinner now, I think. Will have washed up and be reading or knitting or quilting beside the tall living room lamp.

'As well as you'd expect, Em. I didn't read your letter about Dad until yesterday. I'm in Washington. The letter followed me here, but I only just got it.'

'I wondered why I hadn't heard from you.'

'I'm sorry, Em.'

'You're the only one now, Bas.'

'I lit a candle for him yesterday.'

'That's good, Bas. That's good.'

A newspaper truck drives past – the rumble of its tyres on the bitumen as it approaches, then its roar and the glass of the phone box vibrating as it goes past. We both wait until it is gone.

'Did you sell?'

Now the static, an ocean and two continents of it.

'I've got a buyer,' she says uncertainly. 'It hasn't gone through yet, but . . .'

'It's the right thing to do, Em, the right thing. I'm glad that's what you're doing.'

'Yes . . . well . . .'

'How are *you*, Em?'

So simple, yet such a hard question to find once you lose it. I couldn't have asked it yesterday.

'OK, all things considered . . . no . . . no, that's not true. I'm lonely, Bas. I miss him.'

My stomach clutches.

'I would have come back if it hadn't happened so suddenly. I would have liked to have seen him. He suffered a lot in his life.'

'Yes, he did.'

'I'm sorry . . .'

'But he didn't blame you, Bas,' she says quickly. 'You know that, don't you?'

The silence. What else might come to the surface?

'Are you there, Bas?'

I close my eyes. There is no sun rising, no waking city, no receiver pressed hard against the side of my head.

'He didn't blame you for anything, Bas. He would've liked the chance to tell you that. I know he would.'

EIGHT

Antonio Vasari has set a chair against the workshop wall for me. He works his mallet and chisel with speed and intensity, faster than I've ever seen. It is loud too. Silence can be terrifying, so I listen with relief to the sound of his mallet and his chisel, the limestone chips scattering on the floor or crunching under the soles of his boots, the operas he whistles. Antonio offers me tea when he rests midmorning, and makes sandwiches with smoked ham from the fridge when he breaks for lunch.

'Your brother?' he asks, shaking his cap as he steps back from his work. I've been drifting, and look at him without answering, unsure whether I've heard him right.

'You say your brother was killed. What happen?'

It is what the Beards want. *You. Go. Tell.* It is what I have resisted. I shake my head.

'No?' he says. 'Maybe I misunderstand. I thought you said you had a brother.'

I am trapped.

'Yes,' I say finally. And I begin.

Ignited, I talk on and on, trembling, laying it bare.

Antonio gasps and shakes his head, and murmurs, 'Dear God, *no.*' But when Jack is dead and it is Islam I accuse – as I quote the Qur'an, and demonstrate my proofs, and check he understands and test him to see what alliance there might be between us – he grows quiet.

The master carver rises from his chair and turns on the electric jug and puts teabags into two cups he lifts off the shelf.

He sits again and raises his cup of tea to his lips and takes a sip.

'This table here,' he says, touching it, 'is good for stories. Good stories. Bad stories. Many years, and many stories. It is good for telling.'

'What happened to my brother is not just a story. It is terrible. *Evil!* The greatest of evils, the worst of evils.'

He pauses a long time.

'Yes,' he says, looking me evenly in the eyes, 'it is a very terrible story.'

'You want?' Antonio asks one morning, gesturing to the stone.

I stare at him.

'You ever carve limestone before?'

I shake my head. Can he guess how long it's been since I've carved *anything*?

'You try.'

My heart quickens, and I feel a rising panic. I freeze. I am always freezing.

As a child, I'd wander along the foot of the sandstone cliffs in the early morning, inspecting the rocks which had come off when the temperature fell during the night, and which the next day lay split open on the ground. I'd collect the larger grains of quartz and fill a jar with them, then pour water in and place the jar on my bedroom windowsill. Every morning the crystals would glint and glitter and I believed each new dawn was a thing of wonder.

Sandstone is the stone of light and dark. It is rough, is only ever fresh cut from the ground, *just* broken free, and in that very moment of liberation is already crumbling, once again, back into the earth.

'It can't be polished like marble,' my father used to say. 'And this is its majesty, because in its roughness sandstone casts shadows marble never can.'

He could sell stone, my father.

'Sandstone refuses to be dressed up, it can't be made pretty like marble, is never cold, never distant. It is alive in ways all those marble museum pieces can only long to be.'

And as a boy I learnt how to drill a row of holes, insert a feather-and-pin in each, then move across the row of them with a mallet, tapping them one by one like a percussionist – till the stone splits and what is unnecessary falls away. I learnt how to make sandstone smooth like young skin, or pocked like a turbulent sea. I could shape rock into animals or trees or letters or numerals, any pattern under the sun. I knew how to use a rust seam, which fissures would hold and which would split. I knew how stone moved, *our* sandstone. I could transform our hills, the very earth on which we walked, from which we were born.

'You want to try?'

I breathe. I nod.

Antonio disappears from the workshop for a few moments and returns with a small limestone block that he sets before me. Then he puts his hands on my shoulders and turns me towards the shelves where his tools lie: an air hammer and a pointing machine, and coffee cans filled with rasps and chisels lined neatly on a shelf, their sharpened blades towards the wall.

'Take anything you want.'

But when Antonio realises I'm unable to choose, he selects a chisel and mallet himself and places them in my hands.

Sophe is in my pocket, the pressure of her resting against my leg.

No matter how gentle you are, there is always that first touch of chisel on stone, when stone resists. Then you ready yourself, prepare to force yourself upon the stone. It is a sacred moment of doubt. I learned to trust it years ago. Without it, there would be mere butchery.

The first strike.

'Be confident,' I hear Antonio whisper. 'You must tame your stone.'

Riddle, master, slave, servant, or lover.

The stone is your judge.

I raise my arm and strike.

NINE

Antonio sets me tasks, small ones at first, satisfying himself at every step. That I know how to find the bottom of a block, that I can make a surface flat, carve letters and cut leaves. That I know how to 'find the dark', as he calls it, in the light smooth texture of the limestone.

'I think I can use you,' he says eventually. 'Not much. A few jobs. A few dollars, that's all.'

He sets me up in a caravan in the backyard of his brother Gianni's house in a modest part of the city, a little too far from the cathedral to rely on the buses. Gianni is older than Antonio and was once also a carver, but his body is now shrinking. Under his dyed black hair his eyes are filmy, and he probably needs company as much as I need a bed.

I accept the bike Gianni tells me he hasn't ridden in years and cycle through the city's streets in the bright, early hours of the day, pushing the last uphill stretch to the church. Leaning the bike on the inside wall of the workshop, I slip off the small backpack which holds my statuette.

Antonio tells me the cathedral was consecrated just a few years ago, once the major carvings – the altar reredos and the creation tympanum and the trumeau statues – were in place, and every crocket on every finial on every pinnacle had been carved and mounted on the cathedral's steeples.

'But it is not complete,' Antonio says. 'It will be a hundred years before it is complete.'

There are still grotesques to be added, bosses to be mounted, and carvings that need embellishment. Events that need memorialising, some past and some yet to come. 'Every great cathedral needs its resident master carver,' he says.

Whatever Antonio entrusts to me I do: a small lily or an unobtrusive rose, some minor flourish. He teaches me to use the pointing machine – how to transfer the dimensions of a plaster model across to the stone, measurement by measurement. All those martyrs and missionaries who've first been shaped in clay by their sculptor, then cast in plaster and set before Antonio for him to recreate in stone. For months I rough pieces out for him to take over and bring to completion. My hands blister and callous, but they are returning to life.

I watch him finish a wreath of lilies at the feet of a saint, and nod in awe.

He smiles.

'I always have trouble with flowers,' he says looking up at me, pausing. 'The damn bees get in the way!'

Then he slaps me on the shoulder and laughs heartily. The kindness of that invitation.

But when at lunch or over tea, or at the end of a day's embellishing, I try turning the talk to Islam. Antonio waves me away, or ignores me, or tells me the floor needs sweeping.

If I grow angry he only closes his eyes and lifts his finger to his lips.

'Shhh,' he says, 'shhh, now.'

As if I am a baby.

'Not here. We need to work.'

When someone knocks the hands off a statue in the apse, we carry it down the aisle and out the door like stretcher-bearers.

'Do you know who did it?' I ask the cathedral dean, a tall, thin man, as he follows us into the workshop. The final approval for every design of every cathedral carving lies with him.

'We have no idea at all, Mr Adams,' he says. 'Some people think it is a political statement. A statue of George Washington in the Cathedral Church of St John the Divine in New York was damaged the other day and a dollar bill with Washington's defaced head was left on it. But we really don't know. There are so many reasons for damaging a statue.'

'The Muslims blew up the giant Buddhas in Afghanistan!'

'The *Taliban*,' he corrects. 'Yes, and the Vandals destroyed the gods of Rome when they invaded, and Cromwell's soldiers took the noses off Catholic saints all over England, and statues of vanquished kings and presidents throughout history are torn down and replaced by their conquerors. Yes, yes, yes, Mr Adams. But it's more likely to have been a tourist looking for a souvenir, or a young buck acting out a dare, or some poor mentally ill soul. Do you know the story of the fellow who damaged the *Pieta* at St Peters?'

I grit my teeth. I know more about the *Pieta* than the dean ever will, but say nothing and endure his lecture.

'If it's the devil you look for,' Antonio whispers to me when the dean has finished, 'you look in the wrong place.'

We return the statue to its nook weeks later, with new hands, the cracks invisible.

Antonio sets lessons for me. I sharpen tools I've never used before and carve flowers I've never smelt. I complete all the tasks I'm asked, even begin anticipating them before Antonio speaks. I collect fallen chisels from the floor to save Antonio's aging back, carry the stone for him, learn his rhythms.

Slowly I feel the stone of myself breaking. Deposits of soil accumulate in the fresh cracks in my spirit. I feel earth and leaf-litter and drops of rain, all the wetness and warmth of life returning. It is a new remembering.

'Very good,' Antonio says.

We sit at Gianni's dinner table to celebrate the first anniversary of my arrival. The red-and-white checked tablecloth I found in one of Gianni's kitchen drawers makes it look like we're sitting in a restaurant, something special. It is still summer and the light outside lingers. Heat rises from the spaghetti mounds as I serve it onto our three plates.

'Yes,' Gianni agrees. '*Buonissimo!*'

'I'm no cook,' I say, 'but . . .'

They can't know the effort slicing the onions took, even now.

'No, no. Is good. Truly . . . Maybe not as good as a woman's . . .' and he winks and laughs, 'but good for drinking wine.'

Gianni has closed his eyes. I've come to understand the death of his wife four years ago is a shadow he can't step out from under, no matter what his brother tries. But for Antonio it is different. His 'life of women', he calls it, each touching him equally. Whether deeply or not, I can't tell.

He lifts his glass.

'To women!' he toasts.

Our glasses chink.

'To wine!' Gianni says.

'To carving,' I say, and raise my glass.

TEN

Suddenly, one late summer day, there is vindication.

We see and hear nothing. We don't even know it has happened until late in the morning when a group of breathless nuns in dishevelled habits knock on the windowpane. I follow Antonio out of the workshop and high up into the central tower of the cathedral and we look to the south-west where the nuns tell us a plane has crashed into the Pentagon on the banks of the river below. There are no flames from here, no visible embers. But smoke. Inexhaustible clouds of it spill from the opened building all afternoon, rising, catching on the breeze, filling the high blue sky.

'What did I tell you, Antonio? What did I tell you? It's *exactly* what I've been saying.'

'Softer!' Antonio barks. 'You need the feel. Where is the feel?'

'They hate us, Antonio.'

'Your hands need to be soft, Bas. Tender. You can't carve when you're angry.'

I step back from the stone.

'It could have been the cathedral.'

'It wasn't.'

'Next time it might be. All these great carvings of yours might be destroyed in an instant.'

'That is the risk of sculpting, my friend, the risk of carving. Is there anything riskier? You risk making a mistake and breaking the stone. You risk people not liking your carving. You risk someone destroying what you create. You take those risks.'

'Pah! Your head is in the sand, old man!'

I throw down my chisel.

All those people I've accosted about Islam – the factory hands I've stood beside in production lines in the cities that cling to the Great Lakes, my drinking buddies, the old men on park benches, the buskers pausing between songs to tune their guitars, the mothers with their children on overnight Greyhound buses, Gianni, Antonio – all of them must finally understand. He isn't mad after all, they'll say, remembering me, shaking their heads at themselves, wishing they'd listened. Each of those Muslims I've confronted in the street or the aisles of supermarkets will know now the reason for my wrath – will understand it was my duty – that there is something rotten in their faith that needs rooting out, defeating.

Em writes, begging me to come home.

'It's too dangerous,' she pleads.

But there is nowhere I'd prefer to be.

★

Us or them, the president says. There is no need. We've already come together in a great sigh of relief now that we've found the cause for everything we've sensed was fracturing around us.

I start skipping the workshop, become unreliable, spend whole days instead in the great library reading the newspapers, a country-full of *Bugles* and *Posts* and *Standards*. In the first week alone bricks and stones are thrown through windows of Islamic Centers in Starkville and Tidewater and Lexington, a Molotov cocktail is hurled at the Denton mosque, a pick-up driven into the one at Tallahassee. *USA* and *no forgiveness* and *terrorist* are painted in bright red letters outside the homes of imams across the country. In Greater Toledo the stained glass window of the Islamic Center with its *God is Great* lettering is smashed by a bullet. My soaring heart, this strange elation. In bar after Washington bar I quote the verses of the Qur'an I've memorised, turning my trick into an endless supply of drinks.

Still, I wake at night in my caravan, trembling. Because the agitation of *Allahu Akbar* in my blood remains. I wake from heavy dreams come back to torment me despite everything: all the years and all the miles, my late apprenticeship, the planes, these heady months of Islam bared. Despite it all, the nightmare of spilt blood returns, of Sophe and Jack. Of me turning and fleeing. *Look, see, remember*. The Beards are my companions still.

And yet, and yet.

ELEVEN

'You come back or what?'

It's been a full week this time since I was last at the workshop. Antonio finds me with Gianni in his lounge room. He is exasperated but I don't answer. It is midmorning and the sun is shining thinly through the curtained windows. It will not strengthen, I know that by now. Winter has fallen, fast and hard. Sometimes I sleep on the sofa in front of the flickering television screen because it is warmer than in the caravan, and Gianni goes to bed early most nights.

The brothers greet each other with kisses on their cheeks. Gianni points to the television. There are street protests in Rome against the war the American president has started in Afghanistan and Gianni leans forward, reading aloud the protesters' placards, first in Italian then translating them into English for my benefit. He shakes his fist towards the screen, and his face reddens.

'They are foolish. They do not understand.'

He is old.

Antonio watches with us in silence for fifteen minutes, before turning to me.

'What you think you do, Bas?' he tries again.

Even now the glue is dissolving. More slowly here than else-where, but the intensity fades with each passing month. Our memories are short and we are easily distracted. I've been down to the rallies to try to understand: much of the anger and the hatred now looks contrived. The footage of the planes and the towers is no longer shown. The War On Terror, the Department of Homeland Security, the Rules of Engagement, Enemy Combatants and Enemy Non-Combatants – the voice of each new government spokesman grows more hollow.

'It's a clash of civilisations, Antonio.'

Metal barricades hold the crowd of demonstrators from spill-ing onto the cobbled streets as politicians' cars make their way to the Palazzo Montecitorio to debate Italy's involvement in the war.

'So they say.'

'We fight or die.'

The sweet inevitability of that simple proposition.

'You a sculptor or you a soldier, Bas?'

'We're all soldiers now, Antonio. In one way or another.'

Gianni asks Antonio over his shoulder if he wants a coffee, but then forgets he's asked as we watch a young woman swing her leg over the barricade.

'No, Bas. Is not true. You know it is not true. Your own brother.'

Ah, Jack. How close Jack is. Jack who turned his back.

'Does it matter any more, Antonio?' I say.

'You decide, my friend, you decide. But hurry. Tomorrow. You tell me. I need a carver.'

TWELVE

The night before he left, after our father had gone to bed, Jack was examining the posters on my walls, all the sculptures I might one day carve. How knowing and comfortable Jack was in that silence, how unbearable it was for me.

'So when're you off?' I asked, to draw him away from my dreams and vulnerabilities.

'Three weeks.'

'So, Africa,' I said as he gazed at a large photo of the *Winged Victory of Samothrace*. Did he see more in that one inspection than I had in all my months of contemplation?

'You got it,' he said, intent on the marble goddess: the great span of her wings, the detail of each feather, her thrusting breast, the flesh beneath the seaspray-pressed robes, her bared thigh.

'What happened to her?'

'She was lost for two thousand years before they found her, half-buried, on a Greek island. Her arms came off when they shipped her to France, but no one knows what happened to her head.'

'What do you think she looked like, Bas? Her face?'

'I don't think about it. It doesn't matter. She's perfect as she is. Trying to imagine her features would ruin her.'

He turned to look at me.

'What *have* you been thinking about then, Bas?'

That question of his. But I didn't answer, just sat there dumbly, my heart running on and on and on.

'Come on then,' Jack said eventually, 'let's have a shot.'

As we left the house he took the air rifle our father gave him one birthday from its mount on the laundry wall and slipped a box of pellets into his pocket. We helped each other over the barbed-wire fence at the back of the yard, Jack parting the strands for me to climb through, then me for Jack, the barbs glinting in the moonlight.

On the other side of the fence was the paddock of anthills, rising from the earth one after another, high as a man, like sentinels guarding the forest and the sandstone ridges beyond. There must have been a hundred of them – all those abandoned towers and their inhabitants disappeared, never to return, as if an entire civilisation had vanished and forsaken its monuments.

Jack picked up a can we'd left on the ground last time we were out there, and placed it on top of one of the mounds. At forty paces we stopped, and turned. I hadn't fired a shot since before Jack left home for the army, and pellet after pellet thudded into the compacted earth, or flew off into the night. I handed him back the gun. It must have been strange for him, I thought, after all the army's sophisticated weaponry. It took him a few shots till he got his range, worked out the corrections he'd need to make.

'So, Bas,' he said after he'd nailed three in a row and I'd reset the can for him each time, 'what do you want to do with yourself then?'

'Sculpt.' I said it aloud, tentatively.

'Sculpt?'

'Yeah.'

From somewhere in the forest a mopoke sounded. *Oom Oom Oom Oom Oom.* I used to think they were owls when I was a kid. Until Jack set me straight.

'Sculpt?' Jack asked again.

'Yep,' I said. I would hold. I had to.

'Bas,' Jack replied, sighing, 'you've got to get out of here.'

'Huh?'

'There's nothing here for you, Bas. Absolutely nothing. It'll swallow you in the end. You've got to leave, Bas. My brotherly advice to you – leave.'

The shock – realising then *he* would not be coming back. That my father's hopes for Jack and the quarry were doomed. Jack was turning his back on us, maybe forever.

'There's no life here, Bas. No one can survive it.'

I lie on my bunk in the caravan. The curtains gust coldly and a sharp beam of light from the house next door wakes me. I shudder from the chill and sit up to close the window. My statuette of Sophe on the shelf above my head is illuminated by the sudden light. My angel.

The Beards could not have been immune to her beauty, I think, and the thought startles me. Even *they* must have recognised it: Sophe's soft skin, the line of her throat, her sweeping hair and the perfection of her face. Her natural gracefulness. If *anyone* was God's messenger, it was Sophe. The Beards must have known that, *must have.* Yet still they sacrificed her.

THIRTEEN

'You come back?'

'Yes, Antonio, I am back. And I am sorry, if I . . . let you down.'

'Is OK.' He looks at me, those steady eyes of his which have seen so much. 'Here at the cathedral, the sculptor is the creator, not the carver. But we carvers *also* give life. Long life. You know, the sculptor create with his clay. And then when he make his plaster cast – that is the death. And the carving . . . my work . . .'

Antonio lays his hand on the piece before him.

'. . . *that* is the resurrection.'

He smiles.

'You see, I am in the resurrection business.'

I show him my palms, then touch my breast and my forehead as I speak, the words strange on my tongue. 'I want to try again, Antonio. Please.'

He sighs.

'You want tea?'

I shake my head, but he puts on a pot, and when he asks a second time as he's pouring one for himself I accept.

'My father,' he says, 'did both. He sculpt the clay and *then* he carve the marble.'

'Your father taught you to carve?'

I feel my failure, that I have not asked him this before.

'And his father taught him. Seven generations. We lived near the Carrara quarries – you know? We carved the same marble Michelangelo did. My grandfather had a studio on the *corso* in our village. I went back not so long ago. The building is still there. Is not a studio no more, but I knew. I could tell. I look through the window and imagine what it was like. My grandfather . . . my father . . . all those carvers . . . all that marble.'

'But . . . you came to America?'

'My father, he followed the stone. My brother too. The stone yards in New York were filled with Italians! After that they needed stone carvers and cutters down here – you been to the Capitol?'

I shake my head.

'My father is there. Everywhere. He carved the pediments above the House, all the figures, all the stories there. He carved the goddess of peace with the boy at her feet. The boy has a flame in his hands. You think you might burn yourself! See the olive tree behind the goddess. My father's friends told me you want to eat the olives!'

I return Antonio's smile.

'He once carve a memorial for a little girl who drown in the river: a cloud of butterflies and a bell with a tiny clapper at the end of a chain. A miracle! It moves if you touch it, like a real bell.'

'And your brother?'

'You know him. You tell me.'

I think of Gianni's bent shoulders and his paunch and his silent mourning for his wife. I shake my head.

'He was good too, and he and I – we work here at the cathedral together. But the stone did not speak to him. Not like our father.'

He is silent.

'You hear the stone, Bas?'

'I just want a block to sculpt.'

Antonio fixes his cap on his head and stands.

'Come with me.'

He leads me out through the door on the other side of the workshop into the stone yard where sometimes I go to smoke. It is filled with blocks of limestone, some already cut and waiting to be lifted onto Antonio's bench inside. There are finished carvings too: a finial, some gargoyles, a cherub or two. Other flawed blocks have been abandoned after only a few chisel strokes. Clouds of breath follow Antonio as he moves between the rows, running his fingers along the winter stone.

'Here,' he calls out from the farthest corner of the yard. Our breath mingles in the air when I join him, our shoulders almost touching. Before us is a large piece, a metre and a half high, stained from the weather.

'He is good. He is sweet,' Antonio says. 'You take him.'

FOURTEEN

To care for someone like this, casting breath into stone for them. The solace of it. Laying bare her head and shoulders with my point chisel, her breasts beneath her robes, her waist. Constantly brushing the chips away. Moving closer with a claw chisel, nearer still with a flat. Each evening when my work for Antonio is done I carve until I am spent.

She is constant. The redeeming stone remains firm.

During the day I force myself to produce wreaths, to be attentive to Antonio and the roughing out that must be done, setting and resetting the pointing machine, and marking the pieces for Antonio to take up and finish off. He senses my distraction and keeps me busier than before. I sweep the floor three and four times a day, freshen the chisels for him, and in the long hours am sent away from the workshop on dubious errands – to pass messages to the dean, or buy small orders of materials, or guide lorries with their fresh blocks to the back gate of the stone yard.

When I am in the workshop I cannot concentrate. This new presence in the room, standing alone on her bench, a white sheet draped over her. There is change, a new shape to the room, new emotion. When I whisper to myself, the answers are different. There is a new spirit with us. Does Antonio feel the change too?

The banter between Antonio and me. All our easy cups of tea, our shared bread and meat. His voice, and his singing. And in the open windows, a sparrow on the sill. My coursing blood. I think he is right. That it is a terrible thing to carve angry. That anger may become trapped in the stone. I cannot do that to Sophe.

To begin, I light a candle at the end of the day and honour her in the softness. Her veil is pulled back from her head and rests on her shoulders, and her hair flows from her forehead in waves. She allows me to tuck loose strands behind her ear. Her skin glows. In answer to my whispers, she smiles. We are sitting on a patterned carpet and the winds puff against the tent-flaps, then suck them out again. A child's hand appears in the doorway. Then another, and another. A dozen small palms with fingers stretched out, their bodies hidden from us behind the canvas wall. The hands wave and their fingers wiggle – Sophe laughs and so do I, and the laughter brings out the hiding children who spill into the tent, rolling over each other towards us, all arms and legs and joy.

The dean enters the workshop unexpectedly one afternoon to speak with Antonio about the cathedral's sculptures.

'What is this?' he asks when he sees my covered stone.

'It is mine, Dean.'

'And what is it?'

'I work on it at night. After I have finished my work here. Not during the day.'

He waves me away and lifts the sheet. My heart startles.

'Who is she?'

'An angel.'

'I can see that.' He bends close, but not touching. 'She is really yours?' the dean says, facing me.

'Yes.'

He turns to Antonio.

'Is it you who teach him, Mr Vasari?'

'He sculpt before, Dean.'

The dean replaces the sheet.

'Why don't you give him whatever time he needs, Mr Vasari?'

Antonio and I work together in that space, each on our own pieces, the sounds of our chisels and hammers conversing. My agitation seems to fall away. Slowly – imperceptibly – the Beards cease their crowding, stop trying to inhabit the space between my chisel strokes, step back.

Late one morning I look up from Sophe. Antonio's tools have been silent too long and he is leaning heavily on his banker, as if his arm is holding all his weight. When I reach him, sweat is pouring off his forehead, great beads of it, more than the morning's exertion.

'Here, old man,' I say softly and bring a chair across for him, 'sit.'

His skin burns. I fetch him a glass of water which he sips, though even raising it to his lips is an effort.

'How do you feel?'

'I come down with something,' he murmurs.

He is shaking by the time Gianni collects him.

Antonio was working to a deadline, an unveiling the dean has already announced for next month. I take up his hammer. Feel its weight. Feel the way Antonio's hand has shaped the handle to

275

itself over the years, feel him in it. At Antonio's bench is the saint he left, the holy man's bare legs and unfinished sandalled feet. Tentatively, ever so tentatively, I set Sophe aside and begin.

I report to Antonio in the evenings at his bedside. Gianni nurses him in the spare room at his house. The virus is a nasty strain of flu, but Antonio is strong. Gianni lays cool, damp facecloths on his forehead. Picks the blankets off the floor when he kicks them away in delirium, folding them neatly until his brother begins once again to shiver. I tell Antonio not to worry, that I will finish his piece in time. He nods, though in his illness he does not seem to understand.

I carve the writhing serpent beneath the saint's foot. Its head is upturned. Even as it struggles to free itself, it wants to know the man who will subdue it.

When the fever breaks, and the long sleep which follows is over, Antonio comes with me to the workshop. He unlocks the studio door and disciplines himself not to look immediately. Rather he goes through his routine as if nothing has changed: flicks on the light switch, opens the windows for fresh air, puts on the jug of water. Finally he approaches his bench and the saint. Antonio leans forward to touch his limestone, moves around it, face close, before bringing his weathered left hand up to rest across his chin. I watch as he stands there weeping softly, until he turns and kisses me silently, one cheek then the other.

It's close now. Night and day, I am sanding by candlelight, with a dozen large beeswax candles on stands of varying heights. Sophe moves in the warm glow and I lean in to her. The line of her neck. The stillness of her head, its serenity. The down on her arms glowing from the hammam. Her breast rising and falling with her heart.

When I am done for the night I wet my forefinger and thumb with spittle and snuff the flames. There is hiss and smoke, and the wax is warm and sweet. Sophe darkens, candle by candle, until she loses all definition. The walls of the workshop are stark, and the windows appear like tombstones in the night. Is this the blood-room once again, that same dark?

I close the workshop door and lock it. Mount my bike. Feel the cold on my cheek as I coast down the hill.

'Remember,' Antonio says at my side, 'if you any good, you know when to stop. A bad carver, he can't help himself. He work until he loses everything: the light, the dark, the breath of the stone. A bad carver, he can kill a piece.'

In the candlelight I begin again to remember my childhood. I am drawn back beyond the workshop, and Antonio, and the Beards. Beyond Sophe even. Back and back. At the base of the sandstone cliffs, there are shards of sandstone, purple and grey, bigger than my small hands. Jack leaps from boulder to boulder ahead of me. 'Here,' he calls out, 'here's one you'll like, Bas.' And he skips back towards me, holding up a piece of quartz. My father's voice is there too, behind me, rolling deep along the cliff-face, and I stop and wait for him to join us. The quartz is sparkling as Jack turns it over and over, catching the light. My father laughs, and his footsteps are close, and I see his shape from out of the corner of my eye. But the hand that reaches out and rests on my shoulder is not his. I feel the warm hand, and tilt my neck so my cheek is pressed against it, that soft hand of my mother.

★

Finally I wipe the last dust from her cheekbones and her nose, and finish her with water, smoothing her flesh with carborundum, softening her, gently rubbing her close, trickling water from a watering can across her hair, down her face, off her shoulderblades.

'Is good,' Antonio says.

He cups her cheek gently in the palm of his hand, and lingers, looking at her.

'Is beautiful, your angel. Very beautiful.'

He feels the back of her head, and follows the long folds of her robes with his fingers, feeling their texture.

'Is bad luck to touch an angel's wings, you know, when you finish?'

I nod.

I feel something like satisfaction, perhaps even pride, but it is only passing. This is not Sophe, I know that. Know, ultimately, that the moment of my statue's completion is also the moment of my failure.

'Now,' he says, turning to me. 'Now what?'

I shrug. I am exhausted.

'Now your brother? Are you ready to carve your brother?'

I see him. I see me. I see my hands on his shoulders, Jack on the edge of a desert precipice. *The beauty*, he whispers, *the beauty*. I see my brother there at his mountain abyss, turning, that longing in his eyes.

'No,' I groan. 'No.'

FIFTEEN

'Am I going to lose you again?' Antonio says when the bombs go off in Bali.

How can I know? I feel nothing of the rush I felt after the planes, none of the same inexplicable excitement. But if I have to answer him, I will break.

I sit with Gianni and Antonio and watch the bodies go home. Medical evacuation planes flying into Darwin and Perth and Sydney, my cities. So many interviews with so many relatives of the dead. That strange accent on the television which Gianni tells me is mine. And journalists moving between hospital beds, interviewing doctors and nurses and embassy officials. I watch it all, every interview, with every survivor.

Em, I know, will be watching from the living room back at The Springs.

Their faces are broken by grief. New lines cracking open before our eyes. But *they* have each other, I see, the survivors and relatives of the Bali bombing.

There's solidarity, and in some of them another quality. Some aura, beyond either anger or acceptance. Something *gained*. That's how it strikes me – that something has been received by them. And they carry it *for* us whether they want to or not. We recognise a part of ourselves when we look at them, that which they bear for us. Perhaps that is all we see.

A girl in her early twenties is interviewed, the sister of a surfer who's been killed. Though exhausted, she is composed. The journalist's questions are respectful, just enough to draw the young woman on, and she does her duty, calmly expressing her family's grief to the world. Then, suddenly, she snaps and her composure turns to rage. The trigger isn't the visceral horror she is revisiting, but a slip of the journalist's tongue – her brother's name is not John, but *Josh*. The woman is transformed, unleashed: her brother's name is the one detail that matters. The *only* thing that matters. If that is wrong, if his name is not acknowledged, if history won't accord her brother that small dignity, then *nothing* matters. Nothing. The dead man Josh's sister sets herself upon the journalist in primal anger – the enormity of the world there before her, all of its insensitivity, how small her brother might become, her single duty to protect him from that.

'I'm going back,' I say to Antonio.

When he doesn't turn I switch off the transistor radio on the bench, and repeat it.

'I'm not deaf yet,' he says.

He continues polishing the stone before him, his squinting eyes closer to the piece than when he'd first taken me in two years ago.

'I'm sorry, Antonio.'

He takes a deep breath and his shoulders straighten and he swings around to face me.

'Is good, Bas. Is right.'

He clasps me to himself.

'And your angel, Bas?'

'She is yours.'

SIXTEEN

I land in Sydney, its soft sandstone cliffs crumbling into the water. The beauty and the sadness of that. There's anxiety too, not so very different from how it felt when I touched down in Africa all those years ago, though in reverse. This foreign land I'm returning home to. Do I have anything to declare? No. No, I am far too tentative, unsure still about what I've learned. Everything feels unsettled, and if not exactly false, then not yet true: the shuddering vibrations of the carousel as I lift my bag off its dark-curving scales, the slippery bank notes from the Bureau de Change, the different smell of the exhaust fumes in the street. My accent is all around me, but how much the customs officials and shopkeepers and radio announcers and hotel receptionists are a mirror of myself I can't yet tell.

I hitch my way up the inland route, so many eucalypts rushing past after so long. Forests and wildlife corridors and paddock boundaries filled with them. They bring flashes of Africa. All those desert towns with their men hacking off branches with crude axes for fuel and their women stripping the leaves to dry. Swathes of ringbarked gum trees appear on either side of the highway, stretching for miles, an honour guard of skeletons in the midday sun. But I can't think like that.

'What about those Bali bombers?' I ask the truckie who drives me through the middle hours of the night.

'Pricks,' he says, his thick tattooed arms hugging the steering wheel high above the road. He has a moustache and wears a cap from one of the rugby league teams whose name I've forgotten.

'They call it a holy war,' I say.

'Well, they can get stuffed. Those kids who were killed were just minding their own business, enjoying themselves. End of year footy tours. *Christ!* So you can get yourself bombed just for having a drink these days! Could have been you or me.'

'. . . you or me . . .' I repeat, turning the words over in my mouth.

'Fuck oath.'

'Been over there yourself?'

'Was thinking about it, but not now. Too dangerous. Better off staying home. Best country on earth, anyway, ours. God's own.'

'You reckon?' I say, not meaning anything by it, just tired. But he turns his head to face me.

'Don't you?'

It's some sort of challenge, but I can't remember how to read it. If ever I knew.

'My brother was killed.' I answer.

'Bali?'

'No, Africa. You wouldn't have heard about it. Ten years ago. Same thing, though – Islamic fanatics. Before it all got really crazy.'

'Fuck. Sorry to hear that, mate.'

He puts a country music disc into the CD player as the truck rumbles on. It is a peace, of sorts. An hour or so later he pulls into a truck layby.

'I need some sleep. Thirty minutes, that's all.'

He climbs into the bunk at the rear of the cabin.

I step down from the truck and out onto the road. The head-lights of another semi are growing in the south, though the breeze is against it so I can't yet hear the engine. Leaving the bitumen I lever myself over a fence and into a paddock. The grass is shin-high, and though the moon is old, I can still make out the shapes of cattle beneath a pepperina in the far corner. One of the beasts detects me on the wind, rises to its feet, and groans. The truck from the south roars past. The Hereford looks across at me after it has gone, but is soon reassured. It drops its massive head, and folds its legs back to the ground. The sound of the truck becomes a purr in the distance, growing fainter.

Only now do I look up at the sky and see the Southern Cross. I close one eye, reach out my arm and trace its shape with my forefinger. I see the two pointers. I see familiar Orion and his star-studded belt. I think, what else? I say to myself: look, imag-ine. I close both eyes tight. I count to a hundred and when I open them the night is a blur. Before the stars settle back into place I see dust storms swirl around the Milky Way. I see trees and tents and towers. I see camel heads and serpents' eyes. Boulders and burn-ing bushes. I see human figures and I see angels' wings. I start to hum, some song I can't yet remember.

The driver honks his horn, and I make my way back to the truck.

The last of my lifts is down the Great Dividing Range from Toowoomba with some students on their way to Brisbane. They want to talk but I have to save myself. It is still morning. Their little car hurtles down the range, gathering speed, passing slower vehi-cles. The range was so high before I left, so imposing back then.

We pass Table Top and its crown of swaying grass, before they drop me off at the rest stop on the western outskirts of The Springs.

The three old picnic tables set into their concrete slabs in the shade of the camphor laurels are exactly as I remember them. A young couple is changing a baby on one of the tables. I pull my hat closer over my head in case they recognise me – an irrational fear given how long I've been away and that they're probably just passing through themselves anyway. I sling my bag over my shoulder, and set off on the thirty-minute walk to the cemetery.

How much returning is there in a life? Though this isn't exactly a homecoming – I've denied too many too much for that, including Em. Especially Em. And because my father has already died, there can be no prodigal son. I think of Michelangelo's life in Rome, and his great longing to return home to Florence. How when he did, it was too late, and it was just his body that was carted back along a narrow highway in a covered wagon. Of the two of us, Jack left first, but I stayed away longer. It may not yet be too late for me, I think. One can think too much.

The clouds are thickening, folding one upon the other, much earlier in the day than normal. This is something I know without needing to remember. A breeze starts up, blowing into my face. There are no cars on the back road, so I walk down the middle of the bitumen, the table-drains half full from recent rain. I take my shoes off at the weir, wade through, then dry my feet with my socks on the other side. I pass three or four small farms, their spring veg-etables already in, then, getting closer, I reach the overgrown oval, and the intersection and the blue road sign pointing to the cemetery.

The wind is gusting now. I know exactly where to go. I pass through the cemetery gate and step between the names of all the other local families towards mine.

I hear a tinkling, but it vanishes in the strengthening wind. I step forward again. Another tinkling, closer. I turn – as glass sprays across the surface of a tomb, the crystals still settling. A vase shattered by a gust, and its plastic flowers spread like votive fingers on the sandstone. Then, there before me, are my three graves. Mum in the centre, Jack and my father either side of her. How little space they occupy in the earth.

I read my father's inscription, the words Em has selected for history: *John Adams. 1937–2001. Husband of Catherine, deceased, and Miriam. Father of Jack, deceased, and Sebastian.* That surprise. I haven't expected to read my own name in the stone, *our* stone. Because I recognise the grain and the colour immediately, and know not just that it's come from our quarry, but know exactly which ridge it's been cut from, this last stone. Then, below the facts, carved by the hand of a local mason I'm sure to know: *Out beyond ideas of wrongdoing and rightdoing is a field. I'll meet you there.*

I kneel on the ground in the whistling wind. A pee-wee blows out of the branch of a bunya pine and careens past, riding the mad gust. For a long time I kneel. I watch a trail of ants make its way into a crack in Jack's gravestone as the sky darkens. Big, heavy drops of rain fall hard on my back, then stop. I take the statuette of Sophe from my bag, and stand her on Jack's grave, positioning her in the middle of the ant trail. I watch their confusion, see them bump into each other, turn, rise on their legs, and scramble over each other before finding some order and detouring around Sophe to continue their march out of the rain.

When kneeling grows uncomfortable I shift position and sit on the grass, leaning back on my arms. Sheets of rain hang like silver curtains in the south. I eat a sandwich I bought from a café in Toowoomba, then lie on the ground, using my bag as a pillow. I look up at the great brooding sky above me. Its dark underbelly doesn't split but passes slowly overhead, and I am washed in purple light.

SEVENTEEN

When I wake I'm hungry again. I rise, and sling my bag across my shoulder. I follow the road where it crosses back over the creek, then climb the bank to the town.

In the railway store the cigarettes are displayed exactly as they always have been, the sweets beneath the counter the same collection of cobbers and bullets and jubes I knew as a kid. There is even a handwritten list of prices pressed between countertop and glass like there always was, and I wonder how much the cost of a sausage roll or a bacon-and-egg burger has risen in the years I've been away.

'Just a pie, thanks,' I say to the woman behind the counter. She is big and fleshy and seems to lean, rather than sit, on the stool beneath her body.

'That storm was close wasn't it?' she says cheerfully. 'Not that we need any more rain. The country's looking pretty good, isn't it?'

'It's green alright.'

She peers at me and furrows her brow, before turning to the pie oven and sliding open the door. She reaches in with a pair of tongs, lifts a pie out and pops it into a brown paper bag as she must have done a thousand times.

'Sauce with that?'

'Thanks.'

She slips a plastic tub of tomato sauce into the bag. Before I'd left The Springs she would have poured it over the pie out of a bottle, and it would have been no extra cost.

'You're Jack Adams's brother, aren't you?' she says, and I realise she's the same storekeeper who ran the shop ten years ago.

'Yes, I am.'

The silence that follows seems to suck all air and space and time into it, a void I'm powerless to fill. I can do nothing but wait for whatever is at the bottom.

'Terrible what happened,' she says, eventually.

I wonder what the town knows, what it imagines. What story my father told about Jack and about me. Whether it was true what Em had said, that he didn't blame me. When a full minute passes I take my pie and thank her, and quietly make for the door.

'Just terrible,' she says again, a blessing of sorts as I'm moving away.

I nod and step from the doorway down onto the footpath.

'Good to see you, Sebastian,' she calls out after me.

I sit on the wooden bench out the front of the store. The timber is worn smooth from years of people buying their flavoured milk and drinking it there under the awning. I lived an entire childhood in The Springs, and never sat on that bench: it was owned by others, Jack and his mates, their throne. I look out now at the town.

Em's descriptions over the years have been good. It's as if I've already registered the changes to the streetscape while I've been away. The two-storey Criterion Hotel is still there on the right with its red corrugated-iron roof and a sign for counter lunches between 12 and 2 o'clock. It's a miracle fire hasn't yet taken it like it has most of the old pubs in most of the towns in the valley. To the left is the post-office and the RSL club. Directly opposite me, running away to the south where the storm clouds are breaking up over the Border Range, is Railway Street with its grassed median strip and its line of jacarandas sewn at regular intervals all the way to the highway. Pride of place, at the start of the jacaranda avenue, a stone's throw across the intersection at the dead centre of town, is The Springs' war memorial: a large tapered sandstone obelisk with a sphere mounted at its top.

As I finish my pie and rise from the bench a man pushes open the swinging doors of the public bar of the Criterion and steps down onto the footpath. He is small and wiry and leans his elbow on the outside window-ledge as he stands in the verandah's shade and looks out across the intersection towards me.

I crumple the brown paper bag and drop it in the rubbish bin and cross the road to the monument. I read the names of the dead. All our wars are there, most of our families. I begin walking around the memorial, half-looking for Jack's name.

The man across the road straightens, then takes a few slow steps, moving to a verandah post where he repositions himself, leaning his shoulder hard against the timber, his arms folded, half of him in sunlight now. I lift my head to look at the ball of sandstone balanced upon the names of wars and men. I see then, for the first time, that it is not merely a sphere, but is planet Earth itself, hewn from local stone. The continents are smooth – Africa and America and Australia – but the oceans are rough, pocked by hundreds upon hundreds of light chisel strokes, the sculptor's turbulent seas. He's done well, I think, has captured the movement nicely, found the dark.

The man watching me steps out onto the street, no more hurried than the sun across the sky. I wait at the memorial as he ambles across the intersection, my back turned against his approach. When he steps up off the bitumen onto the grass and is just a few feet away, he stops. I can hear him breathing, but still I don't turn. I stay facing the memorial until ignoring him becomes, itself, a challenge.

'What do you think you're doing?' he says, an even drawl, no curiosity in it, something else. I turn and now that he's closer I recognise him and know his daughter in the store has rung through to the pub. He was one of my father's old drinking mates, used to drive trucks for the munitions factory and had been on committees around town. His wife ran the cent-sale out of the hall each year, my only memory of her a faded mosaic of floral dresses, thick ankles and musk perfume. His daughter in the shop was one of three girls, all older than Jack and me.

'Reading the names,' I say.

'What do you want to do that for?'

'Just interested.'

'You . . . looking . . . for . . . anyone . . . in . . . particular?'

He says each word with an impossible slowness, eternity between them.

'No. Just interested . . . Generally.'

It isn't my answer he weighs, but me. He puts me on some set of scales and I know I am heavy. Whatever else he has on the other side. Does one ever know?

'There are some bloody fine names up there, mate. Bloody fine names.'

He lets it sit, his judgement. I understand it. I feel it too in that hard moment. That I deserted both the town and my father. That my father lost both his boys. And now that I'm back it might be all too late. But I know this too: it isn't my fault I've survived.

EIGHTEEN

I stand outside the front gate and see for the first time the garden beds Em described in her letters, notice that the rainwater gauge has been moved to the side fence, and that the mailbox is new, its copper numerals still untarnished. Em isn't home yet, will still be at the hospital. I take a deep breath and make my way down the driveway beside the house.

I guess my gear will be in the garage, and sure enough when I swing its doors open to let in the light, I find it all packed away in a corner – a stack of taped cardboard boxes covered in dust and stained by years of possums. I slit the masking tape of the first box with my pocketknife and peel back the flaps. As I lift a mallet out a cascade of cockroach droppings falls off its head and patters back into the box. My chisels and pins are there too. My gloves and chalk and goggles. A decade-old dust mask disintegrates at my touch and the spare teeth I bought for my claw chisel just before I left are now rusted. I fold down the flaps of the box and step back out into the afternoon sun.

I blink and I blink until I see it.

My great unfinished block of sandstone is exactly where I'd left it down by the back fence. It is still cloaked by its tarpaulin – a frayed and weathered shroud, the colour leeched out of it now. I kick away the four bricks that have held down the corners of the tarp, their rectangular shapes pressed deep into the earth after the weight of so many years. I grasp the tarp-edge in both hands and pull it back in one quick movement.

His shoulder! The shock of that muscle and that bone struggling to get out, powerful still. Desperate, forceful. The layer of mould that has grown over the stone is a mere patina of age. Is nothing. That youthful, urgent shoulder still pushes forward, that exact moment of exertion I'd left all those years before. That primal creature, his unwearied head and neck, his rusted necklace, his thrusting vitality. I run my hand along his nape. I place my palms upon his spine and feel his grain beneath my fingers. I find chisel marks and know them as mine. I press my cheek against his flank, the sun on his back once again and know, now, it is done. Is complete. Was, in fact, perfect a long time ago.

A sculptor should know when to stop.

I climb the back fence, skirt the paddock of termite mounds, and enter the bush. I need to be immersed in it, loud around me. I crunch among the eucalypts, those same sounds, all the buzzing and rustling and crackling bark and leaf-litter underfoot just as I remembered it. As I dreamed it. Wrens flit between branches, flashes of blue. A willie wagtail drops to the ground for the briefest of moments before darting away in a flurry of wing and tail. Somewhere a kookaburra. I pull a eucalypt leaf, long and succulent, from a branch, break it and hold it to my nostrils, something of Jack in its scent.

A long, thin strip of bark peels off a gum beside me and crashes to the forest floor. I reach for the tree's newly exposed flesh and find it soft on my fingertips. I trace the scribbly tracks hidden till now beneath the bark. Their different texture, the henna-dark trails of some unknown insect winding back and forth across the tree's bare skin. Both the symmetry and the chaos of its pattern.

I come out again into the paddock of anthills, and the rusting cans lying scattered in the grass at the feet of the tallest of them. I run my hand over the mounds, all that compacted earth, the feel of them on my palm, crumbling now. The ten thousand suns these mud towers have stood beneath, the storms, the winds. Yes, all things collapse, I think, in time. Eroded by the sky's mercy. And the earth's compassion, and the breath of God who refuses to emerge from rock and soil, but abides there like truth itself, near inseparable. As near as I am likely to get.

There are holes where Jack and I practised our aim with his air rifle. I finger them, looking for pellets, but can't get deep enough. I am working at one of the holes with my pocketknife in the falling light, all my concentration on the task, when I hear a sound behind me, a creak. I turn. And there at the fence, caught in my gaze, is Em.

She has a hand on the top of the timber fence-post, one foot on the bottom strand of barbed wire, and is utterly still. She is so small. The narrow shoulders I remember, the points of them as sharp as ever. Her wrist is thin. Her hair has greyed and is now cut short. But there is something beyond the years, something in her face I see even from here, something in the stillness of her eyes. As if her body has been transformed and is composed of a new substance: some form of sadness, solid and formidable. We remain there for what seems an eternity, me standing motionless beside the anthill, Em frozen with her hand on the fence-post. This long act of recognition, of trying to fit so many things into their proper place.

The kookaburra sings out again from deep in the bush, breaking the stillness.

'Hang on,' I call and I move towards her, 'let me . . .'

When I get to the fence I push my boot down on the bottom strand of wire, taking the tension from her. I pull the next strand up as far as I can, opening a gap. Em bends her back low and steps through, careful not to catch her uniform on a barb.

'Thanks.'

She is strong, I realise as she straightens and we stand beside each other there in the afternoon field. It is me who feels small.

'When did you arrive?' she asks.

'This morning.'

'I would have left the key out if . . .'

But she knows it is unnecessary and lets it fall away.

'Here you are, Bas,' she says eventually. 'Here you are.'

'Here we are, Em,' I answer, smiling. 'Out in a paddock beyond right and wrong.'

Her eyes begin to shine, and I reach for her, and fold her to me and grasp her tight.

AUTHOR'S NOTE

This is a work of fiction.

In the 1990s, however, a United Nations peacekeeping force was established in Western Sahara, refugee camps arose on the border between Western Sahara and Algeria, and Algeria itself was beset by internal conflict. This novel has been informed by those events.

The letter on p. 247 was, with only minor changes, written by an Algerian family in 1996 after an event similar to the one depicted in this novel. The letter was taken from John W. Kiser's *The Monks of Tibhirine*, published by St Martin's Press Griffin. Much earlier, in 1918, a French priest named Charles de Foucauld, formerly a legionnaire, was killed at Tamanrasset in the remote Sahara. That priest is mentioned in this work, and some of Jack's journal writings have been sourced from Foucauld's letters, translations of which appear in Robert Ellsberg's *Charles de Foucauld*, published by Orbis Books. Inspiration for the master carver of Washington National Cathedral and for dialogue in Chapter Thirteen, Part Three, was drawn partly from Marjorie Hunt's excellent non-fiction work *The Stone Carvers: Master Craftsmen of*

Washington National Cathedral, published by Smithsonian Books. The line 'Out beyond ideas . . .' on p. 286 is by Rumi, the translated version by Coleman Barks. The quotations from the Qur'an are from the English version by Marmaduke Pickthall in the Everyman's Library edition.

For their great generosity, I am indebted to Sarah Bendall, Steve Foley, Fiona Guthrie, Rhyl Hinwood, Peter Jensen, Justin Malbon, Jenny-Maree Marshall, Simon Moran, Dirk Moses, Alicia Toohey and Natasha Ziebell. Any errors and all responsibility are, of course, my own.

At UQP Madonna Duffy, John Hunter, Rebecca Roberts and all the team have been unstintingly marvellous, for which I am grateful. And my special gratitude to my editor, Judith Lukin-Amundsen.

Most of all, my deepest thanks are to Alisa.